Enid Blyton

THE
NAUGHTIEST
GIRL
COLLECTION 2

Other Enid Blyton School Stories Collections

The St Clare's Collection 1:
The Twins • The O'Sullivan Twins • Summer Term

The St Clare's Collection 2:
Second Form • Third Form • Kitty

The St Clare's Collection 3:
Claudine • Fifth Formers • Sixth Form

The Malory Towers Collection 1:
First Term • Second Form • Third Year

The Malory Towers Collection 2:
Upper Fourth • In the Fifth • Last Term

The Malory Towers Collection 3:
New Term • Summer Term • Winter Term

The Malory Towers Collection 4:
Fun and Games • Secrets • Goodbye

The Naughtiest Girl Collection 1:
In the School • Again • Is a Monitor

The Naughtiest Girl Collection 2:
Here's … • Keeps a Secret • Helps a Friend • Saves the Day

The Naughtiest Girl Collection 3:
Well Done • Wants to Win • Marches On

Enid Blyton

THE NAUGHTIEST GIRL COLLECTION 2

Written by Enid Blyton:
Here's the Naughtiest Girl

Written by Anne Digby:
The Naughtiest Girl Keeps a Secret
The Naughtiest Girl Helps a Friend
The Naughtiest Girl Saves the Day

Illustrated by Kate Hindley

**Hodder
Children's
Books**

HODDER CHILDREN'S BOOKS

Here's The Naughtiest Girl first published in Great Britain in 1942 by George Newnes
The Naughtiest Girl Keeps a Secret first published in Great Britain in 1999 by Hodder and Stoughton
The Naughtiest Girl Helps a Friend first published in Great Britain in 1999 by Hodder and Stoughton
The Naughtiest Girl Saves the Day first published in Great Britain in 1999 by Hodder and Stoughton
The Naughtiest Girl Collection 2 first published in 2015

9 10

A CIP catalogue record for this book is available from the British Library.

ISBN 978 1 444 92486 2

Printed and bound in Great Britain by Clays Ltd, Elcograf S.p.A.

The paper and board used in this book are made from wood from responsible sources.

Hodder Children's Books
An imprint of Hachette Children's Group
Part of Hodder and Stoughton
Carmelite House
50 Victoria Embankment
London EC4Y 0DZ

An Hachette UK Company
www.hachette.co.uk
www.hachettechildrens.co.uk

CONTENTS

Here's
THE NAUGHTIEST
GIRL

WHYTELEAFE

CHAO · ET · PERTINACIA

CONTENTS

CHAPTER ONE

BACK AT WHYTELEAFE SCHOOL

IT WAS the summer term at Whyteleafe School. All the children were back again – Elizabeth, Julian, Harry, John, Martin, Rosemary and the rest. They rushed round the school excitedly, glad to be back.

'Summer term! My favourite term!' said Elizabeth Allen, pleased. 'Hi, Julian – come and look at my new tennis racket!'

Julian came over, humming a little song. His green eyes twinkled at Elizabeth. 'Hallo,' he said. 'What are you going to be this term, Elizabeth? Naughtiest girl in the school? Best girl? Silliest?'

Elizabeth laughed and gave Julian a punch. 'I'm a monitor, as you jolly well know,' she said. 'I'm going to do my best, and be a monitor all the term – not be chucked out in the middle, as I was last term. What about *you*?'

'Oh, I'm going to do my best, too – but I've got all sorts of bests,' said Julian, grinning. 'I'll beat you at work this term, for one thing – and I'll beat you at

1

tennis – and I'll beat you at thinking out a few little tricks to make life cheerful – and . . .'

'Oh, Julian – I *hope* you'll think of a few tricks,' said Elizabeth. 'But please don't put sneezing powder in the pages of my books again – honestly, it's awful to *have* to keep on and on sneezing without stopping.'

'Right,' said Julian, 'I'll make a note of it!'

Elizabeth was just going to say something more when she caught sight of a boy in the distance. He was so like Julian that she stared in surprise. Same black untidy hair, same green eyes – but what a sulky face!

'Look – there's somebody who looks very like you,' said Elizabeth. 'He must be a new boy.'

Julian turned. 'Yes – that's a cousin of mine. He's got rather a big opinion of himself, as you'll soon find out. He didn't want to come to Whyteleafe School at all.'

'Why ever not?' said Elizabeth, who simply couldn't *imagine* anyone not wanting to come.

'Well – he's not very fond of *me*,' said Julian. 'He doesn't like people who can do things better than he can – and he'll be in our form.'

'And when you use *your* brains you'll be top whenever you want to!' said Elizabeth. 'Even against me!'

'That's easy,' said Julian, and got another punch. 'But, quite seriously, Elizabeth, go slow with Patrick –

he can be very spiteful. Don't play the heavy monitor with him too soon or too much.'

'I shall tick him off if he doesn't toe the line,' said Elizabeth at once. 'How will he behave, do you think?'

'A bit like *you* behaved when you first came!' said Julian, twinkling at her. 'Don't you remember? You were the Naughtiest Girl in the School – and you meant to be, too! The things you did!'

Elizabeth went bright pink. 'You needn't keep reminding me of that first term,' she said. 'I was awful. I just can't think how I could have behaved like that.'

'Well, I wasn't there then,' said Julian, 'but I've heard plenty about it. I bet you'll always be known as the Naughtiest Girl, even if you go on being a monitor for the rest of your school days and end up as Head-Girl!'

'Gosh – I'd never be that,' said Elizabeth. 'Whoever heard of a Naughtiest Girl ending up as Head? Here comes your cousin, Julian.'

Julian swung round. 'Hallo, Patrick,' he said. 'Finding your way about a bit? This is Elizabeth. She's a friend of mine and if you want any help in anything, go to her, because she's a monitor.'

'I'm not likely to go to any friend of yours for help!' said Patrick in a high and mighty voice. 'And, by the way, you don't need to spread around the news that

3

I'm your cousin – I'm not really proud of having you for a cousin! Too swollen-headed for my taste!'

He went off, hands in pockets. Julian glared after him. 'If he wasn't new I'd shake him till his teeth rattled!' he said.

Elizabeth was indignant, too. 'What a cheek from a new boy!' she said. 'Well, he won't cheek *me*! If he does I'll report him.'

A bell rang just then, and everyone hurried in to a meal. Elizabeth scrambled for her place at table. She beamed round at everyone. How good it was to be back among all her friends! John Terry grinned at her across the table.

'Going to help in the garden this term?' he called. 'Have you seen all the seeds that have come up since last term? We shall have a fine show this summer.'

John was partly responsible for the gardens of the school. He loved gardening and was very good at it. Elizabeth nodded back at him. 'Yes – of course I'll help. I love messing about in the garden.'

Elizabeth was going to be busy this term! She meant to ride each day on one of the school ponies. She meant to practise her tennis hard and get into one of the school teams. She meant to help John with the gardens. She was determined to beat Julian as top of the form whenever she could, and that meant a lot of hard work – and she meant to be a good monitor.

Somebody else meant to beat Julian, too! That was Patrick, his cousin. Patrick was jealous of Julian – he had always been glad when he had heard that his cousin didn't work hard at school, and had continually been bottom. He knew that Julian had good brains, and it pleased him that he hadn't used them.

All the same, he hadn't wanted to go to Whyteleafe School. 'Mixed boys and girls!' he thought, scornfully. 'I'd rather go to an all-boys' school. Look at that Elizabeth now – fancy me having to take orders from a girl! Well – I shan't pay much attention to *her*, anyway!'

He set himself to make a good impression on the others in his form. He entered into everything, and because he was good at games, and could be very comical when he tried, he was soon well-liked.

He hadn't Julian's gift of making extraordinary noises – but how he wished he had! Julian could cluck exactly like a hen laying an egg – he could buzz like a blue-bottle fly, drone like a bumble-bee, and make very strange noises like nothing at all.

Patrick had often tried to imitate noises, but he couldn't. For one thing everyone knew he was making them, and that gave the game away.

'Nobody ever knows that Julian is doing the noises,' thought Patrick enviously. 'Last Christmas, when he came to us for a party, he imitated a dog whining, and we all hunted round the house for ages – and though I looked and looked at Julian, I *couldn't* see a single movement of his mouth or throat.'

Patrick soon found that Whyteleafe wasn't at all the 'sissy' kind of school he had expected. His class worked hard and played hard, practically every boy or girl had a hobby, and if anything went wrong it was reported at the big Meeting held by the school each week.

This was a kind of Parliament, at which everything was discussed frankly by the children themselves. Complaints were heard, grumbles were made and set right, money was distributed evenly, plans were made.

Rita and William, the head-boy and head-girl, presided. If punishments had to be meted out, they said what they were to be. Twelve monitors sat on the platform with them – a kind of jury, Elizabeth always thought. She was very proud to be on the platform, sitting alongside the twelve other monitors.

At first Patrick had been pleased to hear that he was to be in Julian's form. He had frequently heard his father and mother say what a pity it was that a boy with good brains like Julian should so often be bottom. He didn't know that the term before Julian had begun to use his brains well, and could always be top of the form if he wanted to be!

So it was a shock to him to find that in the first week's marks Julian was top, Elizabeth was second, and he was tied third with somebody else.

'I thought you made a point of being at the bottom of the form,' he said to Julian. 'Or so I always heard.'

'You heard right,' said Julian, quite amiably. 'I just didn't happen to want to be top, that was all. But I do now. Did *you* want to be top, Patrick? Bad luck that I happen to be using my brains this term, isn't it?'

Patrick turned away. All right – he'd work harder still. He wasn't going to play second fiddle to Julian. He pondered over his tennis. He was good at that. He would take special coaching and practise hard – Julian wasn't much good at tennis! It would do him good to be taken down a peg!

Then one day he came up against Elizabeth. She was the only person in the form he didn't try to be nice to. She was Julian's friend and a monitor – that was enough for Patrick! He hardly ever addressed a word to her, and if ever she came up to a group he was with he walked away.

Elizabeth laughed at first, but soon it infuriated her. She longed to pull him up for something, but the chance didn't come for three weeks.

Then a notice was put on the board for a meeting. 'Meeting of the Garden Committee, at five o'clock

7

sharp,' said the notice. 'All the first form must attend as well, as volunteers are wanted to help with the weeding.'

Patrick was in the first form. He saw the notice and ignored it. Why should he go? He wasn't interested in gardening, he hated weeding, and he certainly wasn't going to volunteer to do anything in the gardens!

He went off to have a quiet practice by himself, taking his racket and tennis balls with him. There was a wall at the side of the school against which he could hit the balls and strike them continually on the rebound.

So, when the meeting gathered, Patrick was not there! John, who was in charge, looked round. 'Are we all here?' he said.

'No. Patrick isn't,' said Elizabeth at once. 'I bet I know where he is, too! Practising hitting balls against the side-wall. I saw him pass the window with his racket.'

'Oh! Well, he's got to come,' said John. 'You are a monitor, Elizabeth. Fetch him, will you?'

'Right,' said Elizabeth, pleased at being able to make Patrick 'toe the line' for once. 'I can hear the thud-thud of the balls against the wall now. I'll bring him along at once!'

And off she went, quite sure she could make Patrick obey her!

CHAPTER TWO

PATRICK COMES UP AGAINST ELIZABETH

ELIZABETH HURRIED round to the side of the school. Thud, thud, thud, she heard the balls being hit regularly against the wall.

She turned the corner and called out to Patrick. 'Hey! You're supposed to be at the Garden Meeting. You'd better come at once.'

'Get out of my way, please,' said Patrick. 'I'm practising.'

Elizabeth glared. 'John sent me,' she said.

'All right. I send you back,' said Patrick, almost hitting Elizabeth with one of the balls, as he sent it against the wall near her.

'Don't be an idiot,' said Elizabeth, trying not to lose her temper. 'You know I'm a monitor, don't you? Well, you've *got* to come when you're told. It's no good having monitors unless they're obeyed, you know that.'

'I'm not obeying a girl,' said Patrick. 'Do go away.

PATRICK COMES UP AGAINST ELIZABETH

I shall get annoyed with you in a minute.'

Elizabeth promptly proceeded to get even more annoyed with the infuriating Patrick. She rushed at him and wrenched away his racket. He was so taken by surprise that he let it slip out of his hands.

Then Elizabeth raced away at top speed with it! Patrick tore after her in a rage. Elizabeth turned a corner and deftly threw the racket into the middle of a bush. Then on she went without stopping, back to the Meeting.

She arrived there, panting. Before she could say a word to the startled Meeting, Patrick arrived, too, fuming. 'Where's my racket? How *dare* you snatch it like that? Elizabeth, what have you done with my racket?'

Elizabeth said nothing. John looked surprised, but pointed to a seat. 'Sit down, Patrick,' he said. 'We've been waiting for you?'

'I haven't come to your silly Meeting,' said Patrick, furiously. 'I've come after Elizabeth for my racket!'

'*Sit down*,' ordered John. 'You're at the Meeting now, and here you'll stay. You won't get your racket till the Meeting is over – and not then if you don't behave yourself!'

Patrick was so surprised at John's determined voice that he sat down. He looked all round for his racket, making up his mind to snatch it and go. But he couldn't see it, which was not surprising, as it was still outside in the bushes!

Patrick didn't hear a word of the Meeting. He glared at Elizabeth's triumphant face. He scowled at the little smile on Julian's. Julian was amused at Elizabeth's method of bringing his unwilling cousin to the Meeting, and he wondered where she had put the racket.

Elizabeth forgot about Patrick in her interest in the Meeting. She was very fond of gardening, and John regarded her as one of his right-hand helpers. He kept consulting her, and she was pleased.

She didn't notice that the sky had clouded over and that it had begun to rain. It was only when it suddenly pelted against the window that she looked out and saw the torrents of rain that were falling. Even then she didn't think about the racket outside in the bushes.

She didn't think of it till the Meeting was over. Then John turned to the bored and sulky Patrick. 'Now you can have your racket back from Elizabeth,' he said. 'And please remember if a Meeting of the whole form is arranged, you've got to come to it.'

Patrick scowled. Elizabeth suddenly remembered where she had put his racket – in the middle of the bushes. Goodness – had it got wet in the rain? She knew it was a new racket, and that Patrick was intensely proud of it.

PATRICK COMES UP AGAINST ELIZABETH

She wished she could go and get it out of the bushes and dry it before she gave it to Patrick. But he gave her no chance to do that. He followed close at her heels when she went out of the room. She walked out of the garden door and went to the wet bushes. It was still pouring with rain. She fished out the soaked racket.

Patrick stared at it in horror and anger. 'You beast! You flung my new racket there in the pouring rain! It'll be ruined.'

'It wasn't raining when I put it there, you know it wasn't,' said Elizabeth.

'Well, why didn't you go out and get it when the rain began?' said Patrick furiously. 'You left it there on purpose! You *meant* the rain to spoil it! Just like a girl!'

'I *didn't* mean to spoil it!' said Elizabeth angrily. 'I didn't even notice it was raining till nearly the end of the Meeting – and then I forgot all about your racket. It's your fault for not coming to the Meeting, so that I had to fetch you!'

Patrick was wiping the strings with his handkerchief. He was trembling with rage and disappointment. His lovely new racket!

'I hate you for this,' he said. 'Now you'll go and laugh about it with Julian, and be glad you've ruined my racket – there wasn't a better one in the school! You'll both be glad it's spoilt!'

13

'Patrick, don't be silly,' said Elizabeth. 'Look – I'm very sorry I didn't think of your racket being out in the rain. If I'd remembered it, I'd have gone to get it at once. And of *course* Julian and I won't be glad if it's spoilt.'

'Yes, you will. I detest you both,' said Patrick, his face bright red, and his green eyes flaming like Julian's did when he was angry. 'I'll get even with you! You're just exactly the kind of mean, catty girl I'd expect my cocky cousin to be friends with!'

He tucked his racket under his arm, and walked off in a rage, the rain still pouring down as he went. Elizabeth shook back her wet curls. Blow! What an idiot she had been to forget the racket when it began to rain. She really was sorry about that.

Julian met her as she went back. 'Gosh, you *are* wet!' he said. 'What happened? Where did you put his racket? *Not* out in the rain, I hope!'

'Yes, I did – but I didn't mean to,' said Elizabeth, soberly, and she told Julian what had happened, and what Patrick had said. 'He never liked me before, Julian, and now he's really furious with me. He hates you, too, doesn't he? Oh, dear, I do hope he won't do anything silly now. He really looked as if he'd like to hit me with his racket!'

'He probably would have if he hadn't thought his

14

racket would be hurt more than you would!' said Julian. 'Cheer up – what can he do to pay you back – or me either? Nothing that matters. Come on into the gym – there'll be games going on there.'

Patrick made a great fuss about his precious racket. He told everyone what had happened. He spoke of having to get all the strings replaced, and when the next School Meeting was held, he actually got up and asked for the money to have his racket completely restrung!

He stood up when William said, 'Any complaints, please?' Anyone could then stand up and lodge a complaint, big or small. Patrick leapt to his feet before anyone else.

'I have a complaint!' he said. 'Against a monitor, Elizabeth Allen. She left my racket out in the rain and it's ruined. I want to ask for money out of the school money-box so that I can pay for it to be restrung.'

'Elizabeth – perhaps you'd like to say something about this,' said William, the head-boy, in surprise.

Elizabeth stood up, feeling embarrassed. She related truthfully what had happened, and added that she was very sorry about the racket being left out in the wet. 'But it wasn't for very long,' she said, 'and I'm sure, William, that it doesn't need restringing.'

'Have you the racket with you?' William asked Patrick. 'No? Well, go and get it. I know a good bit about rackets and I can tell you at once what wants doing.'

Patrick went to get the racket with a very bad grace. He came back and gave it to William. 'Look – there's a string gone already!' he said, pointing to the broken string. Elizabeth stared in dismay.

William examined the racket very carefully. Then he put it down and looked sternly at Patrick. 'That string is not frayed or split,' he said. 'It has been cut. The racket does not need restringing – only that one string needs putting in. Who cut it, Patrick? Tell me that?'

'How should I know?' said Patrick, sulkily.

There was a short silence. 'Now listen,' said William, 'you yourself must pay for that one string being renewed. The rain had nothing to do with its being broken. I think you know that very well. Every other string is perfectly all right. If you still want the whole racket restrung, you can save up the two pounds you are allowed each week, and pay for it yourself – but it will take you more than a term's money!'

Patrick snatched up his racket without a word. He glanced at Elizabeth. She looked scornfully back. So he had actually cut a string in his own racket to try and make out that she had really spoilt it by leaving it for a few minutes in the rain! What a thing to do!

16

PATRICK COMES UP AGAINST ELIZABETH

Patrick made a sudden face at her, and then left the platform with his racket. He passed by Julian and saw a little smile on his face. He almost hit him with the racket! 'I'll pay you both back!' he said in a whisper, and marched right out of the hall.

'Don't call him back,' said Rita, the head-girl, to William. 'He's a new boy. He's got to learn our ways! Now – any more complaints?'

There were none. Nor were there any grumbles. William hammered his fist on the table as a little talking broke out.

'You may dismiss,' he said. 'The Meeting is over.'

Elizabeth sped to Julian. 'Oh, Julian – isn't Patrick MEAN! Did he really cut that string, do you think? It did look exactly as if it had been cut.'

'Of course he did,' said Julian. 'He's an idiot. We'd better look out for him now, Elizabeth. He may really try to pay you back!'

'Pooh! *I'm* not afraid of Patrick,' said Elizabeth. And she wasn't!

CHAPTER THREE

JULIAN'S LITTLE TRICK

PATRICK BROODED over the whole affair. He had a sulky nature; and could not easily forget anything that upset him. He completely ignored Julian and Elizabeth, turning his back on them whenever they came near.

This only amused them, however, and in the end Julian turned the joke against Patrick by calling out warningly whenever he or Elizabeth went near him:

'Be ready to turn your back, Patrick. Here we come again! Hurry up and turn, or you'll see us!'

Patrick tried in vain to think of some big, triumphant way of getting back at Julian and Elizabeth. He was bitterly disappointed that Julian was so good at his class work. His cousin had always been so don't-carish over that, so he had heard, and Patrick had looked forward to crowing over him and being top each week.

But no matter how hard Patrick worked, Julian seemed to be able to work harder! Julian had brilliant brains, found learning easy, and was determined that Patrick should not once beat him in marks.

JULIAN'S LITTLE TRICK

Patrick was second one week – beating Elizabeth. But Julian was still triumphantly top, a full ten marks ahead of Patrick. Miss Ranger, the class mistress, was amazed at the high marks that Julian, Patrick and Elizabeth showed each week! She didn't know how hard they were vying with one another.

Patrick decided to concentrate on tennis, and beat Julian at that. Julian was good, but he wasn't keen on being in any of the school tennis teams. He said it meant too much hard work to keep in practice!

'All the same, Julian, you'd *better* get some practice in,' said Elizabeth, 'because that cousin of yours is getting jolly good. I watched him playing with some boys older than he is, and he was as good as they were. He'll be in one of the top teams if you don't look out – and won't he crow over you! Do, do beat him, Julian.'

'Blow you, Elizabeth,' said Julian, and pretended to sigh heavily. 'What with working like a slave to keep ahead of you and Patrick in class – and now having to tire myself out with tennis, to beat Patrick, my life's not worth living! What about *you* taking him on at tennis?'

'I do try – but he's got a much harder serve than I have,' said Elizabeth, honestly. 'Go on, Julian – you can be *much* better than Patrick, and I'd jump for joy

if you got into the second team, which is what *he* wants to do!'

Julian tried – and Patrick had the disappointment of being well and truly beaten by his cousin when they played against each other two weeks after that! Patrick hadn't realized that Julian had become so good, and he was humiliated and disappointed.

'If he gets into the second team instead of me I'll hit him on the head!' thought Patrick, going off the court with a very gloomy face. 'He doesn't really care about tennis, and I do. He's only doing it to spite me.'

'Jolly good, Julian!' said Elizabeth, giving him a thump on the back as he came whistling off the court, having collected all the balls that Patrick had been too annoyed to pick up. 'Did you see his face? He looked as sick as a hen left out in the rain!'

'Oh well – it's rather a shame really,' said Julian. 'I don't care if I'm good at tennis or not, and he does. But seeing that he only wants to have the pleasure of crowing over me if he beats me, I don't mind beating *him*!'

'Yes – and you *don't* crow!' said Elizabeth. 'I hope you get into the second team and go and play against Hickling Green School, Julian – that's always such a good outing.'

Julian began to get a bit bored with his extra efforts

at lessons and tennis. He was also working very hard at making a model aeroplane, for he was very clever with his hands. All this concentration made him feel suddenly stale.

He began to plan a little pleasure for his form. Strange noises? Something weird up the chimney? He thought hard, and a sudden grin came on his face.

'The chimney! I sit fairly near the fireplace, and I could work something in the chimney. Now – let's see.'

When his classroom was empty, Julian went in cautiously. He crouched down by the chimney and looked up it. It was rather narrow. A broad mantelpiece was over the fireplace, and this Julian examined very carefully. He had noticed last winter that, when the wind was in a certain direction, little eddies of smoke came out from under the mantelpiece. He was looking for the crack from which they must have come.

'There must be a crack or a hole somewhere,' thought Julian, 'or the smoke wouldn't get out from the chimney under the mantelpiece and into the room. Ah – here it is!'

He had found the crack, where the cement had worn away. He took a chisel and made the hole considerably bigger. He poked the chisel some way through, and then decided that the hole was big enough for his purpose.

He took a piece of string and tied a penknife to one end. He poked the knife through the hole, and gave it a push. It clattered into the chimney, fell down and suddenly appeared in the hearth!

'Ha! Good!' said Julian, pleased. He still had hold of the string that went into the hole. He knocked a small tack in on the underside of the wooden mantelpiece and then tied the string to it firmly. He tested it. Yes, it held well.

He undid the knife from the other end of the string, which hung down the chimney into the fireplace. He then disappeared into the corridor and fetched a small bell that was kept there to summon Matron if she was needed in a hurry.

He went back into the classroom and carefully tied the bell to the end of the string that hung down the chimney. Then he undid the other end from the nail, and pulled it, so that the bell was dragged out of sight up the chimney!

Then Julian gave a little tug to the string he held, and a muffled and rather weird tinkle came from up the chimney!

Julian chuckled. He ran the end of the string under the mantelpiece and held it in place by little staples he drove into the wood. The string fell down the side of the fireplace just by his chair. Julian sat down and bent over his desk, holding the end of the string in his hand. He tugged it – and a mournful little jingle came from the inside of the chimney!

'A nice little treat for the class this afternoon,' thought Julian, and tied the string to one leg of his chair.

Miss Ranger took the class that afternoon. It was a geography lesson, rather dull. Julian waited for a moment of silence and then gave the string tied to his chair leg a little tug.

At once it pulled the bell hanging in the chimney and a sudden little jingle sounded in the room. Everyone looked up. Julian did too. He meant to be as surprised as anyone else!

He tugged the string again. Jingle-tinkle-tink went the bell, obligingly.

'What's that noise?' asked Miss Ranger, puzzled. 'It sounds exactly like a bell somewhere. Where is it ringing? Has anyone got a bell with them this afternoon?'

'No, Miss Ranger!' chorused everyone except Julian. He tugged again, and the bell jangled quite loudly.

'Well – it *sounds* up the chimney!' said John. 'But how could a bell ring in the chimney?'

'It couldn't,' said Miss Ranger, firmly. 'So we won't ask you or anyone else to go crawling up the chimney to look for bells there, John. Stand up, everyone, and put

24

your hands above your heads. If anyone has a bell, and can ring it when his hands are above his head, he will be clever!'

Everyone stood with hands above their heads, Julian too. Jingle-jingle-jing! The bell rang again. Julian had managed to get his foot to the string and jerk it! A babble of noise broke out at once.

'Nobody's got a bell and yet it rang again! Miss Ranger, what is it? Miss Ranger, it's peculiar! Where is it, do you suppose? Can't we look for it?'

'No,' said Miss Ranger, firmly, imagining a bevy of excited children crawling over the room and completely ruining the rest of the geography lesson. 'Bell or no bell, we go on with the lesson. Sit!'

They sat and the bell immediately rang a merry peal. 'Take no notice,' commanded Miss Ranger, who was just as puzzled as anyone else, but determined not to show it. 'I have only one more thing to say about this bell – and that is, if I find out that anyone in this class is plaguing us with a jingling bell, I shall do a bit of plaguing myself – and the culprit will be very, very sorry for themselves!'

After that they all settled down, and although the bell rang plaintively at intervals, and the children began to giggle each time, nobody dared to take much notice of it.

As soon as the class was ended and Miss Ranger was safely out of the room, John ran to the chimney. 'It sounded as if it came from here,' he said. 'I know it did!'

He put his hand up the chimney and groped about. Tinkle, jing! He had touched the bell!

'It *is* up here!' he cried. 'I thought so. But how on earth did it get there?' He turned and saw Julian's grinning face. He laughed. 'Julian! It's one of your ridiculous tricks – but HOW did you get the bell hanging there?'

'Easy!' said Julian, and showed the interested class how he had managed it. Only one of them sneered. That was Patrick, of course.

'What a childish trick! I'm sure Miss Ranger will be very scornful about it when I tell her.'

He was immediately pushed down hard on a chair and three or four children pinned him down firmly. 'Sneak! Tell-tale! We'll never speak to you again if you do that.'

'All right, all right. I was only joking,' said Patrick, trying to push them off, afraid of making them dislike him. They let him go.

John had pulled the bell down from the chimney and now it lay on the floor nearby. Patrick gave it a vicious kick, and it slid jangling over the floor. Julian smiled broadly. 'Taking it out on the bell instead of on me, I suppose?' he said. 'Pity you can't see a joke, Patrick.'

The next day a really peculiar thing happened. It was Miss Ranger's class again, this time in maths. All the children were copying sums down from the blackboard, when once more there was a curious noise from the chimney.

Everyone raised their heads and grinned. Was this another trick of old Julian's? But he looked as surprised as they did.

The noise came again, a struggling kind of noise, then came a series of high squeaks, and a little soot fell down the chimney.

'Now whatever is *this*?' said Miss Ranger, exasperated. She suddenly thought of Julian and his tricks. She looked straight at him. 'Julian – is this one of your tricks? Answer me truthfully, please.'

'No, Miss Ranger. It isn't one of my tricks. I can't *imagine* what is going on in the chimney,' said Julian, quite truthfully.

Squeak, squeak, chirri-chirri-chirrup!

Patrick got up. 'Julian's not telling the truth!' he said. 'It was *his* chimney trick yesterday – and it's his trick again today! Look up the chimney and you'll see his trick, Miss Ranger! He's a frightful fibber!'

CHAPTER FOUR

PATRICK IN TROUBLE

THE WHOLE class stared at Patrick in amazement and disgust. Julian shrugged his shoulders. 'I do assure you, Miss Ranger, I haven't the faintest idea what is going on up our chimney,' he said.

'You DO know! You've put something up there again!' cried Patrick, in a fury. 'Just to suck up to the class and make them think you're marvellous!'

'That's enough,' said Miss Ranger. And then, quite suddenly, with another series of squeaks and chirps, something fell down the chimney and came to rest with a little thud on the hearth!

'Chirrup!' it said, feebly. The children stared at it. 'A baby starling – and golly, here comes another!' cried Harry, as a second black little creature arrived beside the other. 'There must have been a starling's nest up the chimney – and these two have wriggled out and fallen down. Poor little things!'

'Sucks to you, Patrick,' said Elizabeth, in delight. 'You can't say that Julian built the starling's nest or

28

turned out the young starlings, can you! Sucks to you!'

'Elizabeth, I don't like that vulgar expression,' said Miss Ranger, coldly. 'John, take those two poor little creatures and put them outside in a bush where perhaps their starling parents may see them and feed them. Patrick, take that scowl off your face.'

'It was Julian who put the bell up the chimney yesterday, anyhow!' blurted out Patrick. 'So what are you going to do about *that*?'

'Nothing,' said Miss Ranger, calmly. 'Sit down in your places, everyone. We are now going on with our lesson – and I must warn you all that I do NOT feel in the mood for any more disturbances, whispers or giggles.'

The children bent over their books, but there were many scornful glances thrown at Patrick. He bent over his book too, kicking himself for thinking that was a trick of Julian's – and for being unable to prevent himself from blurting out about the bell-trick.

He hurried out in front of the others afterwards, afraid that they would take him to task. He ran to get his racket, meaning to go and bang the balls at the side-wall, to work off some of his anger.

But the class followed him, and soon he was surrounded by an angry little company. Elizabeth advanced on him, her eyes gleaming. 'I may as well tell you,' she began, 'that sooner or later complaints will be made about you at the next School Meeting, and—'

'Shut up,' said Patrick, and threw a ball up into the air to hit against the wall. 'Go away, all of you. I'm fed up with this school – and most of all I'm fed up with my grinning, very-very-clever cousin – and with Elizabeth, the cocky, high-and-mighty monitor!'

Elizabeth tried to grab his racket, to make him stop playing about – he should be *made* to listen to what was being said! But Patrick swung it away and then raised it again to hit another ball.

He hit Elizabeth instead! Crack! The racket descended heavily on her right shoulder and she yelled. Julian leapt at Patrick, his face blazing. Coward! To hit a girl!

He caught Patrick by the shoulder, and held him tightly. 'We'll call a Meeting tonight!' he said. 'We'll say that for the rest of this term Patrick shall not play tennis again! We'll confiscate his racket for hitting Elizabeth.'

'Let me go!' said Patrick, fiercely. 'It was an accident – but I'm glad I hit her, all the same. She deserved it! Call your Meeting if you like – I shan't be there! And I'll tell you this, Julian – you're only doing this to keep me out of the second team, because you want to be in it yourself, instead of me!'

He flung Julian off, made a dive under the arms held up to stop him, and tore away at top speed.

'Let him go,' said Rosemary. 'Elizabeth, are you hurt?'

'No. Not really,' said Elizabeth. 'Only bruised. Isn't he a beast, though? Julian, it's bad luck on you to have a cousin like that!'

'We'll send him to Coventry! We won't speak to him for the rest of the term! We'll see that he doesn't touch a racket again!' said several voices.

'Telling a fib about Julian!'

'Wasn't it strange, though, those birds falling down the chimney the very day after Julian had put a bell up there!'

'Jolly decent of Miss Ranger not to say anything more about it when Patrick blurted out the truth,' said John.

A monitor from the second form appeared round the corner. 'I say! What's happening? Didn't you hear the bell, you idiots? You won't get anything to eat if you don't hurry up. I've been sent to find you.'

'Oh goodness – we never even *heard* the bell!' said Elizabeth, still rubbing her shoulder. 'Come on, everyone. All this has made me feel jolly hungry.'

Patrick did not come in to the meal. Miss Ranger did not inquire about him. She knew that he was upset and probably did not want to appear in public just then. Nobody bothered about him. Let him miss his meal if he wanted to. Do him good! That was what most of his class thought.

Elizabeth and Julian did not attempt to call a big School Meeting that night after all. When they had cooled down a bit it seemed rather silly to air the grievances of the first form in front of the whole school.

'After all, the next Meeting is on Saturday,' said Elizabeth. 'If Patrick doesn't behave himself for the rest of the week, we'll make a formal complaint about him then, and deal with him. I don't really believe he *meant* to hit me, Julian.'

'Well, perhaps not,' said Julian. 'He's an unpleasant bit of work, though, isn't he? I wish he hadn't come here. It's hard enough to beat *you* in order to be top of the form – it's getting to be even harder to beat Patrick – and I'm really a bit tired of practising my tennis at every moment, just so that he won't be in the second team!'

'It's jolly good for you to work hard at things!' said Elizabeth, remembering how don't-carish Julian had been the term before. 'I wonder where Patrick is? He hasn't shown up at all.'

'Good thing too,' said Julian. 'I expect he doesn't want to face the form. They'll do to him what he's been doing to you and me – they'll turn their backs whenever he appears!'

'Where did you put his racket?' asked Elizabeth. 'Have you hidden it so that he can't get it?'

'Yes. I've put a note in his desk to say that he can have it back if he apologizes to you,' said Julian. 'Otherwise, he won't have it.'

'Oh, dear – I don't really like all this upset,' said Elizabeth. 'It makes me have feelings that aren't at all suitable to a monitor. Even if Patrick comes and apologizes – and I believe he'd rather lose his racket than do that – I shan't feel like accepting his apology. I might say something rude and begin the upset all over again.'

'Well, do,' said Julian with a grin. 'I've no objection!'

'Come and have a game of tennis,' said Elizabeth. 'Let's slash out at the balls and work some of our crossness out of us. Come on!'

So out they went and were soon hitting the balls with a will. When they had finished they looked about for Patrick. Would he come and apologize? He must have seen the note in his desk by now.

But he was still nowhere to be seen!

CHAPTER FIVE

AT MIDNIGHT

THE CHILDREN were allowed to take their tea into the garden that day and have little picnics in friendly groups. That was always fun. Elizabeth, Julian, John, Harry, Rosemary and Joan found a place in the shade by some bushes.

'Anyone seen Patrick?' asked Elizabeth, biting into bread and honey.

'Yes. I saw him coming out of our classroom,' said John. 'I don't know where he is now though. Having tea by himself somewhere, I expect, brooding over his woes.'

'Oh, well – don't let's think about him any more,' said Elizabeth. 'He's keeping out of our way and I'm not surprised.'

They thought no more about Patrick. Elizabeth went back with the others to fetch her prep and do it out-of-doors that lovely warm evening. But it was difficult to learn French verbs when the swallows swooped and darted in the sky, and bees hummed happily in the flowers around. French verbs didn't go well with swallows and bees.

When they all went up to bed Elizabeth looked round once more for Patrick. She hated to go to bed without making up a quarrel, though she had often done so.

She called to Julian as he went to the boys' dormitory. 'Julian! See if Patrick is in your dormy.'

He wasn't. Julian began to feel a bit worried. Where was the idiot? Sulking somewhere? He debated whether or not to report that Patrick hadn't come up to bed. He decided that he wouldn't – not for a little while, anyhow.

'If I do report him, and he's hiding somewhere, waiting till we're all in bed because he's afraid of being jeered at, he'll get into more trouble,' thought Julian. 'And he'll think I've reported him just for that reason – to get him into a row. Blow him! Well, I'll get into bed, and wait till he comes before I go to sleep.'

He told this to John and Harry, who shared the dormy with him and Patrick. They agreed to do the same as Julian – wait till Patrick came before they went to sleep. 'And we won't rag him at all,' said Harry. 'He's had a pretty poor day.'

But – alas for their good resolves – every boy was

fast asleep before five minutes had gone! The girls fell asleep, too – but Elizabeth kept waking up and wondering about Patrick.

As she turned over for about the twelfth time, she thought she heard a rustling of paper. She sat up in bed and groped for what she had heard. Yes – there *was* a bit of paper somewhere in her bed. It must have slipped down there when she had got in. She pulled it out.

She put on her light and read what was written there. It was a note from Patrick!

'ELIZABETH,

You can believe me or not, but I didn't *mean* to hit you, and I apologize for my racket slipping down on your shoulder like that. It was partly your fault for grabbing at it. I wish I hadn't blurted out about Julian's trick, too, but I said it without thinking.

You won't be bothered with me any more. I'm fed up with Whyteleafe and I'm going away tonight as soon as it's dark. I'm going home. It was mean to take my racket away from me. I would have liked to take it with me. There's no use in staying at Whyteleafe – Julian is determined to out-do me in everything – but the tennis isn't fair, because I really *could* do well at that, and I might have got into the

37

second team.

Nobody likes me now. I don't like anybody either, least of all you. I hope there's a good old upset about me running away – it will serve this beastly school right!

PATRICK'

Elizabeth read this in the greatest horror. She sat staring at the letter in a panic. Patrick must have slid it under the sheet for her to find it when she got into bed, and it had slipped down when she got in. What a pity she hadn't read it hours before – she might have stopped Patrick from being such an idiot as to run away!

She slipped on her dressing-gown and went to Julian's dormy. She put her head round the door and called softly: 'Julian! Julian!'

Julian was a light sleeper. He awoke at once. He went to the door. 'What are you doing here?' he said. 'You'll get into a frightful row.'

'It's about Patrick,' said Elizabeth. 'Come down into our classroom and read a note he's left in my bed. It's urgent, Julian.'

Julian put on his dressing-gown and the two went down into their classroom. They did not dare to switch on the light, but shone their torches on to the note. Julian read it in dismay.

'I say! The fathead! We'll have the police looking for him, and Whyteleafe in the papers, and there'll be a frightful disturbance,' he groaned. 'What in the world are we to do?'

'When do you suppose he went?' whispered Elizabeth. 'He wouldn't go till it was dark, would he? It can't have been dark very long because these summer nights are light for ages. Should we snoop round a bit and see if we can see anything of him?'

'We could. But he'll be gone,' said Julian, feeling most uncomfortable at the thought of having to go and wake the head-master and two head-mistresses, and show them the note. He began to feel that he hadn't come very well out of the affair himself. It was possible that the grown-ups might think him rather mean to have deliberately tried to out-shine Patrick, and not give him a chance to make good at anything.

There was no sign of Patrick, so the two decided most reluctantly to go and tell someone in authority. They made their way down the back stairs of the school, meaning to go through to the hall and up the stairs to where the staff bedrooms were.

And then, as they went down the back stairs, they heard a sound. They stopped. What was that? Where did it come from?

'It's in the cupboard,' whispered Julian. 'Look – over

40

there, where all the sports things are kept. But Patrick can't be there!'

Another sound came from the cupboard – a sound as if the door was being jiggled a little. The two crept up to it. The key was in the lock. Julian did not touch the key, but cautiously turned the handle. The door would not open. It was obviously locked on the outside.

'Whoever's in there is locked in,' whispered Julian. They looked at one another. 'It can't be Patrick. He wouldn't go to this cupboard – it's only got spare sports things in.'

Julian spoke quietly at the crack of the door. 'Who's in here?'

A voice answered at once. 'Who's that? I'm locked in here. I'm Patrick. Let me out.'

Elizabeth clutched at Julian joyfully. So Patrick hadn't gone! Julian was glad, too. He put his mouth to the crack again.

'Patrick. It's me, Julian – and Elizabeth's here, too. We found your note just now. You're an idiot. We are idiots, too, so we're quits.'

There was a silence. 'You let me out at once,' came Patrick's voice, rather shaky.

'All right – on one condition,' said Julian. 'Do you promise to give up your mad idea of running off tonight, and will you go straight to bed?'

41

'No,' said Patrick.

'All right. We're off to bed,' said Julian.

A frantic voice came from inside the cupboard. 'Don't go! It's horrible in here – smelly and lonely and uncomfortable. Let me out. I won't run off. I promise.'

'How did you get locked in here?' asked Julian, still not turning the key.

'Well – I badly wanted to take my racket with me,' said Patrick's voice, 'and I didn't know where it had been hidden. So I looked everywhere. The last place I thought of was this old sports cupboard – but while I was looking someone came along, slammed the door and locked me in.'

'Matron, I expect,' said Julian. 'She's always slamming doors and locking them. Well – I'll let you out.'

He unlocked the door and shone his torch into the cupboard. Patrick was there, blinking, looking very tousled and untidy, and rather white in the face.

Elizabeth felt sorry for him. She slid her arm through his. 'Patrick! I know you didn't mean to hit me! Of *course* I know it. I think we all got silly and excited. We none of us behaved very well.'

'You didn't come to any meals,' said Julian, remembering. 'Aren't you hungry?'

'Yes,' said Patrick going upstairs with them.

'Come and have some of my tuck, then,' said Julian.

'But don't give me away, because we're not supposed to have food at night. Elizabeth, look the other way. Being a monitor, you can't approve!'

'Oh, dear – can't I? But I *do*,' said Elizabeth. 'Patrick, I'll give you back your racket.'

She disappeared. The boys looked at one another. Julian shoved some more biscuits at Patrick. 'I don't *really* want to be in the second team,' said Julian, in a casual, ordinary voice. 'I just thought I would be to show you I *could* be. But all this practising bores me. In any case, you'll always be better than me in that. So go ahead.'

'Oh! Well, thanks,' said Patrick, seeing that this was Julian's way of patching up a quarrel. 'And *I* don't particularly want to slave to be top of the form. You're welcome to that position. We'll – er – split our brains, shall we?'

'Not a bad idea,' said Julian, munching a biscuit himself. 'Easier for us both. Hallo, here's Elizabeth back again.'

Elizabeth came in with the racket.

'Here you are, Patrick – and don't you dare hit me again with it!'

Patrick eagerly took his precious racket. Elizabeth suddenly realized what a tremendous lot he thought of it. She stared at him and he stared back. Then he suddenly smiled.

'Whatever would people think if they saw us all here, munching biscuits at this time of night!' he said. 'Now, don't you go reporting us at the next Meeting, Elizabeth!'

'Come on – we *must* go to bed!' said Julian hearing the clock strike midnight. 'We shall all be bottom of the form if we go on like this – staying up till past midnight!'

They crept upstairs very quietly and said goodnight on the landing. Elizabeth got into bed feeling at peace. Who would have thought things would turn out like this after all? Perhaps Patrick would settle down and be as proud of Whyteleafe as they all were.

Julian got into bed and was asleep at once. Patrick was in bed, too – but he was rather uncomfortable: he had taken his racket with him, feeling that he really couldn't let it out of his sight now; and it was a very hard and knobbly bed-fellow!

'Whyteleafe School's not so bad,' thought Patrick. 'Julian's not so bad, either. And as for Elizabeth, why, she's really quite nice. I'm very much afraid – *very* much afraid – I'm going to like her!'

THE NAUGHTIEST GIRL

Keeps a Secret

WHYTELEAFE

CHAO · ET · PERTINACIA

CONTENTS

CHAPTER ONE

A MESSAGE FROM WILLIAM AND RITA

'IT'S STILL lovely and sunny!' said Elizabeth happily, as she came out of the first form classroom with her friend Julian and his cousin, Patrick.

It was four o'clock in the afternoon. Lessons at Whyteleafe School had finished for the day. Along the corridor, boys and girls were bursting out of other classrooms, laughing and chattering noisily. Soon everyone would change out of school uniform, go to tea, then race off to take part in all their summer term activities.

There was always so much to do at Whyteleafe, thought Elizabeth. She loved it here now. She was still a monitor, though only an honorary one this term. There were no silly quarrels to worry about at present, no misunderstandings, no having to keep her temper. She and Patrick were just starting to get on reasonably well too. At the beginning of term they had been sworn enemies.

'This is my favourite time of year!' Elizabeth told Julian. 'The evenings are so light and long. It gives you time to fit everything in. I think I'll do some gardening later. I'm sure my lettuces need watering . . .'

'You've got to come and watch my tennis match first,' Patrick butted in.

Elizabeth nodded that she would, then continued.

'To think how much I hated it here at the beginning. It seems so strange now. I did everything I could to try and get myself sent home.'

'You mean, last summer, when you were the naughtiest girl in the school?' asked Julian, his green eyes showing his amusement. 'Wish I'd been here then. Poor Elizabeth. You've been trying to live it down ever since.'

'Well, I *have* lived it down,' said Elizabeth firmly.

'She wouldn't be a monitor if she hadn't,' Patrick pointed out. 'Anyway, it wasn't all that strange. Hating it here at the beginning, I mean. Look at me: three weeks ago I couldn't stand the place!'

It was true. Julian's cousin was new this term. And, although the two cousins looked rather alike, their characters were very different. Julian was lively and jokey, full of a self-confidence which came from being so clever and good at everything. He didn't, for example, in the least mind Elizabeth being a monitor. Patrick, when he'd first arrived, had been sullen and lacking in confidence. And he had deeply resented a girl telling him what to do.

'But you do like it here now, don't you, Patrick?' said Elizabeth.

'Not so terrible having a school with girls in it, is it?' said Julian, wryly. 'And you've got your trial for the second tennis team. Already! I call that good going.'

'Yes, not bad.' Patrick flushed with pride. 'Don't you two forget to come and watch me, either. I need supporters.'

'We'll come and support you,' piped up a voice in the corridor, just behind them. It was Arabella Buckley, with a friend. 'We'll come and cheer Patrick on, won't we, Rosemary?'

'Of course we'll come!' said Rosemary, who always agreed with everything Arabella said.

'We'll be there, Patrick,' said Elizabeth quietly. 'You know you can do it. I'm sure you can beat Roger.'

Roger Brown was a big boy, in his last term at Whyteleafe. But even so, he was only clinging on to his place in the school's second team by his fingertips.

Mr Warlow, the sports master, had watched Patrick play. He had also noted how hard the new boy practised each day. So a trial had been arranged.

After tea today, Roger and Patrick were to play

singles against each other. Everybody knew that if Patrick proved to be the stronger player, he would be awarded that precious place in the second team.

'You'll need that special racket of yours though, Patrick,' said Julian. 'Better not let Elizabeth get anywhere near it. You know what she's like.'

He kept a straight face as he said it. For a moment Elizabeth took him seriously.

'Julian Holland, what a hateful thing to say—'

Once, in a fit of rage with Patrick, Elizabeth had caused his lovely new racket to get soaked with rain. She hated to be reminded of it now.

It was Patrick who quickly smoothed things over. 'Don't worry! I'll guard it with my life!' he smiled.

Elizabeth smiled then, too, and the awkward moment passed.

At teatime, she even managed to make a joke at her own expense.

Patrick had changed into his tennis things and come over to join Elizabeth's table, carrying his precious tennis racket. It really was his pride and joy.

'If anything can bring me luck, it's this,' he told John McTavish. 'I'm useless with any other racket.'

'Better not leave it by my chair then, Patrick,' said Elizabeth. 'I think you ought to padlock it to the table leg. You know what I'm like!'

A MESSAGE FROM WILLIAM AND RITA

All the boys and girls at the table laughed. Julian gave Elizabeth's arm an approving pinch. He was pleased to see his friend not taking herself too seriously.

Arabella, however, turned her pretty little doll-like face towards Patrick and smiled primly.

'It wasn't so funny at the time, though, was it, Patrick?' she said.

Elizabeth ground her teeth.

She tried hard to think of something clever to say, to get back at Arabella. But at that moment, someone came hurrying over to their table.

'Elizabeth?'

'Joan!'

Elizabeth was always pleased to see her special friend. But Joan was older and had gone up to the second form quite quickly, so the two girls saw less of each other these days. Elizabeth knew that if she did well at lessons this term she, too, would go up in September. Then she and Joan would be together again. Elizabeth was looking forward to that.

'I've got a message for you,' said Joan softly. She was always quietly spoken. 'It's from William and Rita. They would like you to come along to their study after tea, please.'

Elizabeth frowned in surprise. William and Rita were the head boy and the head girl of Whyteleafe School.

'Are you coming too? Are all the monitors coming?' Elizabeth asked. She was puzzled because there was no school Meeting due for a day or two yet.

Sometimes all the monitors were called in if there was something important to discuss before the Meeting. The Meeting was held once a week. All pupils had to attend. It was a kind of Parliament. At Whyteleafe it was the boys and girls themselves who made many of the important rules and saw that they were applied fairly. When problems arose, they sorted them out themselves. The teachers rarely had to be involved.

'No, they just want you,' said Joan. 'I don't know what it's about.'

Elizabeth rushed through her tea after that. What did William and Rita want to see her about?

'Hey, Monitor, don't gobble your food. You're supposed to set a good example,' teased Julian. 'William and Rita aren't going to disappear down a big hole. They can wait,' he added, carelessly.

'I'll finish up your scrambled egg if you can't manage it all, Elizabeth,' said her friend Kathleen, all smiles and rosy cheeks as usual.

'Would you really like it?' asked Elizabeth, gratefully. 'Cook's given me too much. Then I can slip off and see what they want with me. I haven't done anything bad lately, have I, Kathleen?'

She picked up her remaining chocolate biscuits, put them in her pocket, scraped her chair back, then got up and left the table.

'If you'd done anything bad it would have to wait for the Meeting, Elizabeth!' Julian called after her, 'and the whole school would have to hear about it. You know that's the system here. See you later!'

'Come straight on to the tennis-courts!' Patrick added. 'I'll be playing soon.'

But Elizabeth, hurrying out of the hall, didn't hear them. The chatter and clatter from other tables filled her ears and drowned out the boys' voices.

There was only one thought in her mind at present.

Why had the head boy and girl asked her to come and see them?

CHAPTER TWO

ELIZABETH UPSETS PATRICK

'COME IN,' called the head boy, as Elizabeth tip-tapped nervously on the study door.

It was a lovely, sunny room with a big window. William and Rita were sitting in their armchairs.

Rita pointed to the visitor's armchair. 'Do sit down, Elizabeth.' She was smiling and speaking kindly.

William was smiling, too.

The little girl's heart stopped beating quite so fast. She sat down in the visitor's armchair with its cheerful chintz cover.

'We've got a problem,' explained William. 'We have discussed it with Miss Belle. But now we'd like your advice. We would like to know what you think.'

Miss Belle! Elizabeth's chest swelled with pride. Miss Belle and Miss Best were the joint headmistresses of Whyteleafe School. The children called them The Beauty and The Beast. If Miss Belle were involved in this, then it must be an important matter on which her opinion was being sought.

ELIZABETH UPSETS PATRICK

Rita decided they should get it over quickly.

'The fact is, we shouldn't really have thirteen monitors,' she said. 'It's always been the tradition that we have twelve. And as I'm sure you've noticed at the Meetings this term, Elizabeth, it's almost impossible to get thirteen chairs on the platform. There's always one person practically falling off the end.'

Elizabeth nodded. She *had* noticed that.

It had all come about because, owing to lots of misunderstandings last term, Elizabeth had lost her position as monitor. A second former, Susan, had been elected in her place. But then, at the end of term, when all the misunderstandings had been sorted out, the first form had asked for Elizabeth to be reinstated, as an honorary monitor.

'For once, in a way, we must have an extra one', Miss Belle had agreed. For she knew how much Elizabeth wanted to prove herself a good, wise and sensible monitor, after some of the reckless things she had done.

'It seemed such a lovely idea to have an extra monitor at the time,' continued Rita. 'But we've discussed it with Miss Belle and we're all agreed that it can't be a permanent arrangement.'

William looked straight at Elizabeth.

'We've been wondering whether we should ask Susan to stand down, Elizabeth. What do you think?'

'Poor Susan! That wouldn't be fair!' exclaimed Elizabeth without hesitation. 'She has had hardly any time as a monitor! And she *was* elected by the whole school, with proper votes and everything . . .'

Her voice tailed away. She swallowed very hard. There was no alternative.

'Let *me* stand down,' she said nobly, with a weak, wobbly smile. 'I've had a good turn as a monitor now. I wanted to prove myself—'

'You have certainly done that, Elizabeth,' said Rita.

'Good kid,' said William softly. 'Are you quite sure, Elizabeth? We could ask Susan, you know. She was only elected because of the misunderstandings about your behaviour.'

'I am quite sure,' said Elizabeth, somehow managing to keep that brave, wobbly smile in place. She wanted to rush away now, as fast as she possibly could.

'Well done, Elizabeth,' said Rita. 'William will announce it at this week's Meeting then.'

As Elizabeth left the study, William held open the door for her. He gave her a pat on the back as she went.

'You will be elected monitor again one day, Elizabeth. I am quite sure of that.'

'Thank you, William,' replied Elizabeth, feeling very noble.

She was proud of herself for being so calm and

sensible in front of William and Rita, but as soon as the study door closed behind her, she felt a hot prickling sensation behind her eyes. She was going to cry! She must run somewhere safe, where nobody could see her.

No longer a monitor!

She needed to be alone. She needed time to think, to get over the shock. Where could she go? Where was quiet and unhurried – peaceful?

The school gardens. She often went there when she wanted to think.

She made a beeline for the gardens at once. She shut herself in the farthest greenhouse.

Then she let the tears flow.

'It's not fair!' she sobbed. 'It's not, not fair!'

She forgot all about Patrick and his tennis trial. She forgot that she had promised to come and support him.

Patrick's hopes and dreams had completely slipped her mind.

'Pull yourself together, Elizabeth Allen,' she told herself, some time later. 'Stop being a silly baby. It's perfectly fair and you know it is.'

She dried her eyes as best she could. She put her sodden handkerchief away in her pocket. Then she peeped cautiously through the greenhouse windows.

There were very few people around. There was no

sign of John Terry, the senior boy who ran the school gardens. Good. She did not feel like facing anyone yet, not even John. He was the most kind and understanding of boys, of course. He cared nothing for important positions, monitorships and the like, only for his beloved garden. John was a genius at growing things and at teaching others how to grow them. With his team of volunteers, he helped to provide enough fresh fruit and vegetables to supply the kitchens at Whyteleafe School for much of the year.

Even so, she wanted a little more time on her own.

'Elizabeth,' she told herself, 'you will no longer be a monitor after this week's Meeting. Just get that into your head! It's perfectly fair. And you've got to accept it!'

She felt rather cross with herself for not having foreseen this. It was quite true that since the beginning of term it had been uncomfortable and awkward having an extra chair on the platform at Meetings. She should have offered to stand down earlier! But it was such fun being a monitor, you wanted it to go on forever. So she had simply buried her head in the sand, as an ostrich does when it sees trouble ahead.

'All good things come to an end, Elizabeth,' her last governess used to tell her. 'And sometimes sooner than you expect.'

ELIZABETH UPSETS PATRICK

Elizabeth had never listened to a word that Miss Scott said. She blushed to think how rude she had been. Of all the awful things she had said, not only to Miss Scott but to the long line of governesses before her. Not surprisingly, none of them had ever stayed very long. But now she realized Miss Scott had been speaking sense, after all.

'But Rita says I've proved I can be a good monitor. And William says my turn will come again.'

Elizabeth began to feel more cheerful. It was very warm in the greenhouse. She went and opened the door wide and stood there for a while, gazing out.

The sun was sinking lower. A gentle breeze was making rustling sounds in the blackcurrant bushes. Somewhere a blackbird was singing. A sweet, warm scent wafted from the wallflowers that bordered the nearest vegetable plot. There were butterflies settled there, sharing the flowers with the buzzing bees. In a reverie, Elizabeth found her chocolate biscuits, rather warm and sticky by now. She ate them slowly, a melting mouthful at a time.

'There's more to life than being a monitor,' Elizabeth decided. 'I shall have more time to myself. I must try and get good at lots of things. I shall make myself learn to be a brilliant gardener and grow wonderful things.'

She stared at the neat rows of broad beans that John

and some of the younger boys had planted. How well they seemed to be doing. Although they did need weeding.

Most of Elizabeth's efforts to grow things so far had come to grief, usually because she had forgotten to look after them properly. But she knew that her lettuces were doing well. She closed the greenhouse door behind her and slowly walked round to have a look at them.

'They've grown again!' she exclaimed as she came round the corner.

She had spent some of her own allowance on lettuce seeds. John had told her it was always worth getting the very best quality. She had planted the seeds out in neat rows, watched them grow into tiny lettuces, weeded them carefully once a week. Now she was beginning to get her reward.

The lettuces had suddenly burgeoned. Some of them had formed proper hearts. They were beginning to look like real lettuces. At this rate, they would be ready before half-term. *Her* lettuces would be going into lots of school salads. That thought made Elizabeth feel very proud.

'But they *do* need watering, poor things,' she realized. 'The ground all round them is quite parched looking. I'll go and fill the watering cans.'

The two watering cans were lined up by the garden

tap. Before filling them, Elizabeth turned on the tap and cupped some water in her hands. She washed the chocolate off her hands then doused her face clean. Now nobody would be able to see that she had been crying.

She filled the watering cans but, when she reached her lettuce rows, she stopped. Was there still some heat in the sun? John had once explained to her that watering should be done in the cool of the day, morning or evening.

So Elizabeth set to work weeding between the rows of broad beans, instead. It was hard physical work and it had a wonderfully soothing effect on her. By the time she had finished she felt glowing with good health, and much more at peace with herself. She could face the world now.

'I'm getting quite used to the idea of not being a monitor,' she told herself. 'I shan't tell anyone yet. I'll wait till it's announced at the Meeting. That will give me a bit more time to get really calm and strong about it. I expect Julian will tease me. I hope Arabella doesn't crow.'

The sun was now much cooler. Elizabeth returned to her lettuces and carefully watered each row. She had just finished when John Terry appeared.

There were other boys and girls arriving, too. She could hear their voices beyond the yew hedge.

'That's well done, Elizabeth. Just the right amount of water,' he said. 'You don't want to drown them. They're doing well, aren't they?'

'Do you think so, John?'

'I'll tell you something, though. This is the last time you'll have to water them for a while.' He looked up at the sky. 'This is the end of the sunshine. There's going to be heavy rain for two or three days.'

Like any good gardener, John always took careful notes of the weather forecast.

'Oh. Is there? But it will save me a job, then!' said Elizabeth cheerfully.

'Well, it will save you one job. But it could give you another. You see, Elizabeth—'

'John!' someone shouted.

Before John could finish, a boy came marching over, carrying a garden fork.

'Where exactly do you want this ground turned over?' asked the boy.

'I'll show you in a minute. I just want to explain something to Elizabeth.'

But Elizabeth was staring at the new arrival in dismay. He was a large, heavily-built boy, one of the oldest in the school. He often came and helped in the gardens. He had big feet and big red hands and a gentle face. Elizabeth noticed how pale he looked,

66

as though he were unwell. He was still in his tennis shorts. It was Roger Brown, Patrick's tennis opponent.

The match must be over!

Patrick's tennis trial! It had gone right out of her mind!

'It's all right, John, I've got to dash now!'

Elizabeth started running.

'Tell me another time. I've realized I shouldn't be here!' she called back.

She ran as fast as she could, all the way to the tennis-courts.

Patrick was sitting on a bench near the courts with Julian, surrounded by first formers.

Elizabeth raced towards them, panting for breath.

'Did you win, Patrick?' she shouted.

'Of course he did!' shrilled Arabella.

'Elizabeth!' exclaimed Julian. 'What happened to you? Why didn't you come?'

Elizabeth went very red.

'I forgot,' she said.

'Patrick won!' cried Arabella triumphantly. 'He's going to be in the second team! It made all the difference to him having his friends here, cheering him on. Fancy you just forgetting to come, Elizabeth.'

Elizabeth thought how horrible it sounded, put like that.

She pushed past Arabella to get to Patrick, her hand outstretched. She wanted to shake his hand.

'Congratulations, Patrick. You really deserve to be in the team after all your hard work! I truly meant to come and watch the match. I'm sorry. It's just that, after I'd been to see William and Rita, I had such important things—'

She broke off. She had been going to say 'such important things to think about'. But that sounded bad, too, as though Patrick's tennis trial was *not* important.

In any case, Patrick was ignoring her outstretched hand. He was getting to his feet.

'I've got important things to do as well,' he said. 'Now I'm in the second team, I've got to do some more work on my service action. I'm going to have a good go against the school wall. There's a match on Saturday.'

Without even glancing at Elizabeth, he strode away. There was a sulky expression on his face. He was overjoyed to have beaten Roger and to have won his place in the team. But he had been wondering what had happened to Elizabeth. He had even, in fact, been worrying about her. Whereas she, it seemed, had simply forgotten all about him!

What were these important things, anyway?

Later, he learnt from young Peter what Elizabeth had been doing while his match was in progress. She

had been weeding some vegetable plot in the school gardens. Peter had seen her there.

That was all. Weeding! Even Julian's eyebrows shot up in surprise when Patrick passed on this information.

'She's good at heart though, Patrick,' he shrugged. 'You'll find that out.'

Elizabeth had no intention of confessing to Julian, far less to Patrick, that she had been crying like a baby in the greenhouse. But she would go out of her way to be nice to Patrick, she decided. Then he would soon forget her lapse.

In fact, by cocoa-time that evening, Patrick was already in a mood to forgive Elizabeth and give her another chance. His serving practice had gone well and he was very excited about the match against Woodville on Saturday.

'It's a home match, so you'll have to come and watch,' he told Elizabeth. 'Especially as you're a monitor.'

Elizabeth smiled wryly, thinking of the surprise in store for them all at the weekly Meeting. She chose her words with care.

'Monitor or not,' she said, 'I'll be there.'

CHAPTER THREE

PATRICK MAKES A LITTLE JOKE

IT WAS time for the weekly Meeting. The whole school was required to attend. The boys and girls looked forward to it. It was the day their money was given out. After that, there were always complaints to be heard and interesting things to discuss.

It had been raining for two days and outdoor hobbies had been cancelled, even riding. They were pleased to have the Meeting coming up after tea to liven things up. The weather was supposed to get better by the evening, much to Patrick's relief. He was longing to get more practice before Saturday's match.

All the children trooped into the gym, which doubled as the school hall. In the Easter holidays, a platform had been built at one end for the school's little plays and concerts. It made the Meetings much better, too. There was a long row of chairs up on the platform, facing into the hall. There sat the school's twelve elected monitors, six each side of the head-boy and girl.

William and Rita, in the centre, sat behind a small table. On the table was a Big Book, in which lots of things were written. By the Book lay a small hammer, which they used like a Judge's gavel. They *were* rather like Judges, with their Jury alongside them, Elizabeth always thought. This was not only the school's Parliament, where problems were discussed and rules made, it was also its Court. All complaints of bad behaviour or wrongdoing had to be brought to the Meeting. Problems were aired in public, punishments decided upon if necessary. Above all, boys and girls were made to face up honestly to their faults.

Miss Belle and Miss Best, the joint headmistresses, sat right at the back of the hall, with Mr Johns, the senior master. They rarely took any part in the proceedings and only then if their advice was requested.

Elizabeth had hated the Meetings when she first came to Whyteleafe School. She had thought them a perfectly silly idea. She had since changed her opinion.

But where was she today?

'That's funny,' said Julian, as he filed into the hall with the rest of the first form. He was staring towards the platform. 'Why isn't Elizabeth up there with the other monitors?'

'She must be late,' giggled Belinda.

'But there's no chair up there for her, either.' Julian

was always very quick to notice things. 'It's odd.'

Elizabeth had still not told anybody. It had been too early to tell, she had reasoned. It would come out at the Meeting. She would be quite composed by then. That would be soon enough.

'I wonder what's going on?' mused Julian now.

He did not have to wait long to find out.

All the benches in the hall had filled up. Some of the younger children sat cross-legged on the floor. They were in the junior class, which was below the first form. The babble of whispering and chattering was getting louder and louder.

William stood up and banged the gavel.

'Silence, please.'

There was an instant hush.

'Before the Meeting starts, I have something to say.'

He smiled down at the person who was perched on the very end of a bench, in the front row.

'Stand up, please, Elizabeth. Come up here, on to the platform.'

As she stood up, for all her resolve, Elizabeth found her legs going wobbly. She felt butterflies in her tummy. The whole school was looking at her. She had so hoped that William or Rita would just make the announcement very quickly and quietly. This was awful.

Determined to look dignified, she walked slowly up on to the platform.

Julian and the others watched in surprise. It was their very own Elizabeth. The bold, bad girl. What was all this about?

'For much of last term, Elizabeth was a monitor,' William told the school. 'This term, as a special dispensation, we asked her to stay on for a while – as an honorary monitor. We were so proud of her, weren't we? Well, she has done a really good stint and the time's come for Elizabeth to stand down now. I think we are all agreed that she has been a very fine monitor indeed. I want us all to show our appreciation.'

He gave a brief nod. Rita rose from her chair. Then all twelve monitors on the platform did likewise. As William shook Elizabeth by the hand, the head girl and monitors gave her a standing ovation.

The whole school joined in. With her head held high, Elizabeth came down from the platform. As she walked down the hall to join her own form's benches, children on all sides started cheering loudly. After two days of being cooped up indoors it was good to have an excuse to shout and cheer!

Elizabeth felt weak with relief. The experience had not been humiliating, after all. It had been just the reverse. How tactfully William and Rita had handled it.

PATRICK MAKES A LITTLE JOKE

She felt buoyed up, almost cheerful.

'You dark horse,' whispered Julian, as she sat down beside him. Belinda, Kathleen, even Patrick, they all slapped her on the back. Patrick had reason to know how good a monitor she had been but was secretly relieved. He would never get used to the idea of girls being allowed to boss boys around. This would be better, he felt.

Arabella was clapping politely, for quite the wrong reasons.

Julian squeezed Elizabeth's arm. 'Brave girl!' he hissed, green eyes twinkling. Alone amongst the first formers, he had continued to be curious to know why William and Rita had summoned her the other day. He had been mystified that Elizabeth, usually so talkative, had never referred to it. Now he understood.

Elizabeth simply gave a huge sigh of relief. William was banging his gavel and calling for silence again; time to get on with the Meeting. Thank goodness *that* was all over!

Thomas held up the big money-box now. All the children who had been sent money during the past week had to come forward and drop it inside. After that, every member of the school was handed two pounds from the box, as their spending money for the week.

At Whyteleafe School they did not believe in some children having more money to spend than others. This was the way they shared it out fairly. If any pupil wanted extra money for a special purpose, they had to ask. The Meeting then decided if it was a proper reason.

'Please, I left all my stamps out in the rain and now they're useless,' said Peter, standing up. 'I need to write some letters this week. Can I have some extra money to buy more stamps?'

No, the stamps getting all messy and stuck together was due to Peter's own carelessness, the Meeting decided.

'You'll just have to go without a few sweets this week,' Rita said kindly.

Mary wanted the Florist Shop in the village to send some flowers to her aunt, who was very ill in hospital.

'Request granted,' said the head-boy. 'Thomas, give Mary an extra five pounds from the box.'

After that there were three complaints to be heard. Two were proper complaints and one was silly.

'Arabella Buckley keeps making faces at me in class,' said Daniel Carter. 'She keeps trying to make me laugh. And if I do laugh, I'll get into trouble.'

'That is not a proper complaint,' said William sternly. 'That is just telling tales. Sit down at once, Daniel.'

The first form were making spluttering sounds as they tried not to giggle.

'Try looking the other way, Daniel!' whispered Belinda.

'Arabella's not making faces!' hissed Julian. 'She always looks like that!'

Arabella, who had been feeling so triumphant, turned bright pink. She prided herself on her prettiness.

William banged the table again.

'Before we close the Meeting, some congratulations are in order. Roger, stand up please.'

The big senior boy shambled to his feet. He was embarrassed to be in the limelight. His gentle face, even at the best of times, wore a slightly anxious look. It was just his normal expression.

'As we know,' said William, 'Roger is in the top class and in his last term at Whyteleafe. He has just heard recently that he has won a scholarship to Holyfield School. An academic scholarship. Well done, Roger. Can we give him a round of applause, please?'

As everyone clapped, Roger Brown gave a shy nod then quickly sat down.

'Isn't Holyfield the sporty school?' whispered a second former, to one of his classmates. 'Will he get on all right there?'

Everyone knew he'd lost his place in the second tennis team, to a mere first former.

'They have other people as well,' the friend whispered

back. 'People who are musical or just plain brainy, like Rog. He should be all right!'

The first formers, as they trooped out of the hall, were much more interested in the news about Elizabeth.

'You can be ordinary Elizabeth Allen now,' said Belinda, kindly. 'It will give you more time for riding and everything.'

'Will it feel funny, not being a monitor any more?' asked Kathleen.

'Just for a while, I expect,' replied Elizabeth calmly.

The boys teased her a bit, especially Julian.

'Now you can go straight back to being the naughtiest girl in the school again!' he laughed.

'Never!' retorted Elizabeth. She was standing up to the teasing well.

But then Patrick struck a discordant note.

'Of course, there's no need for you to come and watch me play in the school match now,' he said. 'I won't want you there if you're not an important monitor.'

He was trying to make a joke. But Patrick's jokes were always rather heavy-handed.

His words really stung. For a moment, Arabella and some of the others noted the look of dismay on Elizabeth's face.

By the time the little girl realized that he was not being serious, the main doors had been opened and everybody was whooping and rushing outside. It had stopped raining at last! It was going to be a fine evening.

'Hurray!' cried Patrick. 'I'll go and get my racket and practise my strokes.'

'I must go over to the stables and see the horses!' exclaimed Robert.

People were scattering in all directions.

'My lettuces,' thought Elizabeth. 'I can go and look at them. I'm sure the rain won't have washed them away. They weren't little babies any more. I wonder if they've grown?'

Luckily Elizabeth went and changed into her black wellies first, for there were puddles on all the paths in the school gardens. The big vegetable garden was all muddy and squelchy. She picked her way through the blackcurrant bushes, where the weak sunshine glistened on the wet leaves. Then, on past the dripping yew hedges to where her lettuces lay . . .

She gave a gasp of dismay.

'Oh, no!'

She stood and stared at her rows of lettuce, unable to believe her eyes. Only three days ago they had been such fine specimens, all plumping out nicely and forming hearts. Now they were unrecognizable.

'They're all chewed up. They look horrible—'

UGH! As she bent to touch the nearest plant, a fat

black slug slid off it. Gazing along the rows she saw another slug, then another. They were feasting on her lettuces! They must have been feasting on them for days.

'Elizabeth?'

John Terry appeared, carrying a large white jug.

'Oh, John. Look! Look! Horrible slugs. Big, fat, black ones. They've eaten all my lettuces. They've ruined them!'

He came and put an arm round her shoulders.

'I know,' he said, sadly. He looked down at her disappointed face. 'Poor Elizabeth! This was what I was trying to warn you about the other day, when they said there was rain on the way. If only you hadn't been in such a hurry—'

'You mean you *knew* this might happen?'

'When it's very wet we nearly always get an epidemic of slugs here. There are things you have to do about it.'

'But what, John? I don't understand.' Elizabeth frowned. Oh, *why* had she rushed away the other evening, just to hear about Patrick's silly tennis trial? Why hadn't she stopped and listened to John! 'What *can* you do?'

'Come with me and I'll show you.'

Still carrying the jug, he led her to a warm, sheltered part of the garden. There stood two rows of the finest looking lettuces anyone could hope for. One row consisted of the round variety, the other of the cos variety.

'The slugs have hardly got to them at all!' exclaimed Elizabeth in surprise.

'These are mine,' said John quietly. 'They're extra special, so I've had to take good care of them. We get slugs in this part of the garden, too, though not as many. But look, come along the rows with me and you'll see.'

For the first time, walking down the two rows with John, Elizabeth noticed there were old bowls placed at intervals, six of them in all. They were deep little bowls, old and chipped. Formerly school soup bowls, but long since thrown out. Elizabeth crouched down and peered inside one.

'It's full of dead slugs!' she shrieked.

'They all are,' replied John. 'They've all been drowned! Now, watch what I do, and I'll explain.'

John put down his jug. Then, working quickly, he gathered up the bowls two at a time. He tipped the bowlfuls of slimy, dead slugs on a nearby rubbish heap, then replaced the empty bowls in position.

'Some people put down pellets to kill slugs,' he told her. 'But that can be cruel. Pellets can harm other creatures, too. This way is much better.'

He asked Elizabeth to hand him the jug.

'Is there milk in here?' she asked, sniffing. 'It smells a bit off.'

'It is,' smiled John. 'Cook always has plenty of old milk left over. It doesn't matter if it's a bit sour. I cadge it off her.'

He went round his lettuces, slurping the clotting milk into the emptied bowls.

'The slugs love it. They even prefer it to lettuce. They climb into the bowls and drink till they're fat and bloated. They can't climb out again. They just quietly drown. They feel no pain.'

Elizabeth nodded. She was learning new things all the time.

She went to the rubbish heap and stared with interest at the mound of dead slugs there. It was very satisfying. 'No more eating lettuce for any of *you*,' she thought.

'It does make extra work, though,' sighed John, afterwards. Elizabeth noticed he looked rather tired. 'They say there's going to be a lot more wet weather next week. It's an extra job I could do without. That's what I was trying to explain to you, Elizabeth. That as soon as you stop having to water, there's a new job waiting to be done.'

They stood and looked at Elizabeth's lettuces, at the wreckage.

Elizabeth bit her lip, furious both with the slugs

and with herself. If only she'd stopped and listened to John, her lettuces might still be all right. To make matters worse, she had boasted about them, too. How the first form would laugh if they could see them now.

'You must ask for extra money at the next Meeting,' said John kindly. 'To buy new seeds with. It's not too late for a second planting. They would be ready by August.'

Elizabeth shook her head stubbornly. The next Meeting was a whole week away, August an eternity. It would be the summer holidays. Nobody would be here to see them! If she couldn't watch her *own* lettuces grow and flourish, she would just have to admire John's.

'I've got an idea, John!' she exclaimed suddenly. 'Let me look after *your* lettuces, instead. You've got far too many jobs to do. You look really tired lately. And now you've shown me how to get rid of the slugs—'

'No! Certainly not!' said John sharply.

The little girl was speechless. It was as though she had been slapped.

'Are you going back now, Elizabeth?' he asked, more gently. 'Could you take the jug back to Cook for me, please?'

'No! Take it yourself!' she cried rudely. 'Aren't you frightened I might drop it and break it?'

With that she raced off, boiling with rage.

John, her friend John, was telling her she was useless. Not for one moment was she to be trusted with his precious lettuces! She could have wept with anger.

She was still feeling upset, an hour later.

'Hello, Elizabeth! Where did you disappear to?' asked her friends, as she came into the common room.

It annoyed her that they all looked so cheerful and happy. They were building a castle out of playing cards.

'You're not supposed to use the best playing cards for doing that!' said Elizabeth, before she could stop herself. 'Only the old ones.'

'But it's more fun with these!' laughed Julian.

From the other end of the room, Arabella was listening.

'You're not a monitor any more!' she called out. 'Has it slipped your mind, Elizabeth?'

Elizabeth turned away. She didn't feel like being friendly and sociable this evening. Or being teased.

'I'm tired,' she said, truthfully. 'I'm going to have an early night.'

'Really!' said Arabella, later. 'Did you notice? Elizabeth's face was like a thundercloud. It must be because you made that little joke this afternoon, Patrick. About her not being important and not needing to come to watch the match!'

'Perhaps she's sulking because she's not a monitor any more!' suggested Rosemary.

'Do you really think so?' wondered Patrick.

Across the room, Julian got up, stretched and yawned.

'Don't be stupid,' he said. His eyes were mocking. 'Elizabeth's made of stronger stuff than that. It will be something else, I expect. There will be something else going on in her head.'

He smiled to himself. With Elizabeth, there nearly always was.

CHAPTER FOUR

JOHN TELLS ELIZABETH A SECRET

JULIAN WAS right, of course. Elizabeth went to bed that night still feeling cross about the slugs but even angrier that John had insulted her.

The following morning, in the dining-hall, she chose to ignore him.

'Good morning, Elizabeth,' he said, as they jostled to collect their cornflakes. 'Nice sunny one.'

Lower lip trembling slightly, she deliberately turned her back on him.

Back at her table, all the talk was about the tennis match against Woodville today.

'Isn't it lucky the weather's fine?' said rosy-cheeked Kathleen. 'Don't you think so, Elizabeth?'

Elizabeth said nothing. She could feel herself smouldering again. How could John behave as though nothing had happened?

Everybody noticed how quiet she was.

'I was only joking yesterday, Elizabeth,' Patrick said awkwardly, when breakfast was over. 'You will come and watch the school match, this afternoon, won't you?'

Elizabeth nodded, hardly taking in what he was saying. Her mind was elsewhere.

'Of course, Patrick.'

Then, as she came out of the hall something unexpected happened.

She found John Terry lying in wait for her. He took her firmly by the arm.

'I've got to speak to you, Elizabeth.'

He propelled her round the corner, into the corridor, then gently pushed her into an empty classroom.

'Quick, in here. Nobody must hear.'

Elizabeth was too surprised to protest. Her bad feelings about John began to melt away. What was this all about? What did he want to say to her that was so important?

'Now look, Elizabeth,' he said, once the door was safely closed. 'I didn't mean to upset you last night. You must have thought me really rude and cruel. It was kind of you to offer to look after my plants. But I *had* to shut you up. I was frightened I might give something away.'

'Give something away?' asked Elizabeth, puzzled. But she was already feeling better, much better.

'Look, Elizabeth, can you keep a secret? A really important one. At least, it's important to me. There's not one person in the school knows. Nobody at all.'

Elizabeth began to feel excited and proud.

'Of course I can keep a secret!' she replied.

'Cross your heart and swear to die?'

Elizabeth did so.

'Right. Well, this is the position . . .'

Lowering his voice, he explained everything. He had filled in forms for a competition. He was hoping his two varieties of lettuce would win a very special cup at the Village Show. The Show was in two weeks' time, just before half-term. As well as medals for crafts and wood-working, there was a silver cup for the best produce grown by a young person under sixteen. It could be fruit, flower, plant or vegetable.

John was a modest boy. He was not doing this in the hope of personal glory. That was the last thing on his mind.

'If by any chance my lettuces win the cup, it will be a great honour for the school. The local people sometimes grumble about us and think we have a soft life. This would show them that we don't. That we're not afraid to get our hands dirty and work the soil and grow good things.'

'It would be in the local newspaper as well,' said Elizabeth, feeling excited. 'Then everybody would find out what a good school it is, and that we're allowed to do things for ourselves here . . .'

JOHN TELLS ELIZABETH A SECRET

She paused.

'But why must it be such a secret, John? I'd love to tell everyone—'

'Don't you dare!' he said fiercely. Suddenly Elizabeth realized just how important this was to him. He could not bear the idea of failing. Nor would he be able to bear it for everyone to *know* he had failed. 'If, by any chance, I pull it off and win the cup, I want it to be a *complete surprise*. Now promise again that you'll keep my secret.'

'I promise,' said Elizabeth, solemnly. 'I truly swear.'

'I've only told *you* because I wanted you to know why . . . last night . . . I wanted you to understand.'

'John, I'm so glad you have told me,' said Elizabeth. She looked ashamed. 'And I'm sorry I was so rude and hot-tempered. I do understand now. Of course you couldn't trust me to look after your plants, when it's so important—'

John looked at her in surprise. He interrupted her.

'Oh, Elizabeth, you still don't understand. I suppose I haven't explained properly. I *would* trust you to look after them. You're one of my best young helpers. You make mistakes sometimes, but you learn fast. No, it's not that.'

Elizabeth was beginning to feel a warm glow of happiness spreading through her.

'It's the competition rules,' he said. 'I've signed the entry forms and I had to vouch that whatever I grow will be my own, unaided work. Except for all the help Nature gives me, of course,' he added, smiling. 'Don't you see, Elizabeth? Nobody is allowed to help me with these lettuces in any way. Don't you dare even try to water them for me!'

As they emerged from the empty classroom and went their separate ways, Elizabeth wanted to laugh out loud with happiness. She had completely misjudged John. She had been silly and hot-headed and jumped to conclusions. Now everything was all right again. She was so pleased he had shared his secret with her. She would keep it safe.

Later that morning, Julian asked her to go out riding with him. He noticed how happy she seemed as they trotted along on their ponies, side by side.

'You were like a bear with a sore head earlier!' he remarked lightly. 'Was something the matter?'

'It was just a misunderstanding about something,' replied Elizabeth, cheerfully.

'Oh!' Julian smiled. 'I might have guessed.'

At Elizabeth's dinner table, all the talk was about the afternoon's match against Woodville. The visitors were due to arrive at two o'clock. The first formers were all proud that Patrick was playing in the second team.

JOHN TELLS ELIZABETH A SECRET

'I've got to find my best form!' said Patrick edgily. He was feeling nervous. It was quite understandable. 'I did well in the trial. But if I play badly today it will be me out and Roger back in again!'

'We're all going to come and cheer you on, Patrick,' said Elizabeth.

After dinner, he left early to change into his tennis things. He now had a special badge sewn on his tennis shirt. It was a blue shield which showed that he was a second team player. He kept his precious tennis racket in a special place. He would collect that first before he changed. He was planning to get in a few practice strokes before the match.

The others sat around chatting in the dining-hall. They watched through the big windows as a minibus appeared in the drive.

'Here they come!' said Elizabeth. 'Watching this match is going to be fun.'

'Why are you in such a good mood, all of a sudden?' asked Arabella.

'Am I?' asked Elizabeth. 'Well, it's none of your business, even if I am.'

She stuck her tongue out at Arabella. Not being a monitor and having to set a good example had its compensations sometimes.

'Stop it, you two,' said Kathleen. 'Let's go and bag

places near the courts. We want to have a good view.'

Coming out of the dining-hall, they saw Patrick rushing towards them.

It was such a shock.

He hadn't changed yet. His black hair was completely dishevelled. His face was pale and distraught.

'My tennis racket!' he croaked. 'I've been looking for it everywhere. It's gone. Somebody must have taken it.'

CHAPTER FIVE

ELIZABETH IS ANGRY

PATRICK CONFRONTED Elizabeth. He was extremely agitated.

'Elizabeth, is this some kind of joke?' he asked. 'Have you hidden my racket? If you have, *please* give it back,' he pleaded. 'The match is starting in less than fifteen minutes.'

She stared at him in surprise.

'I don't know what you're talking about, Patrick,' she replied coldly.

'Of course she doesn't!' Julian scolded his cousin. 'As if Elizabeth would hide your racket—'

'What about the time she threw it in the bushes!'

'That was completely different,' replied Julian. 'Look, stop saying stupid things, Patrick. Try to think clearly. You must have mislaid it.' He added: 'If the worst comes to the worst, I'll lend you mine—'

'I don't want your silly old racket!' exploded Patrick. 'Mine's the only one I can play with properly. You know that perfectly well. I haven't mislaid it. It should be on the top shelf in the sports cupboard. Everybody knows that's where I keep it. And it isn't there, I tell you!'

It was such an unexpected thing to happen. The first formers all gathered round him, feeling worried and surprised. They so wanted to see Patrick do well in his first match. They had been looking forward to it.

Meanwhile the two dark-haired, green-eyed cousins squared up to each other as if spoiling for a fight. Kathleen pushed the pair apart.

'Stop quarrelling, for goodness' sake. Let's all try and *do* something.'

'Yes, let's try and find Patrick's racket for him!' exclaimed Belinda.

Julian's anger at his cousin's rudeness suddenly passed. He could see how desperate he looked. He cooled down and took command of the situation.

'Patrick, dash and get changed,' he said, giving him a gentle push. 'You've only just got time! The rest of us will look for the racket. It can't be far away. I'm sure we'll find it.'

With a helpless shrug, Patrick strode off.

Julian organized a search party.

'Martin, while he's in the changing rooms you go and hunt around his dormy. He puts the racket under his bed sometimes, whatever he says. Kathleen, could you come with me? We'll search the sports cupboard.

ELIZABETH IS ANGRY

It might have slipped to the very back of the shelf. Elizabeth, would you go round to the south wall? He spends hours there, practising his strokes. He might have left it behind . . .'

Soon Julian had everybody rushing round the school, hunting for the missing racket, even some of the second formers.

Elizabeth was not quite so forgiving. She felt hot and bothered inside at the way Patrick had insulted her. How dare he suggest that she might play a joke on him, just before his important match? As if she would do something like that, even to her worst enemy.

Nevertheless, she hurried out of the building and made her way to Patrick's favourite spot. He loved to come here, near the shrubbery, and bang tennis balls against the wall, over and over again. Julian had a point. He might have left the racket behind last time.

She ran up and down, looking for it. She even hunted round the corner. But there was no sign of it.

She stared towards the bushes. Was it possible that Patrick had used it to search for a ball? The holly, for example, was very prickly. It was easier to part the leaves with one's racket than use one's hands.

Somewhere in the distance, she could hear children coming outside, calling to one another despondently.

'It's no use! It's definitely not in the building!'

'He must have left it outside somewhere. Let's look round the field!'

If Patrick *had* used the racket to find a ball, reasoned Elizabeth, perhaps something had distracted him. A school bell, even. He might have placed the racket on the ground, rushed off to lessons and then forgotten where he had left it. Well, it was a faint possibility.

She started to comb through the bushes, diligently.

There was still no sign of it.

She came out of the shrubbery, sucking her hand where the holly had pricked her. She stared across the school field towards the tennis-courts. The team from Woodville School had arrived. They were filing on to the court, carrying their tennis rackets. The fifteen minutes was up!

She saw Patrick, in his tennis whites. He was waiting by the entrance to the tennis-courts. He was staring at the ground, the picture of dejection. Elizabeth's heart went out to him. She could hear Julian shouting from a window somewhere—

'It's no use, Patrick. We can't find it. I'll bring my racket out for you. I'm just coming.'

Elizabeth slowly began to circle the school buildings. Rather than go across to watch the match, her eyes searched out every nook and cranny. This was beginning to look very suspicious.

'I was cross with Patrick for talking to me like that,' she thought. 'But, in one way, he was right. Somebody *has* played a horrid joke on him. Somebody's taken his racket and hidden it somewhere. It's the only explanation. Otherwise, surely, one of us would have found it by now? Oh, poor Patrick!'

If only she could find it for him, thought Elizabeth, urgently. Her eyes scanned the big yard at the back of the school kitchens. It was out of bounds, but she crept in and searched around, even peering into some of the dustbins. Where would somebody hide a tennis racket? Not in a dustbin, surely? She was being silly. Where else? She walked through the yard and out into the back drive. She was standing by some parked cars. The Woodville minibus was parked round here, too.

There were garages beyond, most of them open.

'That might be a good place to hide a tennis racket,' decided Elizabeth. 'In one of the teacher's garages. No one would dream of looking in there. Besides, we're not allowed round here.'

Should she go and search them? The situation was desperate.

She looked left and right. There was nobody about. She started to tiptoe past the back of the nearest car. It was Miss Best's car, a rather old-fashioned blue saloon, with shining paintwork and chrome. Miss Best's car always looked immaculate.

'That's funny. She hasn't closed her boot properly!' Elizabeth realized. It was open several inches. She found it hard to imagine the joint headmistress being so careless. She would be leaving the car lights on next. 'I'd better close it for her.'

The little girl took hold of the chrome handle and tried to close the lid of the boot. It would not shut. There was something in the way. She opened the boot wider to see what the obstruction was—

It was a tennis racket.

She pulled it out and looked at it in amazement.

'It's Patrick's!' she gasped. 'How extraordinary.'

Somebody had tried to hide it in the boot of Miss Best's car.

'Well, they haven't succeeded!' she realized, joyfully.

Elizabeth slammed shut the boot. The noise brought Cook to the back door. 'What's Elizabeth doing here?' she wondered. 'I hope she's not being the Naughtiest Girl again.'

But Elizabeth had fled. With Patrick's racket in her hand, she ran all the way to the tennis-courts, her heart beating fast with excitement and triumph.

Patrick and his partner were at the far end of the first court, having a few practice strokes against the opposing pair from Woodville School. The match was

due to start in two minutes' time. Patrick looked a picture of misery as he fluffed a stroke with the borrowed racket. He was by now totally convinced that Elizabeth had hidden his own. Then he heard her voice.

'Patrick!' she shouted, through the wire netting. She was jumping up and down, waving the racket. 'I've found it!'

He raced off the court and came to meet her at the gate. Everybody was watching them.

'Oh, Patrick, isn't it lucky that I've found it in the nick of time?' she began, with a bright smile.

'Very funny, ha, ha. What a coincidence!' he hissed angrily.

He flung Julian's racket down at her feet and snatched his own. His face was like a thundercloud. The last few minutes had been the most miserable of his life. They had been almost unendurable.

'It's not amusing, Elizabeth,' he mouthed at her. 'I think you're beastly. I think this is the meanest trick I've ever come across.'

Elizabeth recoiled. She was speechless.

At that moment, atop the high green umpire's chair, Mr Warlow clapped his hands loudly.

'Time, please!' he called. 'Woodville won the toss and have chosen to serve. Back on court Patrick, please. Let the match begin.'

ELIZABETH IS ANGRY

Elizabeth slowly picked up Julian's racket and walked over to join the other first formers. Belinda and Kathleen had saved her a place on the big grassy bank that overlooked the courts. They slapped her on the back. So did Julian. He took possession of his racket with a wry smile.

'I don't think I'll lend it to *him* again in a hurry.'

'Where ever did you find it?' whispered Kathleen.

'In the boot of Miss Best's car,' replied Elizabeth, dully.

Belinda giggled out loud.

'The Beast's car boot? I don't believe it!'

Sitting just in front of them, Arabella turned her fair head scornfully.

'Don't tell fibs, Elizabeth Allen.'

'But it *was* in the boot of Miss Best's car,' Elizabeth hissed, fiercely. 'It was, it *was*. I looked inside and there it was!'

'You just *happened* to be passing the Beast's car and decided to *look inside the boot*?' asked Rosemary, in disbelief. She was sitting next to Arabella. 'You must have known it was there— You must have!'

'Seeing you'd hidden it there yourself!' suggested Arabella. She spoke primly. 'I think it was really mean to play a trick. And it's even meaner to pretend you didn't, now you feel scared. Now you see how serious it was.

You had half the school looking for that racket! If Patrick plays badly, it will be your fault, Elizabeth.'

'How dare you say that!' gasped Elizabeth.

'Please be quiet, children!' said Miss Ranger, their class teacher, who had just arrived to watch the match. 'You must not talk while play is in progress.'

Arabella studiously turned her well-groomed head away from Elizabeth and focused all her attention on the game. She clapped loudly every time Patrick won a point.

Far from playing badly, Patrick played a brilliant match. With his precious racket safely back in his hands, all his confidence returned. But there was something else. He was fired up with anger at the joke that he believed had been played on him. He turned all that anger into hard, fierce strokes, beating the pair on the other side of the net time after time. He would show Elizabeth Allen a thing or two! She would see what a fine player he was, not someone only fit to have tricks played upon them.

Elizabeth hardly noticed how well Patrick was doing. For it was her turn to feel miserable now. She sat through the match in a blur. She was seething with anger toward Patrick. For Arabella, with her sarcastic comments, she had only contempt.

Soon the match was over. Whyteleafe's second pair

had won by two sets to love! On the court, Patrick was elated. Eileen, his partner, was handing round one of the school biscuit tins. She was hospitality monitor for the day. At Whyteleafe, a different person was chosen to be hospitality monitor at every match. They were given the job of baking sweets, or biscuits, or little cakes, in the days before the match, to offer to all the players afterwards. Patrick was tucking into Eileen's fudge with relish.

He glimpsed the forlorn figure sitting on the bank. For the first time, he wondered if he could possibly have misjudged Elizabeth. It would be terrible if her 'find' had been genuine. He must ask the others about it.

A cheer suddenly went up. Whyteleafe's first team pair had won *their* match as well. Eileen quickly hurried over with the tin, to offer more fudge around. Both matches were over. Whyteleafe had won the fixture.

The news about Patrick's racket had quickly spread. Arabella was claiming that Elizabeth must be telling stories. She was pretending she had found the racket in the Beast's car boot! It was all too far-fetched. Elizabeth had been sulky after Patrick teased her about not being a monitor. She must have decided to get her own back, more likely. The whole thing had got out of hand, so now she was trying to wriggle out of it . . .

Noting the funny looks, Elizabeth's anger deepened.

'Don't worry. *We* believe you,' said Kathleen, sweetly.

But Elizabeth was scrambling to her feet. She had no intention of sitting round watching Arabella stir up mischief. She was even talking to Patrick now, as he came off court. She thought of the tremendous effort she had made to find his tennis racket for him. She had pricked herself. It was outrageous!

She strode away, heading back to school.

Julian caught up with her by the main doors. He grasped her arm.

'Elizabeth!' He grinned. 'Don't get in a huff. You must admit it sounds a tall story, about the car boot. If you and I weren't such good friends, I'm not sure I'd believe you myself.'

'Thanks!'

'You know what Arabella's like. I don't know why she has to stir things up so,' he said, becoming serious for once. 'I'm not sure anyone's taking her seriously.'

'Some of them are.'

'Only the silly ones.'

'Patrick thinks I hid his racket. He will be quite sure of it now.'

'Well, then, he's silly, too. What a chap to have as a cousin. He's an embarrassment sometimes. I'm beginning to wish all over again that he'd never come to Whyteleafe. I was beginning to enjoy myself.'

ELIZABETH IS ANGRY

'I hate him!' exclaimed Elizabeth.

Julian let go of Elizabeth's arm, put his hands in his pockets and frowned to himself. He turned over a small stone with the toe of his shoe. Then he looked her in the eye.

'The simple fact is, Elizabeth, that as you did *not* hide Patrick's racket in the boot of the Beast's car, somebody else did. But who? And why? I think we should go straight round to the car and have a hunt around. We need to look for clues.'

'I can't be bothered!' said Elizabeth, sulkily. 'If someone hates Patrick, it's no more than he deserves. Why should I care!'

'Except it would put you in the clear,' said Julian, calmly.

'I *am* in the clear!' exclaimed Elizabeth. 'I don't have to prove myself to people like Arabella and Patrick. My *real* friends know I wouldn't play such a silly, mean trick and that's good enough for me.'

At that moment some first formers appeared, Arabella amongst them.

Elizabeth turned her back on them and walked away.

She was tired of all this. She did not particularly want to see the rest of her classmates at the moment. Let them chatter away amongst themselves as much as they wished. She would go and do some gardening and enjoy some peace and quiet. She would go to the school gardens and find her dear John Terry and ask him to give her some jobs to do.

But, when she got there, there was no sign of him anywhere.

CHAPTER SIX

JULIAN LOOKS FOR CLUES

ELIZABETH WAS puzzled. She had never known John to be anywhere else but the school gardens on a fine Saturday afternoon. As well as the vegetable gardens, she looked for him in all the usual places: the greenhouses, the tool shed, the potting shed and round by the compost heap. He was nowhere to be found.

After looking for him all over she took a glance at his prize lettuces. They had grown some more and were hearting out nicely. She walked down the two rows, checking the bowls of milk. A few slugs had become trapped in them but there was plenty of room for more. At present, the soil having dried out well, the slimy black creatures had gone to ground. It would need another spell of wet weather to bring them out again in force. At the end of one row, a single dandelion was growing rather closer than it should to a cos lettuce. Elizabeth bent down to pull it out, then suddenly remembered.

She straightened up quickly. She had almost

forgotten. She must do nothing to help John's plants before the competition for the cup, in two weeks' time. No, not even pull out a single weed! It was against the rules. She was proud to be the only person in the whole school who knew John's exciting secret.

'Peter! Sophie! Have you seen John?' she called, as two junior class pupils appeared, carrying little forks and trowels.

'No,' replied Peter. 'Thomas is in charge today.'

'We're going to help put new straw round the tomato plants,' explained Sophie. 'The old straw got all wet. But first we're going to weed round the peas.'

The senior boy appeared then with the wheelbarrow laden with straw.

'That's the trouble when it's been wet,' laughed Thomas. 'It brings on the weeds faster than the things you're really *trying* to grow, don't you think, Elizabeth?'

'Yes.' Not to mention slugs and snails and other undesirables, Elizabeth thought. 'But, Thomas, what's happened to John today? I've been looking for him everywhere.'

'Haven't you heard?'

The big boy stood the wheelbarrow down and walked over to her.

'He's stuck away in the san, poor chap. He's got

German measles or scarletina or something, I've forgotten what. But it's very infectious! He's in a room on his own. Nobody's allowed to go anywhere near him, in case the whole school catches it.'

'Oh, poor John,' Elizabeth gasped.

'It's all right, it's nothing serious. He'll be completely better in a week or ten days. Then Matron will let him out!'

Elizabeth digested the dramatic news. She remembered how tired John had looked the other evening; it must have been because the illness was coming on.

'Until he's let out of San, I'm in charge of the school gardens,' said Thomas proudly. 'And by the way, John gave Matron a message to give me. Nobody is to go near his private patch or touch any of his plants. Strictly forbidden.'

Elizabeth nodded. She knew the reason for that!

Her mind had already turned back to John's lettuces. She glanced at the sky, feeling anxious. A week or ten days! That was such a long time. Supposing it got very wet again and more slugs appeared and needed to be attended to? Or supposing there was a heat wave, with long, hot days and the plants became parched and needed to be watered?

It did not bear thinking about.

'Have you come down to help?' Thomas was asking. 'Would you like to weed some peas, with Sophie and Peter?'

'Oh, please come and help us, Elizabeth,' said Sophie, running over and taking her hand. 'Look how many weeds have grown!'

Elizabeth smiled. 'I'll enjoy that, Sophie!'

After an hour's gardening, Elizabeth felt much better. There was something deeply relaxing about working with the soil, in the gentle sunshine, the sights and sounds and smells of nature all around. It was impossible to feel anxious for long as one listened to the doves cooing in the dovecote, the bees buzzing round the wallflowers.

The following day at breakfast she was pleased to see through the windows that it was another mild day. Would the weather continue like this for the next ten days? With gentle sunshine and just the occasional sharp shower, John's plants would be perfectly safe. Nature would take care of them for him, while he was locked away in the San.

That afternoon she went out riding with Julian again.

'I did go and look for clues yesterday, Elizabeth,' he told her airily. 'After you went off. I wandered over and had a good hunt round the Beast's car.'

They both reined in their ponies.

'Oh? Did you find anything?'

'Just this old crisp packet, blowing about under the car.' He produced a crumpled bag from the pocket of his jeans. It had stars and stripes on it and a picture of Uncle Sam. 'It's an American brand, *Southern Favorits*. Never heard of them, have you?'

Elizabeth glanced at the packet and shook her head.

'It could have blown over from the school dustbins. It doesn't mean anything.'

'True,' agreed Julian. He grinned. 'I've had a thought, though. Do you think the culprit could have been Roger Brown? Trying to upset Patrick, so he could get his place in the second team back?'

Elizabeth frowned and thought about the big, gentle senior boy. She simply could not imagine him creeping around and hiding Patrick's racket.

'Impossible,' she replied.

They looked at each other ruefully.

'In any case,' Elizabeth laughed. 'I'm not sure I care!'

The fact was that Elizabeth and Julian's cousin were no longer on speaking terms. They had simply decided to ignore each other. At the dinner table today, Patrick had been rather full of himself. There was to be another home match next weekend. Whyteleafe would be playing St Faith's and Patrick had been picked for the second team again. After his good performance against

Woodville, his place was beginning to look very secure.

'And Mr Warlow has asked me to be hospitality monitor,' Patrick told Martin, 'as a reward for playing so well. Isn't that an honour!'

'You were brilliant,' said Martin, who was now a great admirer.

'It will be quite a tough match,' said Patrick. 'But the *really* big match will be the one after that, just before half-term.'

'You mean the match against Hickling Green?' said Rosemary, knowledgeably.

Whyteleafe v. Hickling Green was always *the* big tennis fixture of the summer term. The two schools were long-standing rivals.

'Yes,' nodded Patrick. 'A lot of parents come to watch, if they're collecting us at half-term. I've got to play well against St Faith's, to make sure of my place for the big match.'

'I'm sure you will, Patrick,' cooed Arabella. 'Especially now you're keeping your racket safely locked up.'

Nobody else at the table had taken part in this conversation.

Unofficially the class was starting to divide into two factions.

There was a very small faction consisting of Patrick, Arabella, Rosemary and Martin. These four, together with one or two hangers-on, firmly believed that Elizabeth had played a mean trick on Patrick and was refusing to own up. She had not once been called the naughtiest girl in the school for nothing.

A much bigger faction, consisting of Julian, Belinda, Kathleen, and many others, sided firmly with Elizabeth. They felt sure that if by any chance Elizabeth had played a joke, as a former monitor (and such a fine one) she would certainly have owned up.

'As a matter of fact, Julian,' Elizabeth said now, as they turned their ponies to head back to school, 'I really do *not* care. I mean even if it *was* Roger wanting to get his place back in the second team. He deserves it more than Patrick does. He's much more decent than Patrick.'

'Yes.' Julian's green eyes twinkled. His friend was being illogical. 'Of course. And much too decent to have played such a trick in the first place. Well, Elizabeth,' he added airily, 'if you don't care, then why should I?'

There the conversation ended. They trotted briskly back to the school stables. After seeing to the pony, Elizabeth decided to wander down to the school gardens. She had a compulsion to keep an eye on John's project.

'I must just check that the plants are all right,' she thought. 'Even though there's nothing at all I can do about it, if they're not.'

113

The prize lettuces looked as fine as ever. No more slugs had appeared. The few in the bowls remained thoroughly bloated and drowned-looking.

'I suppose there's no chance they can somehow revive?' Elizabeth fussed to herself. 'It would be awful if they're just unconscious and could come back to life again.'

She walked round to the small rubbish heap where John had dumped all the dead creatures before. There was quite a mound of them. She turned them over with a twig, one by one, examining each one carefully. At first she screwed up her nose but she soon got used to them. Poor fat things!

'Yes, they're dead all right,' she thought. 'They're as dead as doornails. So the milk idea really, really works . . .'

'*UGH!*' came a voice at her shoulder.

Elizabeth sprang to her feet guiltily. She turned round.

Sophie was standing right behind her. The child's eyes were round as saucers.

'Why are you playing with those dead slugs, Elizabeth?' she asked, with a shudder.

Elizabeth hurriedly threw the twig away and laughed.

'It's my secret hobby, Sophie!' she joked, 'I like playing with dead slugs.'

'Do you really?' asked the child, solemnly. She had been watching for some time.

'Look here, Sophie,' said Elizabeth briskly. She took her firmly by the hand. 'You know you're not allowed to come wandering down here on your own.'

'I just wanted to look at all the flowers again. They do smell lovely.'

'Well, you're coming back to school with me, right now.'

Sophie was reluctant to leave the flowers. Elizabeth decided to cheer her up.

'I'll teach you a funny song,' she said kindly. 'It's one my governess told me. You can make up any names you like to put in it.'

Soon they were chanting it together, all the way back to school:

What is little Sophie made of? What is little Sophie made of?
Sugar and spice and all things nice
That's what little Sophie is made of!
What is little Patrick made of? What is little Patrick made of?
Slugs and snails and puppy dogs' tails
That's what little Patrick is made of!

At the main doors, they parted, with peals of laughter. Sophie liked the song. She would use it for skipping!

Elizabeth felt cheerful, too. She loved being at Whyteleafe School, in spite of the fact that she was no longer a monitor. She and Julian had been for such a good ride. And John's lettuces were looking fine. They were looking better than ever.

But the next day, the rains came back.

CHAPTER SEVEN

ELIZABETH MAKES UP HER MIND

'WILL YOU please be so kind as to stop staring at me, Elizabeth?' requested Mam'zelle during French, the first lesson on Monday morning. 'Will you be so kind as to keep your eyes down and fixed on your work? Do you not know it is very rude to stare? What is the matter with you this morning? Is it that you have never before seen a person eating a biscuit?'

From the rest of the class there came muffled giggles as the boys and girls glanced up from their vocabulary sheets.

'Sorry, Mam'zelle,' Elizabeth apologized. 'I wasn't really staring at you. I was thinking about something else.'

'You will think about your French vocabulary while you are sitting in my lesson, if you please, Elizabeth.'

Elizabeth lowered her head obediently. She pored studiously over her word sheet. Mam'zelle had given them ten minutes to learn some vocabulary while she herself marked some second form essays over by the big window. Then there would be a test.

Elizabeth had not even noticed that Mam'zelle was eating a biscuit, it was such a commonplace. The temperamental French teacher carried her school biscuit tin everywhere, full of Cook's home-made oatmeal biscuits. She needed them, she had explained to Miss Belle and Miss Best, to counteract the nervous dyspepsia she suffered when taking lessons. It helped to keep her digestive system calm. Everybody knew that. So naturally, first thing on Monday morning out had come the biscuit tin.

'I wish they would keep the *rest* of her calm,' Elizabeth sighed to herself. She was embarrassed to have received a scolding in front of the whole class.

The little girl had been staring not at Mam'zelle but at the window panes beyond. There were large raindrops splattering on to them. Drip-drop. Drip-drop. They were getting louder and larger by the minute. Elizabeth had found it difficult not to watch the rain. Was this just the beginning or would it soon stop?

The rain did not stop. It poured down relentlessly until the middle of the afternoon.

'This will bring the slugs out again, for sure,' Elizabeth thought, in despair. 'And with none of us able to do a thing about it.'

She now felt deeply anxious about John's project once again. The glimmerings of a plan began to form in the back of her mind.

After tea that day, when the rain had stopped, she walked down to the village with her friend, Joan. The children were only allowed to go to the village in pairs.

'What are you going to buy at the shops today, Elizabeth?' asked the second former.

'I'm going to get some sweets for John Terry,' she replied. She still had fifty pence left, even after paying Belinda back for some stamps she had borrowed. She had been planning to save the fifty pence but this was more important. 'John must be so miserable on his own in the san, day after day.'

'You are a very kind person, Elizabeth,' said Joan quietly, linking arms with her best friend as they walked along. 'Susan thinks so, too.'

'Susan?'

'Yes. William and Rita told her how you stood down as an honorary monitor, so that she could have a proper turn. I was so proud of you when I heard that. You were being such a fine monitor.'

Elizabeth felt noble again. Then, she suddenly blushed.

'Oh, Elizabeth, you've gone all red!' laughed Joan. 'I didn't mean to embarrass you.'

'It's not that,' confessed Elizabeth. 'The fact is, I'm quite pleased I'm *not* a monitor at the moment. I'm planning to do something rather un-monitorish. I wish I could explain to you but I can't. It's to do with somebody else's secret, you see.'

'Try not to get into any scrapes, then. But I am sure you will have a good reason, for whatever it is you are planning to do.'

'I have got a good reason,' Elizabeth told herself an hour later, as she crept through the grounds towards the school sanitorium. John's sweets were in her hand. 'I only hope his room is one of the ground floor ones. And I only hope Matron doesn't see me!'

Unluckily for Elizabeth, the very first window she peered through found her looking straight into Matron's face!

Matron was sitting at her desk in her office and she looked up in surprise when she heard a rustle of bushes. Then she saw Elizabeth's face at the window. She quickly opened the window wide and leaned out.

'Goodness gracious, Elizabeth Allen, you gave me such a scare!' she exclaimed. 'What are you doing, creeping round here like a burglar?'

Elizabeth was mortified.

'I wanted to give John a wave through his window but I didn't know which room,' she said hurriedly. 'I was going to wave these sweets at him to cheer him up. I went and bought them for him after tea.'

'You won't be waving through any window at John for a while, you silly girl. He's upstairs and he's tucked up in bed fast asleep. He has to stay in complete isolation you know, Elizabeth. Just until the rash has gone and his temperature's back to normal.'

However, Matron took the sweets for him. Before closing the window on Elizabeth she spoke much more gently.

'Everybody knows John's in quarantine! But you've got a good heart. It *will* cheer him up to know someone's come over with some sweets. He's been a real misery today, I can tell you. Fussing on about the rain and his blessed garden. A drop of rain, I ask you! It must be the fever, I expect.'

Elizabeth slipped away feeling worse than ever. Her plan had come to nothing. Poor John! She had been so hoping she might get the chance to talk to him through the window. To tell him she thought that the competition rules were plain silly now and he must be prepared to let her help him a little bit. But she had been caught by Matron straight away!

Her feet began to drag as she struggled with her conscience for a while.

It was very difficult to come to a decision. But it was

the thought of John lying on his sick bed, fretting and unhappy, that finally persuaded her.

'John's so great – I've got to help him. The competition rules *are* silly now. I've got to look after his plants for him, without his knowing. And without anybody else knowing, either. Nobody need *ever* know, not even John himself!' she realized. 'All that will happen is he'll still win the special cup for the school, just as he's always hoped!'

Elizabeth broke into a run. Her mind made up, there was no time to lose. Recklessly, she ran immediately across to the school kitchens and found Cook.

'A jug of milk, Elizabeth? Whatever do you want a whole jugful for?'

'Oh, drat!' thought Elizabeth.

Then, looking through the side windows, she saw Fluff, the school cat, sitting outside on the low wall.

'I think Fluff looks thirsty,' she said, not untruthfully.

'Fluff always looks thirsty,' laughed Cook. 'Well, you're not going to give him a whole jugful. I'll pour some in a bowl for you.'

She found an old bowl under the middle sink and filled it from a jug.

'Off you go. And when you see Patrick could you give him a message? Tell him I shall have some more cooking chocolate on Thursday, if he wants to make his crispy cakes then.'

Elizabeth slipped out of the side door, walked straight past Fluff and headed for the school gardens. She carried the bowl carefully, for Cook had been generous. She did not notice Fluff stretch, yawn and decide to follow her.

'I don't suppose this will be nearly enough, but at least it's a start,' thought Elizabeth, eagerly. She glanced around, anxious not to be seen.

Luckily the grounds were deserted.

In fact, it was getting so late that Elizabeth should have been indoors. This was the time of evening when the first formers were expected to read or play quietly in the common room.

'I wonder what's happened to Elizabeth?' Belinda was saying. 'I haven't seen her.'

'Perhaps she has a piano lesson,' shrugged Julian, in his casual way.

'No, that isn't today,' said Kathleen.

'If you ask me,' Arabella intervened, 'Elizabeth is not exactly sociable these days. It's the shock of not being a monitor any more, I suppose.'

'*If* we ask you, we will be very interested to hear what you have to say,' replied Julian. 'But as we haven't asked you, we are not.'

Elizabeth tiptoed through the school gardens and

found John's vegetable patch. The ground was squelchy. She placed the bowl of milk carefully on the path and went to examine his salad plants.

It was such a relief to be doing something positive at last. From the moment she had made the decision to help John in secret, a weight had lifted from her mind. There was nothing worse than sitting around, worrying and feeling helpless. This was going to be much more fun.

Half expecting to see the hearty green leaves ravaged by slugs, as her own had been, she was cheered to find them still intact.

She smiled as she thought of what Cook had said about Patrick and the cooking chocolate. Patrick had been going around saying it was sissy to have to make sweets or something, just because he was to be hospitality monitor at the St Faith's match on Saturday. A girl ought to make them and let him have the honour of handing them round. Even Arabella had drawn the line at that. In that case, he boasted, he would get hold of some of those biscuits like Mam'zelle's. But secretly he was making something, after all!

Well, it would be difficult for *her* to give him the message. They were still not speaking. She would have to ask one of the others to tell him.

Elizabeth's mind turned back to the slug situation.

Looking in the six bowls, one by one, she found that a lot more slugs were now trapped in them. The soil was very wet after today's rain and this had brought them out again.

'Two of the bowls are nearly full!' she realized. 'Although the other four are all right.'

How lucky that she had got some milk from Cook straight away. There would be just enough to sort out the two nearly-full bowls. Screwing up her nose, she carried them both over to the little rubbish pile and tipped them out on to the waiting slug mound. That was goodbye to some more fat slugs!

She came back, bent down and replaced the empty bowls in position.

'Now to get the milk and tip half in each,' she thought. Then she stopped. As she had straightened up, she had felt something rubbing against her legs. There came a loud purring sound.

She looked down.

'Fluff!' she exclaimed. Then she saw the traces of milk on his mouth and whiskers. 'Oh, no!' squealed Elizabeth.

She ran over to find her milk.

The bowl was empty.

The big cat with the fluffy face had drunk every last drop.

Elizabeth trudged back to the school kitchens with the empty bowl, feeling a sense of despair. Why did things have to go wrong? She had tried to help John but in fact she had made matters worse. There had been six working slug traps and now there were only four. She had put two of them out of action. As those two bowls were now empty, the creatures would just ignore them. The four remaining bowls would not suffice very much longer. Given more rain, John's lettuces would soon be getting devoured! Oh, what should she do now?

The kitchens were deserted. Cook and her helpers had finished for the day. All the washing up had been done, the floor swabbed down. Elizabeth crept over to the middle sink, carefully washed and dried the old bowl, then replaced it in the cupboard below. About to leave, she noticed that someone had carelessly left the pantry door ajar. She walked over to close it. It was a beautifully cool room, with a stone-flagged floor and marble shelves. Staring inside, Elizabeth glimpsed a long row of large jugs, each with a little square of muslin draped over the top.

On an impulse she slipped in, and peered inside the nearest jug.

It was full of milk. They all were. It was the milk for the children's breakfast cereal. As it was cool this evening, one of Cook's helpers had set them up in readiness for the morning.

'Tons and tons of milk!' realized Elizabeth. She picked up the near jug. It was quite heavy. 'Oh, nobody would ever miss one jug, would they? Not just one!'

It was a reckless thing to do. It was very hot-headed of Elizabeth.

She left with the jug, stealing along the corridors as quickly as she could without spilling the milk inside. She would hide the big jug in her bedside locker!

As she turned a corner, she paused. The common-room door was wide open and she would have to pass it before she could get up the stairs.

The only thing she could do was to make a dash for it!

'Elizabeth!' her friends cried, as she flashed by.

They crowded to the door, only to see her back view disappearing upstairs.

'Aren't you coming in?' they shouted.

'I'm sleepy, I'm going to bed!' came the muffled reply.

A minute later, she was on her knees in the dormitory by her bedside locker. She cleared a space for the jug of milk, placed it inside, then closed the cupboard door. Nobody ever looked in people's lockers. They were private.

To get her breath back, she flung herself on the bed and lay staring at the ceiling.

'What have I done?' she thought, feeling surprised at herself. 'Well, there's no going back now.'

Slowly, very slowly, a feeling of relief crept over her. It could rain as much as it liked this week. The slugs could come marching out if they wanted to. She had plenty of ammunition now. She would be ready for them!

But as so often happens in the scheme of things, there *was* no more heavy rain that week! The ground dried out nicely. Weather conditions for growing prize lettuce turned out to be quite perfect!

Elizabeth continued to keep a watchful eye on them and was thankful. Great secrecy and stealth would have been required, to help them along. Roger, no longer in the tennis team, was always working in the gardens these fine evenings, as was Thomas.

The large jug of milk remained hidden in her locker, untouched and, in time, forgotten.

So when a second former stood up at the next school Meeting, her words gave Elizabeth a shock.

'Please, I have a complaint. On Tuesday morning, when our table went up to collect our jug of milk, there was none left. Cook said staff always fill the right number of jugs, so one table must have been greedy and taken two. We had to share a jug with the next table and we all had a measly amount of milk on our cornflakes. I think the table that took two jugs of milk ought to own up.'

William and Rita, as Judges, looked around the crowded hall.

'Did any table help themselves to an extra jug of milk on Tuesday morning?' asked Rita pleasantly. 'If so, would they please own up now?'

There was silence.

The head boy and girl waited patiently for a few moments. There were rows of blank faces. It was obvious that no one was going to stand up.

At a nod from Rita, William looked relieved and banged the gavel on the little table.

'Very well,' he announced, with a smile. 'I think on this occasion we can be quite sure that one of the kitchen staff *did* make a little mistake. None of us is perfect! You must put the matter behind you, Chloe, and not be the last table to collect its milk next time!'

The whole school laughed.

Elizabeth felt very hot. As soon as the Meeting ended, she had to rush outside and gulp in some fresh air.

She had never in her life not owned up to something before. She felt terribly guilty. But how could she explain to the Meeting about the missing jug of milk without giving John's secret away?

ELIZABETH MAKES UP HER MIND

She went for a walk in the grounds, to calm herself down.

Meanwhile, in the dormitory she shared with some of the other girls a mystery was being investigated.

'I've noticed the funny smell for days,' said Jenny. 'But it's suddenly much worse. It's really bad today.'

'It seems to be coming from Elizabeth's locker!' exclaimed Belinda, sniffing around. 'Do you think we ought to look inside? I'm sure she wouldn't mind.'

When Elizabeth entered the dormitory, she found a crowd of girls waiting for her. Belinda was holding a large, empty milk jug in her hands. She had washed all the sour milk down the sink.

'So someone did take a jug of milk, after all,' said Jenny. 'And it was you, Elizabeth. What did you take it for? It had all gone sour. You hadn't even drunk any!'

Elizabeth just stared at the empty jug in dismay and said nothing.

'Why didn't you own up at the Meeting?' asked Kathleen, looking upset.

'We've stuck by you all this time, Elizabeth!' exclaimed Belinda, who felt betrayed. 'But is it true what some people have been saying? That you do things and don't own up to them. That you can't be bothered to be good now you're not a monitor any more?'

'*Please* explain,' begged Kathleen.

'I can't explain, Kathleen!' Elizabeth blurted out. 'I just can't.'

Rosemary was standing in the doorway listening.

'Arabella has been right about you all along!' she said smugly.

Elizabeth rushed past her and away down the corridor. She was feeling confused and upset.

She had done something wrong. Now she had been found out.

Even Belinda and Kathleen and Jenny were starting to turn against her.

But she had only been trying to keep a secret.

She was thankful that the weekend lay ahead and she would not have to face the whole class again before Monday. She would spend some time with Joan.

First, in the morning, she would have a private talk with Julian.

CHAPTER EIGHT

A PRIVATE LETTER ARRIVES

JULIAN WAS full of good advice the next morning.

'You're in a tight corner, Elizabeth, all because of this silly secret!' he said. 'Whatever is it? Has someone been asking you to make them some cheese? You can't keep that secret for long, it makes such a pong!'

His green eyes were laughing and full of mischief. Everything happened to Elizabeth!

'Of course not,' she replied. 'And if they were, I wouldn't be able to tell you. But it's something much more important than that. And I've crossed my heart and sworn to die.'

'I know that. And so you can't go and confess to William and Rita, which is what the whole class expects you to do,' smiled Julian, wryly. 'Even if you *could* confess, it wouldn't help much. The damage is done!'

'I know,' nodded Elizabeth. 'Now everybody thinks that I played that trick on Patrick. That I hid his racket and was scared to own up about that, as well. That's the thing I can't bear!'

'It's known as giving a dog a bad name,' said Julian. He patted her brown curly hair. 'Oh, poor bad, bold girl. Woof! Woof!'

'It's not funny,' protested Elizabeth. 'I didn't mind it when only two or three people sided with Patrick but now *everyone* does. And the way Patrick looked at me this morning! I don't think he was *really* sure that I hid his racket, it was just Arabella winding him up. But now he's convinced!'

'Isn't it about time we found out who really did?' asked Julian quietly.

'Yes!' agreed Elizabeth. 'And I'm sorry, Julian. I didn't take it seriously before. I was proud and silly. I was just so cross, that's all. To think I was the one who had gone to all that trouble and *found* his beastly racket for him! But now I see I *do* have to put myself in the clear over that. It might even be – well – nicer for Patrick, too,' she admitted, ruefully. 'Oh, poor Patrick.'

Julian had very little time for his cousin but now he looked thoughtful.

'Yes. I suppose so. He *was* pretty upset that you didn't come and watch his tennis trial. Then he must have thought you really disliked him – enough to play a mean trick just before his first match. Not very nice for him. I hadn't really thought about it much from

Patrick's point of view,' he admitted, airily.

'Nor me,' agreed Elizabeth.

She tried to concentrate hard. She thought of the crisp packet Julian had found, *Southern Favorits*.

'Arabella's parents are in America,' she said, tentatively. 'That's why she's come to Whyteleafe. You don't think it's possible they send her goodies, like crisps and things?'

'She never hands them round, if they do,' frowned Julian. 'Besides, where's the motive? We have to find a motive.'

'Well, maybe to get me into trouble,' suggested Elizabeth.

'But she could never have planned it that *you* would find the racket!'

'Maybe that was just a bonus?' sighed Elizabeth.

'The whole thing seems too imaginative for Arabella,' Julian replied rather drily. 'Still. Interesting about her parents being in America. I didn't know that. Would you like to search her dormy?'

'Yes. This afternoon!' nodded Elizabeth. 'While she's safely at the match!'

Elizabeth had already decided not to watch the match against St Faith's this afternoon. She preferred to avoid her classmates at present. It was too horrid, the looks she was starting to get. She had arranged to go to the village with Joan, instead. But Arabella would be at the match, no doubt sitting in the front row.

'The perfect opportunity!' agreed Julian, as they walked back to school together.

'I'll look in her desk, as well,' said Elizabeth, excitedly. 'What will you do, Julian?'

'I shall be at the tennis match,' replied Julian, casually. 'Watching points.'

When she returned indoors, Elizabeth found an envelope in her pigeon-hole. It was firmly sealed and marked *Elizabeth Allen PRIVATE*.

She ran along to the girl's cloakroom and locked herself in a cubicle. Then she opened the envelope to see what was inside.

It was a note from John Terry. He had smuggled it out of the san with the help of one of the school cleaners!

Dear Elizabeth,

Thanks for the sweets. I am feeling much better and have enjoyed them. I shall be out of my 'prison' in a few more days, just in time for that IMPORTANT THING I am going to do. But I am dead worried. It says on the radio there will be heavy rain from Monday onwards. Please keep a close eye next week. Remember do NOT do anything to help them along or we will break the rules. But I have an important job for you.

If they start getting attacked, please dig the very best specimens out of the ground. Wrap them in newspaper and hide them in the potting shed. There is a big, cool cupboard in there on the north-facing wall. Do NOT let anyone see you or they will ask questions. Thank you, special helper . . .
Your grateful friend
JOHN
P.S. When you have read this note, destroy it completely.

Elizabeth carefully memorized the note. Then with trembling fingers, she tore it in into tiny pieces, dropped it down the lavatory pan and flushed it clean away.

It was so exciting to have received a secret message from John. Now she could only feel grateful that all her efforts to help the plants along had come to nothing. No rules had been broken, after all. John would have been angry, if he had ever found out.

But at last, with the lettuces almost ready to pull, he had given her a very important job to do. He was placing his trust in her to do it well. After that, he would soon be back in charge again, thank goodness. He would take his prize lettuces to the village show and win the cup and bring honour to the school! She took her place at dinner with her head held high.

Patrick and Eileen won their match again, although it was a much closer result than against Woodville, the week before. As Patrick proudly handed round his chocolate crispy cakes to the visitors from St Faith's, Miss Ranger and her class clapped and cheered loudly.

'Oh, well done, Patrick!' shouted Arabella. She turned to Julian. 'Wasn't your cousin marvellous?'

'Was he?' asked Julian.

He had not been following the rallies closely.

He had spent most of the time studying the spectators, watching one face in particular.

Elizabeth, meanwhile, had found nothing of interest amongst Arabella's things.

She had been shocked to see how many clothes and pairs of shoes the spoilt little rich girl had smuggled back to school this term, even though it was against the rules. They were hidden under her bed. But of packets of American crisps, or indeed anything American, there was no sign.

'I'd feel rather sorry for her, if I didn't dislike her so much,' thought Elizabeth, her searches completed. She felt guilty for prying, now. 'It must be horrid being the oldest in the class and nearly always coming bottom and having your parents so far away.'

She went off to meet Joan and go to the village. She was lucky to have such a real and special friend, she decided. Arabella's friend Rosemary was very weak and just toadied to her.

Later she said to Julian:

'I'm afraid I drew a blank. How about you?'

'I spent most of the match watching Roger Brown's face,' replied Julian. 'And he looked pretty miserable, even when Patrick and Eileen were winning. It was written all over his face, even when his hands were clapping!'

'Upset to see Patrick playing well again? But that would be only natural,' mused Elizabeth. 'He must be secretly hoping to get his place in the team back. It's the big match next week against Hickling Green, when lots of parents come. He might have wanted to play in that and now it looks like being Patrick again.'

'I agree,' said Julian. 'It certainly doesn't prove he's done anything wrong.'

Neither of them wanted to think that about Roger.

'All the same,' sighed Julian, 'I think we should try and keep an eye on him.'

By Sunday night, Elizabeth remembered there was something else she would need to keep an eye on. This time, with John Terry's permission.

It had started to rain again.

It rained all that night and when they trailed into French on Monday morning, it was still raining.

'The lettuces have been doing so brilliantly,' thought Elizabeth. 'But there's still time for them to be ruined. I may have to start pulling them by tomorrow. I'll go down and have a look at them after tea today. Even if I have to take my umbrella with me!'

But Elizabeth never got the chance.

Something terrible happened in the French lesson that morning, something truly amazing.

They were all sitting at their desks, their heads bent over their books as they copied down a passage from the blackboard. Mam'zelle quietly opened her biscuit tin and slid her hand inside to pull out her first biscuit of the week, then—

'*Aaaaagh!*'

She screamed, and dropped the tin.

She had pulled out a handful of dead slugs.

CHAPTER NINE

THE MEETING DECIDES
TO PUNISH ELIZABETH

MAM'ZELLE LEAPT to her feet, flinging the slugs away in horror. One hit Arabella on the nose and she screamed as well. The tin had clattered noisily to the floor, scattering dead slugs everywhere and a few snails, too.

The classroom door was flung open and Miss Belle appeared.

'Whatever's the matter—?'

'This is the matter, very very *very* much the matter!' cried Mam'zelle, picking a slug off her skirt and holding it at arm's length, between thumb and forefinger, before letting it drop to the floor with the others. 'Look what horrible things have been put in my tin. There are some very wicked children in this class. They think they make everybody laugh—'

Some of the class were indeed stuffing their fists in their mouths. The way Arabella had screamed! And Mam'zelle had looked so funny, holding up the slug like that . . .

141

One look from Miss Belle quelled their laughter. She was angry.

'Martin, go and find a school cleaner to come and clear up this mess at once for Mam'zelle. The rest of the class sit in silence.'

After Mam'zelle returned from washing her hands, Miss Belle gazed at the children for a few moments.

'Whoever was responsible for that silly trick is to come and own up at dinner-time. That will be all.'

The class was very subdued after that. Elizabeth frowned in deep puzzlement, wondering how the mound of slugs on John's rubbish heap could have found their way into Mam'zelle's biscuit tin.

Was there a practical joker at work? Had the same person hidden Patrick's tennis racket?

'Well, Roger can't have done this,' she whispered to Julian, at dinner-time. 'There's no possible motive!'

'And can you see Arabella dare even look at a slug? I can't!' Julian whispered back. He was as puzzled as Elizabeth.

Miss Belle, Miss Best and Mr Johns were puzzled, too. Nobody from the first form came to own up, as requested. The culprit must be elsewhere.

They asked the head boy and girl to call a special Meeting.

It took place immediately after tea, the same day.

THE MEETING DECIDES TO PUNISH . . .

'I hope the culprit owns up quickly,' whispered Belinda, as they filed into the hall. 'I want to play my new record in the common room.'

'I was hoping for a game of tennis but it's still raining,' said Kathleen. 'I wonder who managed to get into the kitchens and get their hands on Mam'zelle's biscuit tin? At least it doesn't seem to have been anybody in our class.'

'Unless it was another of Elizabeth's little jokes,' said Jenny, unhappily. 'And she's refusing to own up again.'

'Oh, I hope not,' said Belinda, biting her lip.

Of course, the rest of the form, especially Rosemary and Arabella, had been whispering about that possibility all day. Now they waited in keen anticipation to see what would happen at the Meeting.

Elizabeth was already in the hall, seated next to Julian. Her head was held high. She well knew what some of them were thinking but she was confident that the truth would come out at the special Meeting. She was impatient for it to start. After that she would get on with the important job of examining John's plants for him.

The school monitors were seated on the platform, with the head boy and girl. They all looked very serious. So did Miss Belle and Miss Best and Mr Johns, observing from the back of the hall.

The entire school was keyed up. A special Meeting was a rare event.

William banged the little hammer.

'I hope this matter can be dealt with quickly,' he told the assembly.

He explained, for the benefit of those who did not know (by now very few of them), exactly what had taken place during the first form French lesson.

He gazed around the hall, slowly and carefully.

'The simple fact is that *somebody* in this hall invented this foolish joke. It is quite unfair that the first form should be the only ones under suspicion. Rita and I therefore ask the person responsible to stand up now and own up. The Meeting will then decide what their punishment should be.'

He waited.

There was a breathless hush.

'Will the person please stand up?' he repeated.

He waited again. Still there was no movement in the hall.

William frowned. Then, quietly he consulted Rita and all the monitors. A minute later he came back and banged the gavel, to stem the tide of whispering in the hall.

'Silence, please. As you know, at Whyteleafe School we do not believe in tale telling. But if the person

144

will not own up, we must get to the bottom of this in some other way. If anybody has any information, if they know anything at all that can shed some light on this, will they please stand up?'

Arabella could barely restrain herself, thinking of the previous incidents. She glanced at Patrick. But he gave a quick shake of the head and stared at the floor.

There then came a sound from the front of the hall. A member of the junior class, who had been sitting cross-legged on the floor, was scrambling to her feet. It was Sophie.

'What do you want to say, Sophie?' asked Rita, gently.

'I know where the person must have stolen the dead slugs from,' she said, importantly. 'They must have stolen them from Elizabeth.'

Elizabeth had a sinking feeling in the pit of her stomach. She could hear her classmates giving little gasps.

'From *Elizabeth*?' asked Rita.

'She's got a special place where she keeps them in the school garden,' explained Sophie. 'She likes playing with them sometimes, don't you, Elizabeth?' asked the child, in all innocence, at the same time turning round to look for Elizabeth.

'You may sit down now, Sophie,' said William.

'Elizabeth, stand up, please.'

Elizabeth did so, her cheeks aflame. Even Julian was looking at her in surprise.

'Is this true?' asked William. 'That you own some dead slugs?'

'I don't own them,' stated Elizabeth, her voice clear and decisive.

'But you know where there are some? You like playing with them?'

Some of the more senior pupils were snorting and trying not to laugh.

'I do know where there are some,' replied Elizabeth. 'But I don't really play with them. I was just messing about to see if they were properly dead.'

She stopped. If this line of questioning went on much longer, John's secret was bound to come out.

'Some of us might call that playing with them,' commented William.

Now the head girl stood up and took over.

'Elizabeth,' said Rita, gently. She was puzzled beyond belief. 'Please just answer one simple question. Yes or no. Did you put some slugs in Mam'zelle's biscuit tin?'

'No, Rita. I did not,' replied Elizabeth, in a loud, ringing voice. 'Somebody else must have found my slugs. That's what must have happened.'

THE MEETING DECIDES TO PUNISH . . .

That was too much for Arabella. She leapt to her feet.

'Fibber!' she cried indignantly. 'You must have done!'

'That will do, Arabella,' said William, firmly. 'If you have something to say, please address the whole Meeting.'

Arabella took a deep breath. But before she could compose a little speech, Patrick grabbed her arm.

'Shut up and sit down!' he hissed. 'You haven't any proof.'

Arabella subsided.

'Very well, then,' said William, looking troubled. 'The time has come for Rita and I to discuss things with the monitors and to come to a decision.'

Everybody on the platform went into a huddle. In the hall, the children whispered quietly amongst themselves. Julian gave Elizabeth's arm a squeeze.

'Don't they eat snails in France?' he grinned. 'Maybe that's why someone played the trick on Mam'zelle.'

'So what!' Elizabeth hissed back. She was in no mood for Julian's jokes. She was pent up, waiting to hear what the Meeting decided. She could see Joan up on the platform, speaking anxiously. She was quite sure that her best friend would be sticking up for her.

At long last, William returned to the table and banged the gavel.

'We have reached our decision. The two second form monitors are convinced that, whatever quarrels may be going on in the first form, Elizabeth Allen is very honest and has never been afraid to own up to wrongdoing. They know her best, of course, but Rita and I are of the same opinion. We have no evidence that Elizabeth played this trick and she has stated clearly to the whole Meeting that she did not. In due course we will discover the true culprit and until then let their own guilty conscience be their punishment.'

Elizabeth sighed with relief, proud to be a member of a school like Whyteleafe. But then her relief turned to dismay.

'Nevertheless, messing around with dead slugs is not something we would expect of a former monitor. It may even have given someone the idea for the trick played on Mam'zelle this morning. Please stand up again, Elizabeth. We have decided on your punishment.'

Elizabeth stood up, faced the platform and awaited her sentence.

'Until John Terry is released from the san and is able to supervise you again, you are forbidden from the school gardens. They are strictly out of bounds. That must be clearly understood.'

Elizabeth nodded and sat down. Her face was very pale.

THE MEETING DECIDES TO PUNISH . . .

The Meeting ended. Sophie was upset. She had not meant to get Elizabeth into trouble.

'If you ask me, you got off lightly, Elizabeth Allen!' scowled Arabella, as they came out of the hall. 'Who wants to do any gardening in this weather, anyway!'

'Yes, what a swizz!' echoed Rosemary.

Patrick was looking thoughtful. He hurriedly steered Arabella and her friend away from Elizabeth. He badly wanted to have a talk with them.

'Got off lightly?' thought Elizabeth, bitterly, as she stood and watched them go. She could have wept with frustration. She had been banned from the school gardens. She would never dare to defy such a ban, given out by the Meeting in front of the whole school. However unjust she knew it to be.

But it meant that she would be unable to follow John's secret instructions this week. She would be unable to save his prize lettuces for him. All the worry, all the trying to help, all the getting into trouble . . . it would all have been in vain.

The Meeting could not have decided on a worse punishment.

CHAPTER TEN

ARABELLA STIRS UP TROUBLE AGAIN

'COME ON, Rosemary. Let's go and talk to Cook,' said Arabella, the following afternoon. 'You never know, she might have seen something.'

'Do you really think we should?'

'Of course we should. I don't think Elizabeth should be allowed to get away with playing that trick on Mam'zelle! Patrick says we haven't got any proof. Well, let us see if we can find some!'

Arabella was still smarting, even twenty-four hours later, from the conversation that had taken place with Patrick.

The fact was that poor Patrick was rather confused.

He had been rather impressed with Elizabeth's bearing at the special Meeting, with the clearness and candour of her voice. He was sure she had played that mean trick with his tennis racket. He felt she must dislike him very much to have done that and the idea made him miserable.

150

ARABELLA STIRS UP TROUBLE AGAIN

But surely Elizabeth did not dislike Mam'zelle, too? They got on well. Why should she want to play an unkind trick on Mam'zelle? It did not make sense. At the special Meeting, she had seemed to Patrick like someone telling the truth. So could there be an anonymous joker on the loose in the school? Somebody with a rather warped sense of humour, who chose their victims at random? To someone like that, putting his racket in the boot of the Beast's car could have seemed really amusing.

Could it be, reasoned Patrick, that Elizabeth really *had* found his racket for him, in the nick of time, that day? The thought chastened him, remembering the bad things he had said to her. On the other hand, he found it strangely cheering. It would mean that Elizabeth did not dislike him, after all.

'What are you suddenly talking about proof for, Patrick?' Arabella had asked scornfully. 'Have you forgotten about the missing jug of milk? She didn't own up about *that* either. And it was actually found in her locker!'

Patrick had no answer. Yet he had still felt uneasy.

'Let's see what we can find out, Rosemary!' said Arabella, now. She felt excited as they walked over to the school kitchens together. She had discovered that Mam'zelle always left her empty biscuit tin with Cook at weekends, to be replenished for the new week ahead. 'Elizabeth could have got into the kitchens over the weekend and put her slugs inside the tin and shut the lid firmly. Then Mam'zelle could have come to collect her tin soon after. Picked up the tin, felt it was heavy and thought her biscuits were inside! Come to think of it,' frowned Arabella, 'I wonder what happened to the biscuits?'

'That's one of the things we can ask!' said Rosemary, who was not quite following all this.

Cook was on tea break but one of the kitchen helpers, Molly, was there.

'No, I didn't see nobody suspicious, not over the weekend,' she said blankly.

Then Rosemary asked if she had seen any of Mam'zelle's special oatmeal biscuits lying around anywhere.

'Well, isn't it funny you should ask that?' replied Molly, looking unhappy. 'I found them all dumped in the waste bin on Saturday afternoon. I don't think Mam'zelle could have liked the look of them this week. Very wasteful, I thought it was.'

In the waste bin!

'Are you *sure* you didn't see somebody from our form in here, on Saturday?' begged Arabella. 'Some time earlier? Before it was time for Mam'zelle to come to collect her tin? Think hard, Molly!'

'Well, only Patrick, of course,' said Molly. 'He came in to collect the tennis tin. He had made some nice chocolate crispy cakes for the tennis match. It was stood on the table, next to Mam'zelle's. I nearly gave him the wrong one. It's a blue tin, you see, very like hers.'

Arabella gasped out loud. Two blue tins. Of course!

'Thank you, Molly,' she said. 'You've been most helpful. If they didn't take all our money away from us at this school, I would give you a small gift.'

Then, grabbing Rosemary by the hand, she hurried out of the kitchens.

'Where are we going, Arabella?'

'To find Patrick, of course!' cried Arabella, triumphantly.

The rain had stopped for a while. They found Patrick by the south wall, practising his tennis strokes. Arabella was careful not to show her true feelings.

'Patrick, I'm afraid I've got some rather unpleasant news,' she said, sorrowfully.

She told him about the inquiries they had made in the school kitchens.

'So I'm afraid the slugs weren't meant for Mam'zelle, at all, Patrick,' she said, her eyes cast down demurely. 'The person dumped the biscuits and replaced them with slugs because they thought it was the tennis tin. They were playing a mean trick on *you* again, Patrick. Nobody would dare play a trick like that on Mam'zelle.'

Patrick's face turned pale, as the words sunk in.

A vivid picture of how it would have been came to his mind's eye. He, the hospitality monitor, proudly opening the blue tin, proudly offering round to the visiting team from St Faith's . . . the dead slugs! Elizabeth, sitting on the bank, waiting eagerly for this moment. Convulsed with laughter when she saw him humiliated . . .

So Elizabeth really did dislike him then. How he had fooled himself!

The sense of disappointment turned to a sudden rush of blind anger.

'And nobody will dare play a trick like that on *me* again, either!' he raged. 'Especially not Elizabeth Allen. Just wait till I find her.'

He pushed the two girls aside almost rudely and went racing round to the front of the school. Rosemary felt a twinge of anxiety. What was going to happen now?

It was very unfortunate.

Elizabeth was standing at the top of some steps outside the main doors. She was standing on one leg, like a stork, staring into space and thinking about John's

154

lettuces. They were probably being chewed up right now, one by one, and there was nothing she could do . . .

Patrick came round the corner of the building, saw Elizabeth, then charged towards the steps, with his head down like an angry bull. He almost cannoned into Mr Johns on the way. He came bounding up the steps towards Elizabeth, shouting wildly and waving his arms—

'Those slugs and snails were meant for me, weren't they, Elizabeth! You wanted to make me look an idiot. You wanted to get me into trouble—'

His flailing arms caught Elizabeth's right elbow and she overbalanced. With a cry of surprise she found herself slithering all the way down the steps, to crash face downwards into a big muddy puddle at the bottom. She lay there, winded, gasping for breath. Whatever was the matter with Patrick? It had all been a dreadful shock.

Miss Ranger came running over. Both she and Mr Johns helped the girl to her feet. Elizabeth was covered in mud from head to toe. She was clearly shaken and tears were running down both cheeks.

Gently, Miss Ranger took hold of her hand.

Patrick stood, frozen, at the top of the steps, staring down at the scene in dismay.

'I'll see Elizabeth gets a hot bath and some fresh clothes,' said Miss Ranger. 'Oh, poor Elizabeth.'

'And *I* will deal with the boy,' said Mr Johns, angrily. 'Patrick Holland, stay right where you are. I am going to have a word with you.'

As Elizabeth, still shaken and upset, was led indoors by her class teacher, the senior master spoke sternly to Patrick.

'We do not tolerate this sort of behaviour at Whyteleafe.'

'I didn't push her, sir. It was an accident—'

'Yes, because your temper was completely out of control,' replied Mr Johns. 'You behaved like a ruffian.'

'I had good reason to lose my temper!' protested Patrick. 'I've just found out something. Elizabeth tried to do something extremely bad to *me* . . .'

Mr Johns cut him short.

'You will report to the head boy and girl's study in one hour's time,' he said. 'You may put your side of the story *then*. They will be very fair. But I shall be very surprised if you go unpunished, Patrick. Whatever the provocation. Until you are called, please go and wait in your common room.'

Over the next hour, as he paced up and down the first form common room, Patrick gradually began to feel calmer. His classmates had heard about the incident

157

on the school steps. At Matron's insistence, Elizabeth herself had been sent to bed after her hot bath. Luckily she was unhurt, not even a bruise. But it was felt she should rest, have an early night. Now, as his classmates heard about the two blue biscuit tins, and how Elizabeth must have mistaken Mam'zelle's tin for the tennis tin, they began to understand why Patrick had lost his temper.

'I'm sure William and Rita will understand, too,' thought Patrick. 'I don't like telling tales but I will have to explain it all to them. They will see what Elizabeth has been putting me through. It is hateful the way she can dislike me so much!'

However, on his way to their study, he heard running footsteps behind him.

'Patrick!' puffed Kathleen, catching up with him. 'Wait! I've only just heard about it all and what you intend to say to William and Rita. But you can't. It's rubbish. Elizabeth could *not* have thought the oatmeal biscuits were the goodies for the tennis match. She could never have made that mistake. She *knew* you had made some chocolate crispy cakes.'

'How could she know?' asked Patrick. 'I kept it a secret. And besides, we are not even on speaking terms.'

'I know you're not! That's why when Cook gave her a message to give you about the cooking chocolate, she asked *me* to give you the message instead. To pretend that Cook had asked *me* to tell you. Elizabeth would never have put the slugs in the wrong tin. Either somebody from another form did it, or the trick was meant for Mam'zelle after all.'

Patrick's mouth fell open now.

'Thanks, Kathleen,' he croaked. 'Thanks for telling me this.'

He walked into the head boy and girl's study in a bemused state.

When asked to put his side of the story, he could only mumble in embarrassment.

'It was just a misunderstanding. I thought Elizabeth had done something to me . . . but she hadn't. It was wrong of me to lose my temper.'

'You must learn to control it in future, Patrick. You must learn the hard way.'

At breakfast the following morning, everyone at Elizabeth's table was very subdued. They had all heard the upsetting news. Patrick had lost his place in the tennis team. He was forbidden the honour of representing the school against Hickling Green, the most important fixture of the summer. He would have to be replaced by Roger Brown.

Patrick had moved to the farthest end of the table, away from Arabella. While he crunched his cornflakes, he stared at her, moodily.

She never once looked at him. She kept her eyes fixed on her cereal bowl, her face pink with discomfiture.

Even Elizabeth was silent.

Patrick had apologized to her this morning. He had apologized handsomely. But he had lost his place in the second team. Nothing she could say would bring that back for him. As the little girl stared at Patrick's sad, crumpled face, she could only feel sorry for him. Poor Patrick!

John Terry was released from the san that afternoon, a day sooner than expected. The doctor had looked by and pronounced him fit. Luckily, nobody else at Whyteleafe had managed to contract the infection.

It was just before tea. With joy in his heart, after being cooped up for so long, John rushed down to the school gardens. He made straight for the potting shed. He knelt down by the big cupboard and opened the door. He peered inside. He expected to find some fine specimens of lettuce in there, carefully wrapped in newspaper.

The cupboard was empty.

He hurried round to look at his lettuce patch. He stared at his plants in shock. They were almost drowning in pools of water. There were slugs crawling all over them. Most of the plants had been decimated.

'Elizabeth never came and pulled any, even though I wrote to her!' He was deeply disappointed in her. 'She must have forgotten. I'm surprised.'

Deeply anxious, he hurried to the tool shed and found a trowel and some newspaper.

Then he worked his way up and down the two rows, examining each lettuce in turn. His shoes squelched in the mud. From his fine crop, only a single lettuce in each row remained intact. One a round one, the other a cos. With nimble fingers, he gently eased them out of the soil, careful not to damage any of the fine leaves. He wrapped them in newspaper and left them in the cool cupboard in the potting shed.

'They were not the best two,' he thought, in despair. 'They were not the two I would have chosen. I only hope they are going to be good enough. I'll take them to the Church Hall tomorrow. That is the day you are allowed to leave entries.'

He arrived at tea, very late. A big cheer went up. All the children were pleased to see John fit and well again. But Elizabeth saw him shoot her a puzzled look. She feared the worst.

'Are they all ruined?' she whispered, when they found each other after tea.

'Nearly,' he said, with a brief nod. He looked hurt.

But as Elizabeth explained about the Special Meeting, and the dead slugs, and being banned from the school gardens, his face paled.

'Poor Elizabeth! Then . . . Oh! There's nothing else I can do. I shall have to go and explain to William and Rita.'

'But you mustn't, John,' she pleaded. 'You know it's a secret! You always wanted it to be a complete surprise. At least wait and see if you win the cup.'

'I don't expect I will,' he sighed. But he looked at her, gratefully. 'Thanks, Elizabeth. I'll find some way of putting things right for you. I promise.'

Elizabeth nodded. She had complete faith in John Terry.

Things were indeed put right for Elizabeth. It happened in the nicest possible way. John's two remaining lettuces won the cup!

At the last Meeting before half-term, he was called up on to the platform by William and Rita. John held the silver cup aloft for the whole school to see. The children clapped and cheered and drummed their feet on the floor. It was such an honour for the school. There was going to be a photograph in the local newspaper. Everybody would see what fine things they did at Whyteleafe School.

ARABELLA STIRS UP TROUBLE AGAIN

'We have another announcement to make,' said William solemnly, when the cheering had died down. 'On behalf of the Meeting, I want to make a statement. Elizabeth Allen has been seriously misjudged. When Sophie saw her with the dead slugs last week, they had come from John's slug traps. She was worried about John's project, while he was in the san. She knew his secret plan but also that it was against the rules of the competition for him to receive any help. She was simply turning the pests over with a twig, to check that they were properly dead. Stand up, please, Elizabeth.'

Elizabeth rose. With due ceremony, Rita opened the Big Book in which everything that happened at the Meetings was written down. She was holding a pen.

'The Meeting wishes to delete all record of Elizabeth's supposed wrongdoing and punishment. Please accept our apologies for our hasty judgement, Elizabeth.'

As Rita wrote in the Big Book, Elizabeth was given a round of applause.

'So *that's* what you were up to!' whispered Julian, as she sat down. There was an amused light in his eyes. 'Did John use milk in his slug traps? Is that what the jug was for?'

Elizabeth smiled guiltily.

'I didn't use any, though!' she explained, hastily. 'I'm

so glad I didn't. It would have been breaking the competition rules.'

'Our bold, bad girl break any rules?' he mocked. 'Oh, no, never!'

An instant later, they were serious again.

For William had a final announcement to make.

'On one matter, I regret to say, the Book must remain open. We still do not know who played the unkind trick on Mam'zelle. Until the culprit owns up, or the truth comes out in some other way, none of us on this platform can rest.'

Nor could Elizabeth or Julian.

CHAPTER ELEVEN

THE CORRECT CONCLUSION

THE TWO friends longed to know who had really hidden Patrick's racket in the Beast's car boot. It had been at the root of so much trouble for Elizabeth and was still not resolved. Patrick no longer knew what to think. He was so forlorn about losing his place in the school team, through his own stupid behaviour, that he tried not to think about it at all. A few in the class still wondered though.

Julian was by now deeply suspicious of Roger Brown.

Elizabeth was inclined to agree.

'I have to admit it was very clever of Arabella to realize that Mam'zelle's tin looked the same as the tennis tin and that one could be mistaken for the other. I had no idea she had so much brain power. She proved herself a better detective than us.'

'Yes,' agreed Julian. Neither of them knew that it was Molly in the kitchens who had pointed this out. 'Even if Arabella did get the wrong culprit! But you're right,

Elizabeth. I feel quite miffed not to have thought of it myself. It does provide the perfect link with the mystery of the missing tennis racket.'

'Both tricks intended to get Patrick chucked out of the second team,' nodded Elizabeth. 'The first because he would have played so badly without his proper racket. The second to get him in disgrace for playing a stupid joke on St Faith's.'

'And Roger the only chap with a motive,' added Julian.

'Well, he's *got* his place back in the team now, after all,' said Elizabeth. 'Oh, Julian,' she said, impulsively, 'I do think it's such a shame about Patrick. I don't hate him any more. He was so silly letting himself be stirred up by Arabella. She's such a mischief-maker. But I wish he could get his place back from Roger. He's the better player, anyway. I expect we'll lose against Hickling Green now!'

'You are very noble, Elizabeth,' grinned Julian. Then he sighed. 'But how can we prove that Roger's done anything wrong? How can we be sure? Wouldn't he have owned up by now, anyway? He's such a decent chap.'

They both frowned. They had been over the same ground time and time again.

* * *

THE CORRECT CONCLUSION

Soon it was the day of the big match.

Elizabeth and Julian were standing on the upstairs landing, gazing through the big window. Dinner-time was over and the tennis match against Hickling Green was due to start in exactly one hour. Last summer the match had been played away. Elizabeth remembered it was a good outing. This year it was the visitors' turn to come to Whyteleafe. The coach carrying the rival team and supporters would arrive in about forty five minutes' time.

A few Whyteleafe parents were arriving already. Some of the pupils had a half-term exeat. There had been bustle and excitement all day as children packed their cases. Most parents would remain for the big match before driving them home. Elizabeth was staying on at school over half-term for a camp in the grounds. Joan was staying on, too. It would be such fun!

Watching the early cars roll up, Julian concentrated on naming all the different makes. Elizabeth, bored by this, was still fretting about Patrick, and the mystery, and whether Roger had been to blame. She knew that Julian had been keeping a careful eye on the senior boy.

'No, nothing suspicious, I'm afraid,' he reported as Elizabeth returned to the subject, yet again. 'In fact, just the reverse. Each time I watch him, he looks more down-in-the-dumps than ever. It knocks a big hole in our theory, Elizabeth!'

She nodded. They had both noticed it. For someone who had got his place in the second team back, Roger hardly seemed overjoyed. On the day it happened, he was seen walking around school with an anxious frown. And the frown had just got deeper and deeper.

'Did you see him at dinner-time?' continued Julian. 'I thought *Patrick* looked miserable until I saw Roger's face. It just doesn't make sense.'

'And look at him now!' exclaimed Elizabeth, pointing. 'Look, Julian. There he is. I can see him. Look, over by the tennis-courts.'

The big boy had just appeared, wearing his tennis whites. Racket in hand, he had begun pacing up and down, up and down by the empty tennis-courts. He was waiting for the match. He was all ready to begin.

'But there's a whole hour to go yet!' exclaimed Julian. 'What strange behaviour!'

'Julian, why don't you go and talk to him?' asked Elizabeth, suddenly. 'I'll stay here.'

'What, accuse him, you mean?' asked Julian. For a moment his usual sangfroid deserted him. How could he, a mere first former, accuse one of the most senior boys in the school of wrongdoing, without a shred of evidence? 'Don't be silly, Elizabeth. It might just be his nerves.'

THE CORRECT CONCLUSION

'It probably is. Which means he could be grateful for someone to talk to!' exclaimed Elizabeth. 'Of *course* I didn't mean accuse him! But you never know. He might open up a bit. You might find something out. I'll keep out of the way, though, or he'll be on his guard. He knows I got into trouble over the slugs and everything. But you can do it, Julian. You know how grown up you can be!'

Julian smiled. He looked interested.

'It's worth a try,' he said.

He strolled nonchalantly over to the courts. Elizabeth watched from the window.

'Hello, Roger. Want a fruit gum?'

The big boy stopped in mid-pace, close to a wooden bench, blinking. His thoughts were far away. Someone was proffering a tube of sweets, waving it under his nose.

'Oh, hello, Julian.'

'Here, have a fruit gum. Give yourself some energy for the big match.'

'Thanks.' Roger took the sweet and popped it in his mouth.

'Gosh, Roger. You do look nervous.'

'Do I?' He sucked hard on the gum. 'Matter of fact, I am a bit.'

Julian sank down on the wooden bench.

Automatically, Roger sat down beside him. It would seem unfriendly not to. Julian was a nice kid. Very intelligent.

'Well, you can only do your best,' said Julian, comfortingly. 'That's what my mother always says.'

'I wish my father said the same! He says you've always got to play to win. You can't go through life being a loser!' Roger burst out. 'And he should know! There are so many of his old sports cups in our house it takes a week to clean the silver.'

Julian looked at Roger's big, gentle face with sudden interest.

He offered him another fruit gum. It was a black one this time, Julian's favourite, but he felt it might be a good investment.

'Is your father coming to watch you today?' he asked, casually.

'Is he *coming*?' exclaimed Roger. 'He's flying in specially. He's cutting short a business trip. All the time I've been at Whyteleafe he's been longing for me to make the school teams. I tried and tried and never succeeded, till this term. As soon as Dad heard I'd made the second tennis team, he said it was a dream come true and he'd be here to watch me play in the Hickling Green match, no matter what. He thinks I must be a late developer and he says this will just be the beginning of my sports career . . .' There was a desperate look on Roger's face, as he said this. 'As a matter of fact, Julian, I'm pretty scared of letting my father down today. It will break his heart.'

Julian, with his bright, intelligent green eyes, looked at the boy beside him, at his ungainly feet and his large red hands.

'Won't he be pleased when he hears about your academic scholarship?' he ventured.

Roger shook his head. He was deep in thought.

'He thinks sport's more important. He's too old to play sport himself now. He wants to sort of live it through me. He knows about the scholarship already. The news came through just before he left on his last trip.'

'It must have been a bit of a worry for you,' said Julian, treading very carefully, 'when you lost your place in the team for a while?'

'A worry? It was a nightmare!' exclaimed Roger, unguardedly. 'There was no way of letting Dad know. He was already in the States, you see, and there was nowhere I could telephone to stop him flying back today—'

Roger suddenly clammed up. He felt he was letting his tongue run away with him.

Julian was sitting very still. The word 'States' had sent

a little tremor through him. So Roger's father made his business trips to America, then?

Roger was lumbering to his feet.

'Well, that's enough. I can't sit here all day, eating all your fruit gums, can I, Julian?' he said awkwardly. He fished something out of his shorts pocket. 'Here – have a crisp. They're good ones. It's my last packet till Dad gets here.'

He produced an open crisp packet. Julian stared at it. The words on the front said *Southern Favorits*.

'I'm sorry, Roger!' he burst out. He truly did feel sorry for the big, gentle boy. 'I'm sorry. But I've guessed the truth. Even before you offered me a crisp!'

Julian produced the matching packet from his pocket, tattered and crumpled. He had been guarding it carefully, all this time. Just in case. 'You dropped this by Miss Best's car. The time you hid Patrick's racket in her boot. Then, when that didn't work, you tried to play another trick on him with the slugs. He thought Elizabeth had played those tricks. *That's* why he lost his temper with her and why you got your place back. But it should be Patrick playing today, shouldn't it? Not you!'

Roger sank back down on to the bench. He looked anguished.

He buried his face in his hands.

'My father's coming!' he groaned. 'He'll be here soon!

He's flown in from America specially. Please don't give me away,' he begged. 'I was honestly going to confess everything, after half-term, once this match was safely out of the way. I intend to own up at the next Meeting, I promise. But let me play today. Please.'

'I have to go and consult Elizabeth,' said Julian. He suddenly felt desperately torn. 'We'll decide this together.'

'Please let me play!' begged Roger, as Julian walked away.

Elizabeth said that there was no time to lose. They must go and find the head boy and girl and ask their advice. It was much too big a decision to make on their own.

William and Rita, without hesitation, reached the correct conclusion.

'It's all very sad,' said Rita. 'Of course Roger cannot be allowed to play. He has done such bad things but, more to the point, it would solve nothing. He would simply be storing up more misery for himself in the future.'

'His father would expect him to get into teams at his next school,' agreed William. 'The misery would just go on and on forever! Mr Brown must be made to face up to the truth. Just because he was a sporting hero himself, it does not make Roger one. His talents lie in other directions. And he must be brave and tell his father the whole truth.'

Even as they were discussing it, Roger had come to the same conclusion.

Eyes blurred, he set off up the school drive. He would wait at the gates for his father's car. He would tell him the whole truth and ask to be taken home straight away.

William was about to leave the study to find Roger when there came some alarming sounds through the window.

A blaring horn – the scream of car brakes – a cry of pain.

They all rushed outside.

A heavily built man was kneeling on the school drive beside the prone figure of a boy. He had been driving fast. He had raced all the way from London Airport, anxious not to miss any of the match.

'It's Roger!' he cried out to them in horror. 'It's my own son. I've knocked down my own son.'

They all knelt round the boy while Rita rushed off to find Matron.

'Oh, let him be all right. Please let him be all right!' Roger's father kept saying. 'What was the matter with him? He was wandering alone, in such a daze. He was right in the middle of the drive. I couldn't stop in time—'

174

'He was very upset, sir,' Elizabeth said, quietly. 'You see, he knew another boy should be playing in the match today. Somebody much better than him. He cheated to stay in the team, but it wasn't for himself. He did it all for you.'

'For me?' asked Mr Brown. He was stroking his son's head.

'He knows you want him to be good at sport,' said Julian. 'He couldn't face losing his place in the team and letting you down.'

There was a long silence.

'I've been a fool,' said Roger's father, at last. 'Oh, please let him be all right!'

Matron arrived.

'Should we call an ambulance?' asked Mr Brown, looking fearful.

Matron kept everybody back while she examined Roger and took his pulse. Then she looked up, in very great relief.

'Pulse good and strong,' she said. 'No sign of any broken bones. I'm afraid his head must have struck the ground. He's concussed. I think he's just beginning to come round.'

Even as she spoke, Roger began to stir. He groaned once or twice and then opened his eyes and saw that it was his father who was bending over him.

'Dad, I've behaved stupidly, I've let you down. I'm so sorry—'

'Hush,' said his joyful father. He soothed his son's brow. 'I know all about it now. I'm the only one who's behaved stupidly. But I promise you, Roger, things will be very different in the future.'

There was just time for Patrick to change into whites, find his beloved tennis racket and fill the vacant place in the second team. Elizabeth had begged Mr Johns to allow him to play.

He was so happy to be back in the team. But he was sorry to hear that Roger had been knocked over by a car and had had to go to hospital for a check-up. He was very surprised to learn that Roger had been the person behind the beastly tricks, but relieved that none of it had been anything to do with Elizabeth.

So she did not dislike him, after all!

Whyteleafe defeated their old rivals that day, and Patrick put up a very fine performance. There was much cheering and clapping as he came off the court. It was his play that had made all the difference.

Patrick walked up to Elizabeth and in full view of everyone, gave her a big bear hug.

'Will you forgive me for being so beastly?' he asked, in embarrassment. 'It was so clever of you to find my

racket that day. Fancy your noticing that the boot of the Beast's car was open, just a few inches. If you hadn't noticed that, I would have lost my place in the team. Everything would have been completely different.'

Over on the bank, Arabella watched and felt grumpy.

Why did people always end up liking Elizabeth?

Elizabeth just stood in the sunshine and gave a happy little sigh. She was pleased that she was staying on at Whyteleafe over half-term. It was the best school in the whole world.

She thought of all the effort she had put into trying to help John Terry. In the end, he had won the cup and surprised the whole school with no help from her at all! But she was proud to have kept his secret.

The person she had really helped was Patrick. And even that was an accident!

She still didn't know why the racket had been hidden in such an unlikely place. Though she learnt later that Roger had planned, in fact, to hide it in one of the garages – until Mr Leslie, the science master, suddenly appeared on the back drive. Roger, in a panic, had fled, thrusting Patrick's racket into the nearest car boot as he went!

But there was one thing that Elizabeth never did find out. The little song she had taught Sophie, about Patrick being made of slugs and snails and puppy dogs' tails, was the inspiration behind Roger's failed plan with the tennis tin. He had heard Sophie and her friends chanting it as they skipped one day and it had given him his brainwave.

With the Naughtiest Girl around, these unfortunate things just seemed to happen!

THE NAUGHTIEST GIRL

Helps a Friend

CONTENTS

CHAPTER ONE

A BIG RESPONSIBILITY FOR JOAN

'LOOK, JOAN!' exclaimed Elizabeth, as they emerged from behind the stables. 'Look at all the tents! The teachers and the seniors must have put them up for us. There were only bushes and trees and grass and buttercups here this morning. Oh, Joan, I do hope Miss Ranger will let me be in your tent. I'm so proud you've been made a tent monitor!'

The two friends paused, out of breath. Their kitbags, stuffed full of spare clothes and camping equipment, were heavy. They each carried a pillow and a sleeping bag, too. They were making their way from the school buildings across to the camp site. Putting everything down for a moment, they leaned against the stable wall and gazed at the scene beyond.

'To think that's where we'll live for the next few days!' laughed Elizabeth, clapping her hands. 'Oh, won't it be fun? I'm so glad neither of us is going home for half-term. Isn't it just like a little secret village?'

For all children staying on at Whyteleafe School over

half-term, a summer camp had been organized in the school grounds. And this wild corner, beyond the stables, made a perfect camp site. The school tents had been brought out of storage. They were ex-army bell tents. Supported by a central pole, their roofs tapered to a point and they were high enough to stand up in. The tents were dotted along both banks of an old dried-up stream bed. On a washing line, strung between two willow trees, some bright tea-towels billowed gently in the sunshine.

'Why, yes, it does look half like a village,' Joan agreed, quietly. 'The brown tents are like little houses. Except they haven't got any windows in them, of course,' she added. She touched the large torch that was sticking out of the top of her kitbag.

'At least this torch will be useful at night when it gets dark inside.' All the tent monitors had been told to bring a torch – only one was allowed per tent.

That reminded Elizabeth.

'I'll *die* if I haven't been put in your tent!' she repeated. 'I begged and begged Miss Ranger to say I could be. I wonder what she's decided?'

'Hadn't we better go and find out?' asked Joan, with her gentle smile.

'Yes, let's!'

The two friends humped their kitbags over their

shoulders once more. With their pillows and sleeping bags rolled under their arms, they staggered onwards. The ground was uneven here, with large tussocks of grass to step round. But they went as fast as they could. Elizabeth was beginning to feel tense now. Joan, too, looked rather anxious. What would Miss Ranger have decided?

Elizabeth and Joan were best friends. At one time they had been in the first form together. In those days Elizabeth had been called the Naughtiest Girl in the School and Joan had been her only true friend. Joan was older than Elizabeth and had gone up into the second form some time ago. In fact, she was a second form monitor. It meant that the friends saw far less of each other in term time than they used to. It was going to be marvellous fun being at camp together, thought Elizabeth, and even better if she could be in Joan's tent.

Miss Ranger, Elizabeth's form teacher, was to be in charge of the girls at camp, assisted by Rita, the head girl. The boys, whose tents were pitched on the other side of the dried-up stream, would be answerable to Mr Leslie, the science master, and William, the school's head boy.

'You will sleep four girls to a tent,' Miss Ranger had explained to some of them. 'There will be a school monitor, or one of the senior girls, in every tent. She will be known as Tent Monitor. She will be responsible for the happiness and wellbeing of everyone in her tent. As there will be a little junior girl to look after in most of the tents, it will be an important responsibility.'

The boys' side of the camp would be run on similar lines.

'Will we still have Meetings, so we can air our complaints and grumbles?' Arabella Buckley had asked, eagerly. She would have loved to have been a tent monitor herself, able to boss people around. But as there was no hope of that, she was uneasy. 'I mean, if there are any problems that the tent monitor can't solve?'

'Oh, yes, there will be the usual Meetings, with William and Rita in charge,' Miss Ranger had assured her. 'But they will be held in the open air. I hope you can keep them nice and short.'

And now, as the two friends reached the camp site, here was Miss Ranger coming to greet them.

'Hello, Elizabeth. Hello, Joan. You are almost the last to arrive! My goodness, you're certainly heavily laden, Elizabeth. Here, let me take your pillow and sleeping bag.'

'It's my fault we've taken so long, Miss Ranger,' confessed Elizabeth. 'I couldn't decide which books to bring, or whether to bring my yo-yo, and then I couldn't get everything into my kitbag—'

'Never mind!' replied the first form teacher. 'Follow me.'

She led them past the nearest tents and through to a large clearing. Here the ground was level. Ground sheets had been spread out, with bags and bedding piled high. Lots of girls were milling around Rita, the head girl. Rita was holding a list and directing the girls to their various tents. Beyond, a brick barbecue had been built and a fire lit. The delicious smell of toasted muffins mingled with woodsmoke drifted towards Elizabeth. Beyond the barbecue, a camp kitchen had been set up. In fact, it was still being built. Thomas, a senior boy, was banging some stakes into the ground with a mallet, while Mr Leslie sawed some rough planks.

The two friends dumped their things on a ground sheet and gazed round at all the activity with interest.

'This is Camp Centre!' explained Miss Ranger. 'It's a very busy place, as you can see.'

Elizabeth stared across at the list in Rita's hand.

'Please, Miss Ranger, will I be in Joan's tent?' she blurted out.

'Yes, indeed, Elizabeth,' replied the teacher, lightly. 'I've decided that Joan will be the best person to keep you in order.'

The friends exchanged joyful looks.

'Oh, I'm so pleased,' said Joan, quietly. She rarely showed emotions but the relief on her face was unmistakeable. 'I'm sure Elizabeth will be a great help to me.'

'Joan will *not* have to keep me in order, Miss Ranger!' said Elizabeth. Even though the teacher had made the remark lightly, it had stung just a little. She was *not* the Naughtiest Girl any more. She was going to be as good as good could be.

'Of course not,' replied the teacher. 'Joan, may I have a quiet word with you, please? It's just about your junior.'

As the teacher took Joan to one side, Elizabeth went and stood by the kitbags and gazed about her. She was in a happy little dream. She was definitely going in Joan's tent! Life was perfect. It was a sunny day and they had been promised more good weather to come. The sky was completely blue. And how fine the big bell tents looked! Much better than those low ones that you had to crawl into. It would be like living in their own little house!

Which tent would they be given? And which of the younger girls were they being asked to look after? Miss Ranger had warned them there would be a junior in most of the tents.

A BIT RESPONSIBILITY FOR JOAN

'Elizabeth!'

Joan walked across and joined her. The teacher had departed.

'Miss Ranger has told me where our tent is. She says we can just pick up our things and go straight there. You see,' she explained, 'it seems that Teeny's been here quite a while. She's sitting in the tent, waiting to get to know me.'

'Teeny Wilson? Is that who we've got?' asked Elizabeth cheerfully. Noticing that her friend looked rather pale, she added: 'What's the matter, Joan? Teeny won't be any trouble for you to look after. I'm sure she couldn't say boo to a goose!'

Tina Wilson was new at Whyteleafe School this term and small for her age. She was the smallest member of the junior class, which was why everybody called her Teeny. Elizabeth had noticed the timid little girl standing alone at playtime, her spectacles too big for her small, round face.

Miss Ranger had confided to Joan that Teeny was not settling down well at her new school. She seemed rather shy and nervy. She would no doubt find sleeping in a tent rather strange at first, even a little scary. The teacher had reasoned that calm, gentle Joan was exactly the reassuring presence at camp that Teeny needed. She had told Joan as much.

'It's going to be a big responsibility, looking after Teeny,' was all Joan would say.

'No, it isn't. It's going to be fun!' replied Elizabeth, as they headed along the bank towards the last group of tents. 'We'll make sure she has a good time. Am I going to be a big responsibility, too?' she teased her friend. 'I promise I'll be good. You know I'm not the Naughtiest Girl in the School these days!'

Joan barely smiled.

'Ssh,' she said. 'That's our tent at the end. She mustn't hear us talking about her. And, wait Elizabeth, there's something else I have to tell you. Let's put our things down a minute.'

Obediently Elizabeth propped her things up against a willow tree but she was hardly listening.

'What, Joan?' she asked, staring impatiently towards the brown bell tent that was to be their home for the next few days. The flap was partly open. She was longing to peep inside, see what it was like in there, and make friends with Teeny. She and Joan would soon put the little junior at her ease. 'What a glorious position!' she exclaimed. 'We're right in the corner.'

The tent was pitched by the school's high boundary wall. The crumbling old wall's dark red brickwork was almost hidden in places by cascading honeysuckle. Elizabeth could smell the sweet scent, wafting on the

192

warm breeze, even at this distance. By the wall, the bank of the old stream dropped down to where the dried-up water course came to an end at a culvert. The culvert, an old brick-built tunnel, would once have carried the flowing water underground for a short distance. Now the stream bed was just dry, powdery dust and the entrance to the culvert choked with rubble and weeds.

'It's about the other person in our tent,' Joan was saying. 'It's going to be Arabella.'

'Arabella Buckley?'

As Joan's words sunk in, Elizabeth groaned.

'Oh, no, not Arabella!'

Then she suddenly giggled. She was too happy today to let anything dismay her for long. She thought of her rich, spoilt classmate, with her pretty doll-like face. Arabella was always perfectly groomed and thought a great deal of herself.

'Miss High-and-Mighty at camp!' she exclaimed. 'Having to slum it in my tent. Oh, Joan, this should be funny!'

'Now, promise me you two won't quarrel—' began her friend.

'Don't be so tent-monitorish!' laughed Elizabeth. 'It depends how badly Arabella behaves whether we quarrel or not. Come on, Joan, what are we waiting for? Let's go and investigate the tent right now! As long as Arabella doesn't do anything silly and make me lose my temper, there's nothing to fret about!'

She grabbed Joan's hand and bounded towards the last tent.

She was far too excited to notice the frown on her friend's face or to hear her soft reply.

'Knowing Arabella, I'm worried she might.'

And that was not the only thing that Joan was worried about.

CHAPTER TWO

ARABELLA ACCUSES ELIZABETH

AS THE face peered in at her, the tiny, bespectacled girl in the tent gave a nervous start.

'Peep-o! Hello, Teeny!' cried Elizabeth boisterously.

Then she ducked into the tent, followed by Joan.

The small child shrank back into the shadows, just inside the tent. Her hands were shaking a little.

'Oh, I'm sorry,' she apologized. 'You made me jump.'

Teeny was on her own. Arabella had gone off somewhere.

'Isn't it lovely in here?' said Elizabeth, as her eyes got used to the gloom. She danced round the tall, stout tent pole in the centre. 'Look, Joan! You can stand straight and walk around in the middle! Isn't this fun?'

'I've put my things over there,' Teeny was telling Joan, shyly. She pointed to the far side of the tent. 'It's nice and dark and cosy over there. Is that all right, Joan? Am I allowed?'

Joan at once gave permission.

'What a good idea, Teeny,' said Elizabeth. 'I think

I'd like to sleep that side, too. Unless you want to, Joan?'

'Oh, no, I'll be quite happy here,' said Joan sweetly. She was crawling around near the open tent flap, in the very small space that Arabella had left clear. 'I like to be near the fresh air!'

'Arabella's taken up far too much room though,' Elizabeth pointed out. Arabella's sleeping bag was already fully unrolled, with her personal belongings piled all around. 'She's been in and unpacked, then, Teeny?'

'She was here very early,' replied the junior. 'She wanted to bag a good place in the tent, she said. She's gone to get a muffin now. Please, may I go and get one, as well, Joan?'

'Of course, Teeny,' replied Joan, gently. 'Off you go. And while you're out, Elizabeth and I will bring our stuff in and sort it out.'

'We'll get the tent ship-shape!' added Elizabeth, eyeing Arabella's things. There was a glint in her eye. Did Arabella really think she was going to get away with having twice as much space as the rest of them? Not if Elizabeth could help it!

The two friends went outside to collect their belongings. They watched the figure of Teeny hurrying off through the tents, looking this way and that as she went.

'What a jumpy little thing!' observed Elizabeth. 'But she really likes you, Joan. I can tell that already. She really looks up to you.'

'I do believe she does,' agreed Joan.

When the two friends had finished sorting things out, they sat outside the tent in the sunshine to take a rest. It was then that Arabella appeared.

'I've had to move a few of your things, Arabella,' Joan said pleasantly. 'You hadn't left me quite enough room. And would you mind rolling your sleeping bag up, please?'

'Whatever for?' asked the fair-haired girl. 'I've arranged it just how I want it for bedtime tonight.'

'Because it's a camp rule,' replied Joan, quietly. 'Kitbags must be kept packed during daytime and sleeping bags rolled up. With four people using the tent during the day, we have to leave enough space for people to be able to move around.'

'Oh, sorry. I didn't know,' replied Arabella. 'Though I can't think who will want to spend time in the tent during the day, when it's so sunny outside. I certainly won't.'

Giving Elizabeth a rather pointed stare, she ducked into the tent to attend to her sleeping bag. Elizabeth smiled to herself. 'What good news,' she thought.

'Come on, Elizabeth,' said Joan, rising to her feet.

'If we're going to the village, we'd better stroll down there now. I've got my purse.'

'Are you sure we've got time?' asked Elizabeth. Reluctantly, she, too, got to her feet. 'We could always go tomorrow.'

'I've looked at the rota. We've got plenty of time!' replied Joan. 'We're down for Kitchen Duties at six o'clock and that's two whole hours away.'

Joan had discovered that her torch batteries were getting low. She wanted to go to the village and buy some spare ones. It was a strict rule at Whyteleafe School that if pupils wished to walk down to the shops during free time, they must always go in pairs. Naturally, Elizabeth had agreed to accompany Joan. But in truth she would have much preferred to spend the free time exploring the camp site. There was so much jollity and excitement going on. There was going to be a barbecue round the camp fire that evening!

'If you say so—' began Elizabeth.

And then suddenly there came a loud screech from inside the tent.

A moment later, Arabella burst out, hurling her sleeping bag on the ground in front of her.

'What have you put in my sleeping bag, Elizabeth Allen?' she shrieked. 'Take it all out, whatever it is. If you put it in, you can take it out! I suppose I was meant to feel all that stuff in the dark, when I climbed into my sleeping bag at bedtime!'

'How dare you!' exclaimed Elizabeth, in amazement. Her own voice rose in anger. 'Whatever are you talking about? How dare you start screaming at me!'

Girls from nearby tents were now peering out, to see what the rumpus was about.

Arabella turned to Joan, for support.

'When I started to roll my sleeping bag up, it felt all lumpy!' she screeched. 'Then I put my hand inside and there was something all wet and yukky. And there was something prickly, as well. Feel inside, if you don't believe me!' Her voice rose to a high-pitched squeak. 'I'm sure anybody in the *world* would scream at Elizabeth, if she did the same thing to them!'

As Joan bent down to unzip the sleeping bag, Elizabeth could feel herself starting to boil with rage.

She hardly cared what Joan was pulling out of the sleeping bag. A wet sponge, Arabella's hairbrush, a bar of sticky soap, a little nailbrush . . .

'Oh, dear. Poor Arabella,' Joan was saying, rather helplessly. 'Somebody's been playing a joke on you . . .'

Elizabeth was too busy fighting to control her hot temper. Then—

Arabella walked up to Elizabeth!

'I suppose you think it's funny? I suppose you were

really looking forward to watching me get into bed tonight—'

She gave Elizabeth a hard push.

And at that point Elizabeth boiled over.

'Why should I want to bother to play a joke on you, you stupid creature!' she shouted. 'Everybody knows you've got no sense of humour. I don't know anything about your silly sleeping bag—'

'Fibber!'

'I expect you did it yourself to get me into trouble!'

'Fibber! Fibber! Fibber!' shrilled Arabella.

'Don't you dare call me a fibber!'

Elizabeth made a lunge at Arabella while Joan stood there, looking aghast, just as the next-door tent monitor came racing over.

'*Stop it!*' she cried. It was Philippa, one of the senior girls. 'Who's the tent monitor around here? Can't they keep order?'

It was the sight of Joan's ashen face that calmed Elizabeth down. She took a step backwards. Arabella, too, backed away.

'That's better,' nodded Philippa. 'If you've got a disagreement, just learn to settle it in a civilized way.'

She returned to her tent.

Then a tiny figure tiptoed out from behind the nearby willow tree. It was Teeny Wilson.

She looked very white and trembly.

She walked straight up to Arabella.

'Please don't blame Elizabeth,' she said. Her voice was barely more than a whisper. 'It wasn't her who played the joke on you.'

Arabella looked startled.

'Who was it, then?' she asked.

'It was me,' said Teeny.

They all gasped. Then Teeny turned to Elizabeth, miserably.

'It was only going to be a – a bit of fun. I didn't mean somebody else to get the blame.'

Elizabeth stared down at the small upturned face in astonishment.

Arabella's mouth was opening and closing. No words would come out.

'Teeny, some people don't mind jokes and some people hate them,' explained Joan, gently. 'You must please apologize to Arabella at once.'

The child went over and said sorry.

'I suppose you're only a kid,' muttered Arabella. 'But please don't do anything like that again. You will now be so kind as to spread my sleeping bag out in the sun and sit with it until it dries off. When it's completely dry, you will then roll it up and put it back in the tent.'

ARABELLA ACCUSES ELIZABETH

Arabella turned to Elizabeth.

'Sorry,' she said.

'I should think so!' replied Elizabeth.

Flouncing off, Arabella then called back over her shoulder to Joan:

'You could at least have stopped us two shouting at each other. No wonder Philippa didn't know who the tent monitor was supposed to be!'

It was so cruel that it brought tears to Joan's eyes.

As the two friends walked slowly away from the tent together, arm in arm, Elizabeth tried to comfort her.

'Arabella often says unkind things, Joan. You mustn't take any notice of her.'

Elizabeth was thinking hard. Her head was still spinning from the dramatic events of the past few minutes. She was astonished that Teeny had dared to play such a trick on Arabella. Teeny was such a shy, nervous little thing! It didn't make sense, somehow.

But Joan had other things on her mind.

'I can't *help* but take notice of what Arabella said. The truth is, I'm really worried, Elizabeth,' she confessed. 'Teeny looks up to me so and I know she will want to lean on me. I'm quite frightened . . . that I'm not going to make a success of things.'

Joan looked so agitated that Elizabeth's heart went out to her.

She suddenly felt full of remorse that she had teased Joan earlier. She had not taken her friend's worries seriously. She was also very cross with herself for losing her temper with Arabella, however much she had been provoked. Arabella wasn't worth it! Nothing was worth seeing Joan unhappy.

She made a solemn vow.

'Joan, from now on I'm going to be as sweet and good-tempered with Arabella as anything. And I'll help you to make sure that Teeny doesn't do anything silly again, either. You just wait and see. Everyone in the whole camp will soon realize that you're the finest tent monitor there's ever been! I'm going to back you up all the way.'

CHAPTER THREE

JOAN MAKES A SILLY MISTAKE

AS ELIZABETH made her solemn vow, Joan's face lit up with pleasure. Whatever her worries, it was a great comfort to have such a loyal friend.

'Thank you, Elizabeth,' she said, softly. 'And I must try to live up to your hopes of me. I shall try not to let down any of the people in my tent.'

'You will be a fine tent monitor, just you see,' repeated Elizabeth, pleased to see that Joan looked calm and happy again. 'We'll both have to keep an eye on Teeny though, won't we? Do you think she had just *finished* filling Arabella's sleeping bag when we surprised her in the tent? She was right next to it, wasn't she? And her hands shook with fright when we appeared!'

'Why, yes, so they did,' remembered Joan. 'That must have been the reason! I had been warned to expect her to be nervy but—'

'Nobody could be as nervy as that!' agreed Elizabeth.

The two girls were walking along the top of the bank, deep in conversation.

On the opposite bank, where the boys' tents were pitched, some juniors were running along together, laughing and shouting boisterously. The girls gave them hardly a glance.

'Don't you think the whole thing was odd?' continued Elizabeth. 'It was such a strange thing for Teeny to do. She is such an unconfident little thing. Fancy her daring to try to play that trick on Arabella, of all people! You only have to look at Arabella to know that she's not the sort of person to play jokes on.'

'A girl in a higher form, as well!' agreed Joan. 'Yes, it's puzzling. But I wonder if I can guess the reason? Miss Ranger has explained to me that Teeny is desperate to make some friends. Do you think she could have read story books about camping and the jolly jokes friends play on each other? Perhaps she thought we'd all like her and think she was fun and be pleased to have her in the tent?'

'Oh, Joan, that's a clever theory!' exclaimed Elizabeth. Then she began to laugh. 'You mean, perhaps she was trying to *make friends* with Arabella—?'

'Well, at least to break the ice.'

Even Joan began to laugh now, as she saw the funny side.

'The trouble is,' sighed Elizabeth, when they had stopped laughing, 'I can see a flaw in that theory. If

Teeny thought it was such a fun thing to do, why was she looking so scared—'

She got no further.

'*Look out, Joan!*' she cried.

Two figures were hurtling through the air towards them. They had launched themselves from the opposite bank and were heading straight for them!

The girls leapt back only just in time, as the flying figures thudded on to the grass in front of them, sprawled out like starfish.

'Are you all right?' gasped Joan, anxiously.

'Of course they're all right!' said Elizabeth, as a boy and girl from the junior class scrambled to their feet. 'Look where you're going, you two! You nearly landed on top of us.'

Duncan and Kitty smiled cheekily. They were two very tough little juniors, both athletic. Elizabeth glanced at the huge leap they had made and was secretly rather impressed. The two opposing banks of the old stream were high at this point, the drop between them a steep one. Why, she would rather like to try that herself!

'You're lucky you haven't hurt yourselves!' Joan was saying. 'You could have missed your footing.'

'It's easy as pie,' boasted Duncan.

'Well, you're not to do it again,' Joan told them.

'There's a footbridge down by Camp Centre,' Elizabeth pointed out, anxious to give Joan full backing. 'What's wrong with using that?'

'It's the wrong way,' grumbled Kitty, rather sulkily. 'We're going to visit one of the tents up this end.'

'Yes, that's right, we are,' agreed Duncan, looking equally put out. 'We're going to see somebody in our class, aren't we, Kitty?'

'In that case, you should have scrambled down the bank and up the other side,' Joan told them. 'And that's what you must do in future, when you don't want to use the footbridge. Is that understood?'

'Yes, Joan!'

'And turn your collars down neatly!' added Elizabeth, for good measure. 'They look messy turned up like that!'

The two friends scampered off. Joan and Elizabeth watched them for a while.

'Thanks for backing me up,' said Joan, gratefully.

'I think you managed them really well!' replied Elizabeth, turning on her heel then, impatient to be on their way. 'I wonder if we've got time to have a toasted muffin before we go to the village? I can smell them from here!'

'I'm sure we have—' Joan began.

She stopped.

'Look, Elizabeth!' she said, eagerly.

JOAN MAKES A SILLY MISTAKE

'What?' asked Elizabeth, turning back. 'Something interesting?'

'In a way, yes. Look there – can you see our tent?'

Joan was pointing back the way they had come. Through a gap in the tents they could just see their own, nestling under the high brick wall. Teeny was sitting cross-legged outside the tent. She was obediently watching over Arabella's spread-out sleeping bag, waiting for it to dry. And Duncan and Kitty were running up to speak to her!

'Teeny! That's who they were on their way to see!' exclaimed Elizabeth.

'Yes, isn't it good!' said Joan, in relief. 'Teeny must be making some friends, after all.'

'Perhaps we'll be able to stop worrying about her soon,' smiled Elizabeth. 'Let's go and get our muffins now!'

As Elizabeth stood by the camp fire, swallowing delicious mouthfuls of warm muffin, she remembered some words from a famous poem that her father had once read to her. Something about – 'Bliss . . . was it . . . in that dawn to be alive . . .'

This, she decided, was indeed bliss. How she loved it here at Whyteleafe School! How silly she'd been when she had first arrived last summer, trying to get herself sent home by being the Naughtiest Girl in the

School . . . It was such a nuisance that she still had to live down that nickname. She was sorry that Philippa had overheard the quarrel with Arabella. That must have earned her a black mark! But everything was going to be all right now, surely?

Camp Centre was abuzz with activity. Some of the boys had been collecting firewood for the barbecue. Mr Leslie had finished building a fine table in the camp's Kitchen Area. Cook had arrived in her old jeep and boxes of bread rolls were being stacked on the table. Although some of their meals would be eaten in the school building, there was to be a First Night Barbecue outside this evening.

There would be sausages and grilled bacon, eaten in the open air between crusty buttered rolls, and washed down with plenty of orange juice, apple juice or lemonade.

Elizabeth was looking forward to it with great excitement. She turned to the boy standing next to her.

'Poor old Julian, having to go home for half-term!' she told Martin. Julian Holland was her great friend in the first form. 'He has no idea what he's missing!'

'There's plenty of work to do,' replied Martin, who was also in the first form. He could be rather earnest at times. He pointed to the big table. 'You and Joan are doing Kitchen Duty with me and Arabella. We've got all those bread rolls to butter!'

'Have we really?' asked Elizabeth, with interest. She had wondered what job they would be given.

Joan had been talking to Susan, the other second form monitor. They had been in a huddle together over their timetables. All the tent monitors had been given one of the typewritten lists in advance. It was their responsibility to see that the members of their tent were at all times punctual for Camp Duties.

'Elizabeth! Here a minute!' Joan called, as Susan walked away.

As soon as Elizabeth rejoined her friend, she could see that something was wrong.

'I've made a silly mistake,' she said, looking agitated. She handed Elizabeth the timetable and pointed to the first day rota. 'I looked so quickly, I thought that was a 6. But it isn't! It's a 5—'

'So it is,' replied Elizabeth, peering at it. 'It's a bit smudgy. You could easily mistake it for a 6—'

'So we've got to report for Kitchen Duty not at six o'clock but at five!' Joan was saying. 'And that's less than half an hour away!'

'Well, don't look so worried, Joan. We all make mistakes!' said Elizabeth cheerfully. Secretly she felt rather pleased. A trip to the village today had never been high on her list, not when they were still enjoying settling into camp! 'We'll just have to go and get your new torch batteries tomorrow, after all,' she smiled. 'It was lucky you noticed in time—'

'Because I don't want any more black marks against my name!' Elizabeth was thinking privately.

'Oh, don't be feeble, Elizabeth!' interrupted Joan, sharply. 'Of course we must get the batteries today. We can't possibly leave it till tomorrow!'

'But—'

'No "buts"! Come on, quickly, we've got to hurry!'

Joan grabbed hold of her friend's hand and hauled her towards the footbridge which joined up the two halves of the camp.

'If we go up past the boys' tents, there's a short cut through to the back drive! Then it's only a few minutes down to the village. I've got my purse with me!'

'Joan, I don't think we've got enough time!' protested Elizabeth, puffing to keep up with her friend. 'Even if the batteries do run out tonight, it won't really matter, will it?'

'Of course it will!' exclaimed Joan. She seemed in a slight panic. 'Supposing Teeny wakes up in the night and wants something . . . If you're tent monitor, you *must* have a working torch. I'm sure it's one of the rules. Please, Elizabeth!' Joan shot her friend an imploring glance. 'We can run all the way there and all the way back. You know what a fast runner you are! You promised you'd help me to be a good monitor—'

'Of course,' nodded Elizabeth. She could see now that this was really important to Joan. 'Let's run really fast then. Let's break the world speed record!'

They pelted over the wooden footbridge and up the field, past the boys' tents, the summer breeze blowing through their hair. It was really exhilarating, running as fast as this! thought Elizabeth.

But it took them some time to find the short cut through some bushes that led into the school's back drive. The leaves had grown and all the bushes looked the same. By the time they reached the school gates, Elizabeth knew they were not going to make it to the village and back by five o'clock.

CHAPTER FOUR

ELIZABETH REMEMBERS
HER VOW

AS THEY came through the school gates and pounded along by the road, on the grass verge, Elizabeth glanced at her watch with a sinking heart. This was such a mad idea of Joan's. They had not even reached the first corner yet!

But Joan was striding out, keeping just ahead of Elizabeth, her teeth gritted.

Then, rounding the first corner, Elizabeth let out a whoop of joy.

Of course! The garage shop!

'Look, Joan, the garage is open!' she cried out, in relief. 'We won't have to go all the way to the village, after all!'

'I always get my batteries at the hardware store—' began Joan.

'I tell you, the shop at the garage sells them!' protested Elizabeth. 'How silly of me to forget. I went there once with Julian! He needed some for a model he was making.'

Recovering their breath, the girls picked their way through the forecourt of the petrol station. It was very busy indeed today, packed with cars waiting for petrol.

The hopeful look on Joan's face quickly faded when she saw the long queue of people in the garage shop.

'Oh, Elizabeth, it will take all day! Are you sure they sell them? Don't you think it would be better if we just raced straight on to the village—?'

'No, I don't!' said Elizabeth firmly. It was such a warm afternoon. The run had already made her hot and sticky. 'It will be much nicer standing in a queue than running along by the dusty old road. Have you got any spare money, Joan? Perhaps we can get an ice cream as well.'

'I really think we *should* run on—'

But Elizabeth looked resolute and went and stood at the back of the queue. On this matter, at least, she felt that Joan was being unreasonable. Joan had no choice but to come and stand beside her. She could see that Elizabeth had no intention of budging. And, of course, it was strictly forbidden for children to go to the village on their own.

The queue moved at a snail's pace. Joan fretted and

frowned the whole while. At one point, the shop manager disappeared for minutes on end to help a driver who was having trouble with the air machine.

'Sorry about that, folks,' he apologized, when he returned. 'The poor man had a flat tyre!'

When Joan and Elizabeth finally got to the front of the queue, a horrible shock awaited.

'I'm sorry, girls,' said the man, coming back with some batteries. 'These are the only ones we stock here. If you need the bigger ones you'll have to go down to the village.'

Elizabeth could have died of shame!

Joan was wonderfully sporting about it.

'Don't be upset!' she said, sweetly. 'It's no use crying over spilt milk. We'll just have to run all the harder now, won't we?'

Joan had no intention of being defeated. She was still determined to buy her new batteries!

They ran all the way to the hardware shop in the village, where there was no queue at all and the correct batteries were in stock. Then they raced all the way back to school.

They were terribly late.

It was long past five o'clock.

Martin and Arabella had buttered a whole mountain of rolls without them. They were standing by the big

216

table in the Kitchen Area, with the buttered rolls piled high in front of them.

'We were waiting and waiting for you to come!' complained Martin.

'We've just this minute finished. We had to do them all on our own, every single one!' said Arabella. 'It's not fair. You were supposed to be here at five o'clock!' she added, very loudly.

Miss Ranger appeared.

'So there you are, Joan. Where *have* you been this past half-hour?'

She looked very angry.

'I needed some new batteries for my torch, Miss Ranger,' began Joan. 'I'm so sorry, I—'

'That's no excuse, Joan. You know how important it is we keep to the timetable at all times, if camp is to run smoothly. And you a tent monitor! You're supposed to set a good example—'

Arabella was listening in the background, looking smug.

But it was not Arabella's face that Elizabeth was glancing at. It was Joan's. To see the distress on her best friend's face was almost unbearable!

Elizabeth remembered her solemn vow. She pushed herself forward.

'Please, Miss Ranger, it wasn't Joan's fault,' she burst

217

forth. 'It was entirely *my* fault! I made Joan stop at the garage shop and there was a long queue and they didn't have the right batteries! I should have listened to Joan. We should have headed straight for the right shop, in the village, the way she wanted us to, instead of me being so lazy, and then we would have been back here much quicker!'

'I see,' replied the teacher, gazing at Elizabeth and recalling her Naughtiest Girl nickname. For a moment, Elizabeth wondered if she were going to be punished. But then—

'Thank you very much for owning up, Elizabeth,' said Miss Ranger, with a nod. 'That was quite the right thing to do.'

Elizabeth felt a warm glow.

It was worth getting into trouble herself, to have helped Joan. Now nobody would think Joan was a bad tent monitor and Arabella could wipe the smug smile off her face.

But, to Elizabeth's dismay, Miss Ranger turned back to Joan immediately.

And she proceeded to give her a stern lecture.

'You should know by now, Joan, that Elizabeth can be headstrong. And she is younger than you, too. Just because she is your friend, that is no reason to forget that you are also her tent monitor. At camp, where everybody has more freedom, that carries very special responsibilities. You must remember those responsibilities in future and assert your authority at all times.'

For Joan, it was mortifying.

For Elizabeth, it was completely infuriating.

She had got herself into trouble, and earned a black mark, all for nothing! It had not helped to get Joan out of trouble, after all. If anything, it had got her in deeper! It was *not* the outcome that Elizabeth had intended.

The pleased expression on Arabella's face didn't help her temper, either. She would no doubt be spreading the story round the camp with glee.

Was Teeny really going to wake in the night, wondered Elizabeth, as Joan feared? Was Joan *really* going to need those silly new torch batteries? After all, it looked as though Teeny had already made friends with Duncan and Kitty at camp. Now that the junior girl had made some friends of her own, reasoned Elizabeth, she would soon stop being so dependent on Joan. She would stop going around looking so nervous and fearful and Joan would be able to relax!

But Joan did not relax.

She didn't seem to enjoy the barbecue at all. It was not just the telling-off from Miss Ranger. There was more to it than that. Elizabeth felt sure she knew what the reason must be.

Duncan and Kitty had not made friends with Teeny, after all.

CHAPTER FIVE

QUITE A DIFFERENT TEENY

THE OTHER juniors all ignored Teeny. Duncan and Kitty rushed happily around at the barbecue with their friends. None of them took the slightest notice of the little girl.

At one point, Duncan bounded up to Elizabeth, munching a bacon roll, looking cheeky.

'Mr Leslie says we can if we want to, Elizabeth!' he said, through a mouthful of bread.

'Don't speak with your mouth full, Duncan!' said Elizabeth. 'Can do *what* if you want to?'

'While we're at camp!'

'Do what while you're at camp?' repeated Elizabeth.

'Wear our collars up, of course!' he said, and went bounding off again.

As Duncan rejoined his friends, Elizabeth saw that at least five of them were following the same fashion. Their blue school sports shirts were buttoned to the neck and the collars turned up. The rest of the school wore the shirts open-necked, the collars neat and flat.

How silly, thought Elizabeth. She smiled to herself. It must be the latest craze in the junior class. But she had neither noticed nor cared this time. Her eyes were elsewhere, watching Teeny closely. They returned to Teeny now.

What was wrong with the child? She was so nervous and jumpy. She seemed frightened of her own shadow! She stuck close to Joan's side all the time, following her around like a puppy-dog! Poor Joan looked more strained by the minute, weighed down by the responsibility.

Elizabeth felt guilty that she had questioned Joan's decision to get the batteries. Perhaps it really was important, after all. It was Teeny's first night at camp tonight. If she had a bad, sleepless night then Joan would need the torch, to be able to attend to her.

'And if that happens, I shall speak to Miss Ranger about it in the morning!' decided Elizabeth. 'Joan's much too brave to go bleating to Miss Ranger on her own behalf but I shall say something. And then Miss Ranger will realize how important it was for us to run down to the village and how responsible Joan was being!'

That thought cheered Elizabeth up considerably.

A little fantasy ran through her mind in which Teeny was tossing and turning in her sleeping bag that night, until Joan came and sat beside her and held her hand, quietly reading her a story by the light of the torch. The child then dropping off into a deep, contented sleep . . .

Then, in the morning, fantasized Elizabeth, she would find Miss Ranger and quietly explain how wonderful Joan had been and how important it had been that her torch was working. And Miss Ranger would run anxiously to find Joan, to apologize. 'Please forgive me, Joan. What you and Elizabeth did was much more important than buttering bread rolls. I can see you are a very fine tent monitor indeed . . .'

'Elizabeth! There are some sausages left!' cried Kathleen, breaking into the reverie. The rosy-cheeked first former ran over and grabbed Elizabeth's hand. 'Come on, hurry, they'll soon be all gone!'

Elizabeth enjoyed herself after that.

Food tasted so delicious eaten out of doors, around the camp fire. The sweet smell of woodsmoke made her feel thirsty but there were plenty of cold drinks to be had. Elizabeth liked the apple juice best. They were all being spoiled tonight, as a special treat. There was some excitement when little Kitty was stung by a huge bumblebee. But she was very brave and didn't cry at all. Rita took her to the first aid tent, where Matron treated the sting and soon made it better.

After that Mr Lewis, the school music master, came

down to Camp Centre with an accordion which he squeezed and played jolly tunes on. Then they had a sing-song round the dying embers of the fire. It was all very exciting.

At the end of the evening, Elizabeth and Joan each took one of Teeny's hands and led her back to the tent. They were careful to step over the guy ropes of Miss Ranger's tent, on the way. The teacher had her own private tent, a smart little green one.

'It's nice to think we have Miss Ranger so close at hand, isn't it, Teeny?' said Joan.

'I'm not scared,' said Teeny. 'Not when you're going to be in the tent with me, Joan.'

Soon Joan was settling the girl down into her sleeping bag. The juniors had been allowed to stay up late tonight. Teeny Wilson had had a long day.

'It's going to be a busy day tomorrow, Teeny,' said Joan, looking at her timetable. 'After breakfast, we are going to have a Meeting.'

'A proper Meeting, with William and Rita in charge?' asked Teeny, wide-eyed. 'Just like we have in school?'

'That's right,' nodded Joan. 'Except we will sit on ground sheets, in rows, and there won't be a platform. And also Miss Ranger hopes the Meeting will be nice and short. There hasn't been much time for any complaints or grumbles yet, has there?'

'No.' Guiltily the child stole a glance at Arabella's sleeping bag. It was neatly rolled up in the tent now. Arabella had not got back yet. 'No, I suppose not.'

'And tomorrow afternoon, Teeny, we're going on a nature walk over in the woods. I will be in charge of you. We'll take paper bags with us and see how many interesting things we can collect. Won't that be fun?'

Teeny peered over the top of her sleeping bag. Elizabeth thought she saw sudden fear in the child's eyes.

'I don't think I want to go to the woods, Joan. Do we have to go? Couldn't we stay in the tent, instead? I've got my playing cards with me. We could play a game of Snap.'

'No, Teeny.' Joan suddenly sounded very weary. 'We have to keep to the timetable. It's much more fun in the fresh air, anyway! We can play Snap some other time, if it rains.'

Elizabeth felt sorry for her friend. Poor Joan! She had been stuck with Teeny all evening. She took her responsibilities so much to heart.

'Why don't you go off and have a chat with Susan now, Joan?' she suggested nobly. 'I'll stay here and keep Teeny company. Go on!'

'Perhaps I will!' she said, gratefully. 'It would be

rather nice to see Susan. She's promised to lend me a book.'

As Joan ducked away out of the tent, Elizabeth picked up her rolled-up sleeping bag, placed it by Teeny and sat on it.

She was remembering the little day-dream she had had earlier.

'Have you got a favourite book with you, Teeny?' she asked. 'Would you like me to read you a bedtime story?'

It might help Teeny to get to sleep, being read a story, Elizabeth had decided. Though not by torchlight, of course, for it was still light outside and the tent flap was rolled back.

'Ooh, thanks, Elizabeth!'

In the next five minutes, Elizabeth very quickly discovered that her earlier day-dream was certainly not going to come true.

In fact, it could not have been more wide of the mark!

After finding a book and handing it to Elizabeth, the junior girl squirmed down happily into her sleeping bag. She smiled and gave a contented sigh. This was quite a different Teeny. For the first time, all the strain seemed to have left her little face.

'Oh, I do love it in here!' she told Elizabeth. 'It's so

warm and cosy and soon it will be dark. It's going to be lovely snuggled up in my sleeping bag in the dark. I wish I could stay snuggled up in our cosy house like this all the time!'

Elizabeth started to read out loud.

She was only two pages into the story when she heard a very gentle snoring sound. Teeny's eyes were closed. She was already in a deep, sound sleep.

'What a fuss about nothing,' thought Elizabeth. 'Teeny likes it in the tent!'

And Teeny remained sound asleep for the rest of the night.

The only person to enjoy the use of the torch was Joan! She had awoken suddenly, just after it had got dark, and had used her torch to read in bed.

Elizabeth woke in the night to hear Arabella complaining bitterly.

'How are the rest of us supposed to get any sleep with that wretched torch on!' she whispered loudly. 'I don't care if Joan is the tent monitor, it's not fair of her to keep other people awake.'

Bleary-eyed, Elizabeth sat up to see what the fuss was about.

Joan was fast asleep. Her book and torch had fallen from her grasp. The torch had rolled along and was lying next to the book. The torch had been left on, its powerful beam lighting up the tent!

Joan had been reading in bed and had carelessly fallen asleep without switching it off!

'It's all right, Arabella, I'll fix it!' whispered Elizabeth, squirming out of her sleeping bag into the cool night air. She tiptoed across to Joan's side, clicked off the torch, then stumbled her way back through the darkness to her sleeping bag.

As Elizabeth wriggled back into her sleeping bag and fumbled with the zip, she couldn't help feeling cross. Now she was cold!

It suddenly seemed even more ridiculous, all the fuss Joan had made about getting the new torch batteries. Why, they weren't needed at all! Teeny loved it in the tent. She was in a deep, deep sleep. Even Arabella's complaining hadn't woken her.

Meanwhile, Joan had not even been trying to conserve the new batteries. Far from it. She had been really careless.

It was really very lucky that the beam of light had woken up Arabella. Otherwise Joan's precious new batteries, which had caused them so much trouble, would have been completely dead by the morning!

Sometime later that night, Elizabeth was again woken

by Arabella. She was still complaining – and this time more loudly.

'I'm freezing!' came the petulant voice. 'I'm absolutely freezing. Joan, can you hear me? I'm freezing, I tell you.'

Elizabeth blinked and sat up. Joan was awake herself this time. She, too, was sitting up. Only Teeny, at the back of the tent next to Elizabeth, snored on happily.

For a moment, Elizabeth was puzzled. It was the middle of the night, the coldest and darkest time, and yet she could see! Instead of it being pitch dark inside the tent, as it had been earlier, everything was bathed in a pale light. She could see Arabella and Joan clearly, sitting up in their sleeping bags on the other side of the tent.

'You've opened the tent flap!' Arabella accused Joan.

Even as Arabella said it, Elizabeth suddenly realized that the tent flap was rolled back and tied in its daytime position. She could see the moon and the stars outside, hanging in a bright, clear night sky! They were shining into the tent! It was a beautiful sky, thought Elizabeth.

'Teeny needs some fresh air, Arabella,' hissed Joan. 'Please keep your voice down. You'll wake the other two.'

'Fresh air? It's cold! It's coming right on my face.'

'Lie down and go to sleep at once, Arabella,' replied

Joan. 'It's rather stuffy in the tent with four people sleeping in it. As tent monitor, I have decided to open the flap. I am in charge and I must ask you to lie down and go back to sleep.'

'How can I go to sleep—?' began Arabella, her voice getting squeaky. 'I'm right next to it!'

Elizabeth listened, in consternation. It didn't seem to her to be stuffy in the tent, not in the least. But Joan was right, she *was* their tent monitor. Miss Ranger had told her to exert her authority. And now that was exactly what she was doing . . .

On the other hand, whatever the rights and wrongs of it, there was going to be an awful rumpus in a minute if Joan wasn't careful.

'It's all right, Arabella!' hissed Elizabeth. 'We can change places. I don't mind some fresh air. May we change places, Joan?'

'Of course, Elizabeth,' replied her friend, in gratitude. 'Arabella, please go and sleep in Elizabeth's place, now that you've woken her up. And do not wake Teeny up. You've made quite enough noise already.'

Grumbling quietly, Arabella did as she was told.

In her new place, next to the open tent flap, Elizabeth tried to settle down and get warm and go back to sleep.

It took her quite some time.

'I do think Arabella's got a point,' she thought,

shivering slightly. 'It's much too cold here, with the tent flap open. Oh dear. I do hope Joan's not going to find the tent stuffy every night. I didn't think it was stuffy at all!'

Elizabeth slept fitfully and was the last person in the tent to awake next morning. Gentle sunshine was now filtering in through the open tent flap. Joan and Teeny had gone to wash and clean their teeth. Arabella was about to follow suit.

'Fancy offering to sleep there, Elizabeth!' she commented. 'You should have backed me up. We should have insisted that Joan close the flap. I was still cold, even on the other side of the tent. I'm not going to put up with this every night.'

'You may have to. Joan's our tent monitor, not you, Arabella!' said Elizabeth, loyally.

Arabella's mouth set in a thin, stubborn line.

'Have you forgotten there's a Meeting this morning, Elizabeth? I have every intention of making a complaint!'

CHAPTER SIX

ELIZABETH BEGINS TO LOSE PATIENCE

AT WHYTELEAFE School, the children made many decisions for themselves. A weekly Meeting was held, attended by the whole school. The Meeting was run not by the teachers, but by William and Rita, the head boy and girl, assisted by twelve school monitors who sat just behind them.

It was a kind of Parliament. Problems were discussed, rules and regulations made. At the same time, it was a little 'court', too, with William and Rita as the Judges and the monitors, the Jury. Wrongdoing had to be reported. If it were serious, it was written in the Book. The Meeting would then decide what action should be taken. Of course, the joint headmistresses and the senior master always sat at the back of the hall, as observers. But they rarely took any part in the Meetings. The children were expected to face up to their own faults bravely and work out the best way of dealing with them.

Elizabeth had hated the Meetings when she first came to Whyteleafe School. They had made it so difficult for her to be naughty! These days, however, she rather enjoyed them.

But she feared that this morning's Meeting might be less enjoyable than usual.

It would be held at Camp Centre, as soon as the boys and girls had washed up their breakfast things. There had been cornflakes and milk this morning, followed by plenty more buttered rolls, washed down with a mug of hot tea. Each pupil was responsible for their own enamel mug, bowl and plate, as well as their cutlery. They queued at the two stand-pipes set up in the Kitchen Area and swilled their mugs and bowls clean in jets of cold water. Mr Leslie had linked the camp site into the mains water supply, which already ran to the nearby stables.

He had also constructed a simple drainage system which took the waste water down to the empty stream bed. Elizabeth thought it was very clever.

It really was like a secret village here!

On this pleasant, sweet-scented morning, Elizabeth could not bring herself to tell Joan what Arabella had said. She was hoping that Arabella would change her mind. Joan had enough to worry about, for already Teeny was hanging around her again. Gone was the happy, relaxed little thing who had been in the tent last night. She was back to her usual jumpy self, with that funny half-scared look behind the big glasses.

It occurred to Elizabeth that Teeny would not be looking forward to the Meeting, either. She must be wondering if Arabella were going to make a complaint about the sleeping-bag joke, or at the very least, a grumble. As Elizabeth dried up her cereal bowl, flicking a fly away with the tea-towel, she puzzled again about that strange incident.

'Whatever possessed Teeny to try to play such a trick?' she thought. 'I still don't understand it.'

Would Arabella make complaints about both Joan *and* Teeny at the Meeting? Elizabeth was very much hoping that she would think better of it. There she was now, sitting on a log in the sunshine, talking cheerfully to Belinda. She seemed in a good mood. The night was over. It was the nice, warm daytime again!

'I think I'll go and speak to her, and be friendly,' Elizabeth decided, remembering her promise to Joan. 'I'll suggest we ask Joan if the four of us can take a vote about having the tent flap open at nights. That would be a much better way of settling it.'

But before she could get Arabella alone, the whistle blew. It was time for the Meeting.

All the children went and sat in rows, on the ground

sheets. Facing them, William and Rita sat on upturned logs behind a camping table. The Big Book was on the table in front of them. Seated cross-legged alongside them, also facing the audience, were the sixteen tent monitors, Joan amongst them. On canvas chairs, somewhere at the back, sat three grown-ups. Instead of Miss Belle and Miss Best and Mr Johns, as it would have been indoors, it was Miss Ranger, Mr Leslie and Matron. Apart from that, and the fact that they were out of doors (and a great number of children had gone home for half-term) it was just like a proper Meeting! And William even had to bang on the table for silence, as usual. He did this with a wooden mallet used for driving in tent pegs. He had forgotten to bring the gavel.

The Meeting was much shorter than usual.

There was no money to be shared out. That had been done just before half-term. There was only one grumble.

'Please, the zip of my sleeping bag keeps sticking,' said John McTavish. 'It's such a nuisance.'

'Sort it out with your tent monitor. There's probably a piece of lining caught in it!' replied William, at once. 'That's not a proper grumble, John. What can the Meeting possibly do about it?'

Everybody laughed and John hastily sat down.

ELIZABETH BEGINS TO LOSE PATIENCE

But Arabella duly made her complaint, as promised.

Just as Rita was about to close the Meeting, she rose hesitantly to her feet. Elizabeth noticed Teeny blanch. But Arabella had no intention of complaining about the sleeping-bag joke. She had better fish to fry.

'I'm sorry to have to bring this up, William and Rita,' she said, looking her demurest and most doll-like. 'It's really a little embarrassing because it's a complaint about something our tent monitor did last night.'

Elizabeth saw Joan stiffen.

'Very well, Arabella,' said the head girl. 'Let us hear your complaint.'

With considerable dramatic skill, Arabella told the Meeting about the freezing cold draught that had woken her in the night, her shock at finding the tent flap had been tied back and her monitor's insistence that it should remain open for the rest of the night.

William and Rita exchanged uneasy glances. They were well used to Arabella's complaints. Often they were trivial and almost always shrill. But this morning her tone was calm and measured.

'That is a perfectly reasonable complaint, even though it is about a tent monitor,' agreed William. 'Let us first of all hear what Joan has to say. Sit down, please, Arabella.'

Joan seemed to be frozen. There was a helpless

expression on her face. Susan had to give her a nudge, to make her stand up.

'I – I just thought the tent seemed rather stuffy, that's all,' she said feebly. 'I thought perhaps it would be better for the four of us to have some fresh air.'

Elizabeth sat there, curling up with embarrassment on Joan's behalf. Some of the campers were whispering and giving Joan surprised looks. Instead of trying to put up a spirited defence, Joan had made her excuse very lamely. It was almost as though she, herself, thought that what she was saying sounded rather silly!

And for the first time, Elizabeth realized it only too plainly. It *was* silly. It was ridiculous. It had been freezing in that draught last night!

As Joan sat down again, William and Rita asked the rest of the tent monitors to come into a huddle while they debated the issue.

Joan sat apart, looking abject, while the discussion took place. All around Elizabeth there was giggling and chattering, and people saying *Brrrrr*! It always added spice to Meetings when somebody made a proper complaint.

Soon, the tent monitors returned to their places. William banged the mallet on the table.

'Silence, please. We are all agreed that the bell tents are designed to be closed at night. This stops insects flying in. There are adequate fresh-air vents in the canvas. After all, they were made for the British Army's desert campaign! Stand up again, please, Joan.'

Joan did so.

'Arabella's complaint is upheld. If you find the tent a little stuffy, perhaps your sleeping bag is too heavy, Joan,' he added, sympathetically. 'I'm sure Matron might be able to find you a lighter one, if you ask her.'

The Meeting broke up.

Elizabeth hurried over to join Joan and linked arms with her. She hated to see her so upset.

'I should have warned you! Arabella told me she was going to make a complaint but I was hoping she would think better of it.'

'It wouldn't have made any difference, if you had,' said Joan, in a dull voice. 'It was fair enough. Perfectly fair.'

'Oh, then you don't mind if we have the flap closed tonight?' asked Elizabeth, unable to hide her relief.

'It will have to be, won't it?' sighed Joan. 'I can't have some of you feeling cold . . .'

'But Teeny was perfectly all right, Joan!' exclaimed Elizabeth, to cheer her friend up. 'I know you were worried about the tent being stuffy for Teeny's sake. But she slept like a baby, didn't she? She was fine. You didn't even need the torch for her! That's good, isn't it—?'

Elizabeth broke off. Miss Ranger was walking up to them.

The teacher spoke quietly to Joan.

'Let me explain something,' she said. 'I know I told you yesterday that you must always be sure to assert your authority, to show exactly who is tent monitor. But by that I meant you must be sure to keep Elizabeth in order! If you try to assert your authority in an unreasonable way, as you appear to have done with Arabella, then you will lose your tent-mates' respect.'

'Yes, Miss Ranger,' replied Joan.

As the two friends walked back to the tent together, Elizabeth felt helpless. She was so determined that everyone should see what a fine tent monitor Joan was. She had even earned a black mark with Miss Ranger, covering up for her. But she could see Joan's confidence ebbing away in front of her eyes. Had Elizabeth's best efforts all been in vain? Things had certainly got off to a very bad start.

As if to prove Miss Ranger's point, Arabella's respect for Joan was now very low. After the triumph of having her complaint upheld at today's Meeting, there was no stopping her!

When the friends arrived back at the tent, they found her already arranging some of her things round the sides, humming cheerfully. Teeny was with her.

'Thank you for not telling on me at the Meeting,' the junior was saying, gratefully.

'Oh, that's all right, Teeny,' replied Arabella, nonchalantly. 'I think we should have my mirror here, don't you? We can prop it up in the middle, against the tent pole.'

The vain first former had been feeling lost without her favourite mirror. Usually it hung by her bed in the dormitory. If she stood far enough back she could almost get a full-length view in it. She had carefully wrapped it and staggered down to the camp site with it. She had been puzzling ever since whether she would need Joan's permission to put it up in the tent.

'Hey, you can't put a mirror up in here!' protested Elizabeth. 'It'll get in the way. We'll all trip over it.'

'But we *need* a mirror in here, don't we, Joan?' said Arabella, turning to the tent monitor.

Joan hesitated. Without even waiting for her reply, Arabella knelt down by the central tent pole and carefully propped the mirror there. She preened herself in it.

'There!' she said. 'We all want to make sure we look nice, don't we, Teeny? Just because we're at camp, that's no excuse for looking scruffy. I've brought plenty of different clothes—'

'We can see that—' began Elizabeth, hotly. They

241

were stacked all round the sides of the tent. Then she stopped.

She mustn't lose her temper with Arabella. She had promised Joan that. It would only make Joan's life more difficult.

'Please let's have a mirror up in the tent, Joan!' begged Teeny, coming and holding her hand. 'It'll make it more like our little house than ever!'

'You can have it up if you want, Arabella,' decided Joan.

'Oh, thank you, Joan. I was sure you'd agree!' replied Arabella, smiling sweetly.

Elizabeth glowered and left the tent.

Later, Joan apologized to Elizabeth.

'I only agreed to please Teeny,' she said. 'Have you noticed how happy she is in the tent? She's like a different person. It's as though she feels safe when she's in our little house, as she calls it.'

So Joan had realized it, too.

'I wonder why she doesn't mix with the other juniors?' continued Joan. 'Do you think she could be being bullied?'

'I'm sure not,' shrugged Elizabeth. 'She's been at Whyteleafe since the beginning of term. There would have been some sign of it by now. Somebody would have seen something.'

'But there is *something* not right,' sighed Joan.

In her present mood, Elizabeth was not sure if she cared. Far from it being fun to have a little junior to look after in the tent, it had become a problem. Joan, so kind and conscientious, had become a hopeless worrier since being put in charge of Teeny! That was at the root of things. Everything that had gone wrong had been due, in one way or another, to Teeny, decided Elizabeth.

'Drat the little creature,' she thought, crossly. 'I'm beginning to wish Joan had never set eyes on her.'

That afternoon, there was worse to come.

CHAPTER SEVEN

TEENY HAS AN UNHELPFUL FALL

ELIZABETH HAD not slept well that first night but Joan had fared even worse. By the end of the morning, she began to look rather tired. Just how tired Joan was, Elizabeth was soon to discover.

Elizabeth was sitting in the school dining-hall, with Teeny, eating a delicious meal of hot pie, with buttered new potatoes and carrots. It tasted good. The joint heads had decided that every day at one o'clock, the children should come indoors for their main hot meal of the day.

But where was Joan? wondered Elizabeth.

At midday, Rita had announced to the campers that any girl who wished to have a hot shower before lunch could go up to school early. Joan had thought that seemed a fine idea and hurried off. Elizabeth wasn't bothered.

'I'll meet you in the dining-hall, then, Joan. I'll bring Teeny with me.'

'Save me a place! I expect there will be a long queue

for the showers,' was Joan's reply.

Elizabeth had saved Joan a place but her friend had still not appeared. All the other girls were back from their showers and were halfway through lunch! Whatever could have happened to Joan?

'She'll miss out on the first course altogether, if she's not careful,' thought Elizabeth, in alarm. 'The queue for pudding's starting to form now.'

She gobbled down her last new potato and got up from the table.

'I'm just slipping off to find Joan,' she told Teeny. 'Now, you be sure and eat up all your food.'

'She must have forgotten the time,' said Teeny solemnly.

But the showers were silent and deserted. There was no sign of Joan in there. Puzzled, Elizabeth scratched her brown curly head. Where should she look now?

Perhaps Joan had gone to her dormitory, to find something she had forgotten to pack? Perhaps she was having a problem finding it . . .

Elizabeth bounded up the stairs to Joan's dormitory and threw open the door.

'Joan!' she exclaimed, in amazement.

Her friend lay on top of the bed, fast asleep!

'Joan, wake up! Wake up!' Elizabeth shook Joan's shoulder. 'You've fallen asleep! There's delicious hot pie for lunch and you'll miss it, at this rate!'

Joan woke up, looked startled, and sat bolt upright.

'Whatever time is it? I felt so sleepy after my shower. I only meant to have a little nap – oh, Elizabeth! I'm so sorry you've had to come looking for me! The fact is, I didn't sleep very well last night.'

'I wondered where you'd got to!' laughed Elizabeth, in relief.

Except Joan's lack of sleep was no laughing matter, as Elizabeth soon came to discover. On the nature walk in the woods that afternoon, she thought that she had never seen her friend so exhausted. She kept on yawning and there were dark rings under her eyes.

'Poor Joan!' she thought. 'By the look of her, she hardly got a wink of sleep at all in the tent last night. Worrying about Teeny and everything, I suppose.'

Miss Ranger and Mr Leslie had escorted all the boys and girls along the country lane at the back of the school and into the woods. They all walked with the teachers for a time and had fun naming different flowers and watching birds.

Then, brown paper bags were handed out.

'You're all to scatter for half an hour,' smiled Miss Ranger. 'See how many different leaves you can find.' The pretty little woods boasted a splendid variety of trees. 'When we get back to camp, we'll see if we can

247

identify them all. Let's see who can find the most!'

'And no need to go up trees,' said Mr Leslie. 'You will find plenty of leaves growing low down and some on the ground, as well. When I blow the whistle you are all to return here.'

The teachers then reminded all members of the junior class that they must stay close to their tent monitors and obey their orders.

Teeny was full of energy after her good night's sleep. She kept running up to Joan and showing her the leaves she was finding. Elizabeth collected some as well. To her relief, Arabella had decided to go off with Philippa and Mandy, the junior in the next-door tent.

Joan, pleased to see that Teeny was enjoying herself after all, went and sat on a mossy bank. It was beneath an oak tree, in a lovely sunny spot, on the edge of a dell.

'I don't think I can go another step,' she said, leaning back against the tree trunk. 'Let's have a little rest.'

Elizabeth came and sat down beside her. Both girls tilted their faces towards the sun. It was lovely to feel its warmth on their cheeks and to hear the breeze rustling through the leaves of the oak tree. Teeny walked round the tree and found an oak leaf to add to her collection.

'Coming over here with us, Teeny?' called a voice.

Kitty and Duncan appeared on the other side of the

dell. They were waving to Teeny to come and join them, in a friendly fashion.

Elizabeth and Joan glanced at each other eagerly. Yesterday they had been disappointed when Duncan and Kitty's visit to the tent had come to nothing. But surely there could be no mistaking the situation today? The two children were trying to get to know Teeny better.

'Some friends from your class!' said Elizabeth, pleased.

'Would you like to go and play with them?' asked Joan, gently.

The little girl stood motionless. She clenched and unclenched her fists two or three times, as though trying to screw up courage. Then, coming to a decision, she nodded. What a funny, nervous little thing she was, thought Elizabeth.

'Off you go, then!' smiled Joan.

Even as the little girl walked slowly down into the bumpy dell to join her classmates, Joan gave a huge yawn and her eyes closed, thankfully.

'If you don't mind, Elizabeth, I'm going to snatch a nap. Will you keep an eye on them for me?'

'Of course!' replied Elizabeth.

Within moments, Joan had dozed off!

It was so comfortable and warm on the mossy bank,

thought Elizabeth, she would have liked a snooze herself. She closed her eyes and leaned against the huge tree trunk, enjoying the feel of the rough bark in the small of her back. With eyes closed, she could hear the murmur of voices as Duncan, Kitty and Teeny talked together in the dell. What a happy sound, she thought. Was Teeny making a real effort to mix with her classmates, at last?

In her sleepy state, it was a few moments before Elizabeth realized that the murmur of voices was becoming fainter, fading into the distance . . . She opened her eyes instantly, in time to glimpse the three figures disappearing amongst some trees on the other side of the dell.

'I'd better creep after them!' she thought. 'Just to keep an eye on them. I mustn't spoil any fun though, not when Teeny's making friends at last.'

Leaving Joan fast asleep, Elizabeth tiptoed across the dell and into the trees. From the sound of the children's voices, she could tell they had stopped somewhere. As she drew nearer, she darted from tree to tree, in order not to be seen. There was no sign of Kitty's tent monitor, nor of Duncan's.

'The little imps must have given them the slip,' thought Elizabeth, smiling to herself. 'But I don't suppose they can be very far away.'

She pulled up behind some rhododendron bushes and peered through the masses of blossom. Now she had a clear view of the children!

'I'll go first, then Kitty, then you!' Duncan was shouting.

Elizabeth stared. The three juniors were up a tree. They were all sitting astride a long low bough which stretched out horizontally, a few feet above the ground. Duncan was moving into a crouching position.

'Watch me do it, Teeny!' he was shouting. 'It's easy-peasy!'

He jumped from the end of the bough and landed in the long grass below, quite comfortably.

'Now me!' cried Kitty excitedly, bumping along to the end of the bough and doing likewise.

Elizabeth was too far back to stop them.

Besides, it looked a very easy jump and rather fun, she thought. Her main emotion was relief, at the sight of Teeny having fun with her classmates at last!

'Now you, Teeny!' Kitty was calling up. 'Do it just like we did. Dare you!'

The bespectacled junior was bumping out along the bough, very, very slowly. Halfway along, she looked down and seemed to freeze.

'Come on, Teeny!' encouraged Duncan.

From her hiding place, Elizabeth silently urged her

on. 'Yes, come on, Teeny. What have you stopped for? It's easy!' She wanted to shout it out loud. 'Come on, Teeny. You know you can do it!' She could tell from the look on Duncan and Kitty's faces that they wanted Teeny to succeed, too.

'I can't!' Teeny suddenly cried out. 'I can't do it!'

Panic-stricken, she tried to turn round on the bough, to go back the way she had come. Duncan and Kitty were shouting at her . . .

'Don't do that! Don't be a baby!'

'You'll fall if you try that! Don't be such a coward, Teeny!'

Teeny just carried on trying to twist round, getting her legs in a hopeless tangle. She slithered and slipped – and overbalanced.

'Aaah!'

'Teeny!'

Even as Elizabeth was running towards her, Teeny came toppling down off the bough, her glasses flying through the air.

'Teeny! Are you all right?' exclaimed Elizabeth.

Duncan and Kitty looked on in dismay.

Elizabeth helped the little girl to her feet and dusted her down. She was shaken but unhurt.

Elizabeth found her glasses for her.

'Thank you, Elizabeth,' said Teeny, taking them.

She looked very shamefaced. 'I was such a coward! It wasn't Duncan and Kitty's fault.'

'I know it wasn't,' said Elizabeth. 'I saw what happened—'

Duncan and Kitty exchanged relieved glances.

'You should have jumped, Teeny!' Elizabeth told her. 'It was simple. It was silly and dangerous to try to turn back. You'd better not go climbing up trees at all in future.'

The other two juniors were nodding in agreement.

'Shoo away, you two!' Elizabeth said quickly. 'You should be with your tent monitors. Off you go now, and find them! I'll look after Teeny. And don't you go telling the other juniors about this and having them laugh at her. I think we should just pretend it never happened.'

The two children looked at Elizabeth gratefully and scampered off. They had been rather frightened that they might get into trouble, thanks to Teeny being such a coward. But Elizabeth knew that if she were to scold them, it would put them off befriending Teeny another time.

Except, she was not sure that there *would* be another time.

'I think we should give up on Teeny,' she overheard Kitty say.

'But she does like us so,' replied Duncan. 'Shall we just try the . . .'

His voice faded into the distance. It sounded like – '. . . the green ear'.

Elizabeth frowned, puzzled. Whatever was Duncan talking about? Green ear? Try the green ear?

She must have misheard!

Teeny looked so sad as she watched them go. Elizabeth felt sorry for her, in spite of everything. Why did she have to be such a baby and so scared of everything? She was her own worst enemy!

They hurried back and woke Joan, just as Mr Leslie's whistle blew. On the way back to Whyteleafe, Elizabeth whispered to Joan what had happened.

Joan was conscience-stricken.

'I shouldn't have gone to sleep like that! I should have watched the whole time. Oh, thank goodness she wasn't hurt.'

'If she had been, it would have been her own silly fault!' said Elizabeth, crossly. 'Don't fret about Teeny so, Joan. We can forget about it now.'

Unfortunately, it did not prove possible to forget about it.

That evening, Teeny's glasses kept slipping down her nose. She showed them to Arabella, who was in the tent at the time.

'Why, the frames are damaged!' said Arabella knowledgeably. 'Look, there's a little screw missing that should hold the earpiece tight in place. How on earth did that happen?'

'It must have been when I fell out of the tree,' Teeny responded.

'Tree? What tree?' asked Arabella sharply. 'Where was Joan when this happened?' She proceeded to question Teeny carefully.

Joan was upset to find out about the spectacles. She took them straight to Matron, who was confident that Mr Leslie could mend them by morning. Matron also insisted on handing Joan a lightweight sleeping bag.

'I thought you must have come to collect this, Joan! William said you would probably want to try it out tonight.'

'Oh, I'm so pleased you won't have to sleep in the thick one tonight, Joan,' said Arabella, pointedly, when Joan brought it back to the tent. 'It will be so lovely for the rest of us to have the flap closed.'

Joan stared at her, miserably.

A few minutes later, her misery increased tenfold. They were all settled down in their sleeping bags for the night. Patiently, Arabella waited until Teeny was sound asleep. Then she launched forth.

'I was very shocked to find out how Teeny broke her

glasses, Joan,' she whispered indignantly. 'Fancy your just allowing her to run off on her own, like that! Elizabeth tries to cover up for you all the time. But, if you don't mind my saying so, I do think you are turning out to be a hopeless tent monitor!'

Elizabeth ground her teeth in dismay. How very unhelpful of Teeny to be such a coward and to fall and break her glasses! Joan was such a fine tent monitor; she worried about Teeny all the time. How dare Arabella say such things! At the same time, realized Elizabeth, this looked like more trouble for her best friend.

Joan just lay there, rigid, saying nothing.

CHAPTER EIGHT

JOAN TELLS ELIZABETH THE TRUTH

ELIZABETH FOUND it difficult to get to sleep. She was too churned up, feeling exasperated with Teeny, furious with Arabella and above all worried about Joan. She lay there for some time, as outside the dusk slowly faded and the tent grew ever darker.

At last, when it was pitch black inside the tent, her eyes began to close . . .

And suddenly were wide open!

Had she dreamt it just now, or had Joan left the tent?

Surely not. The flap was securely tied; the tent was still in pitch darkness.

'Joan?' she whispered.

There was no reply.

She wriggled out of her sleeping bag and crawled across to Joan's. She felt it with her hands. It was empty. So she hadn't dreamt it!

It was strictly forbidden to leave the tent at night without very good reason. Was Joan feeling ill? Elizabeth lay there for a few minutes, waiting for her friend to return. But Joan did not come back.

'I must go and look for her!' decided Elizabeth, feeling alarmed.

As quietly as possible, she struggled into her dressing-gown, then crawled out of the tent. She was very careful all the while not to disturb Arabella. That would be a disaster!

What *was* Joan up to?

It was a warm night outside. There was more cloud cover than last night but with just enough moonlight to see by. Elizabeth gazed around. Where should she begin to look?

She tiptoed round to the back of the tent, glancing this way and that, her ears attuned for the merest sound.

Down in the cutting, where clumps of grass grew beside the empty stream bed, she could hear the whirring of crickets. Then, suddenly, something else –

A tiny, sobbing sound!

She ran up over the top of the bank, then dropped down the other side.

'Joan!' she whispered.

She could see a forlorn figure down there, in a

dressing-gown, huddled up near the culvert that led beneath the boundary wall. Her shoulders were gently heaving. In some alarm, Elizabeth ran to her and placed an arm round her shoulders.

'Joan, what are you sitting down here for?' she whispered. 'Why ever aren't you in the tent?'

'I can't go back in there!' Joan sobbed quietly. 'I keep trying to pluck up courage but I can't. It's pitch black in there, you see, Elizabeth.'

'Joan, I don't understand—'

'I'm so ashamed,' sobbed Joan. 'I can't bear anyone in the world to know. Not even you, Elizabeth . . .'

But now she blurted out the truth.

'I didn't want the torch batteries for Teeny. I wanted them for my own sake. Then, when I realized none of you wanted the torch on, I lay awake for hours, terrified. That's why I opened the tent flap in the end. Not for Teeny's sake. It was for myself. I just knew I would never sleep if I couldn't have any light in the tent. Elizabeth, I can't get to sleep if it's pitch dark. Never, ever!'

'Oh, Joan!' gasped Elizabeth, struggling to take all this in.

Her friend was frightened of the dark! Elizabeth would never have guessed it. How well Joan had kept her secret!

JOAN TELLS ELIZABETH THE TRUTH

'But, Joan, how can you get to sleep in the dormitory at nights?'

'Because there's always a light in the corridor. The teachers always leave it on for us, don't they? So a nice crack of light comes under the door and that's all I need, Elizabeth. As long as I can see some light, I'm all right.'

'Poor Joan!' whispered Elizabeth. She took her handkerchief out of her dressing gown pocket and dried her friend's eyes for her. 'You mustn't cry. It's not your fault! Can't we explain to somebody about it?'

'How can we?' asked Joan in despair. 'First of all, I can't bear anyone to know. You *must* understand that, Elizabeth. And secondly, they would never let me be tent monitor. How can they allow someone who's frightened of the dark to be in charge of a junior? Especially a nervy little thing like Teeny. The poor child looks up to me so. If she found out about my silly fears, she would be frightened, too. It would put the idea into her head that the dark is something scary when it's not. What sort of example would I be setting?'

At the mention of Teeny's name, Elizabeth felt a moment's annoyance. Oh, no, not Teeny again!

But then, of course, it dawned on her.

She had been blaming Teeny quite unfairly. All the things that had gone wrong so far had not been Teeny's fault, after all. Even the accident with the glasses this afternoon would never have happened if Joan had had a proper night's sleep and been awake enough to look after her!

The root of it all, Elizabeth was forced to admit to herself, was Joan's secret fear. Teeny had not been to blame.

'I'm afraid if we told anybody, there would be only one outcome,' Joan was saying, calmly. In spite of everything, it had given her comfort to confide in Elizabeth at last. 'I would probably be asked to sleep up at school at nights. And Arabella would probably be made tent monitor in my place.'

Elizabeth realized that this was true.

Now, at once, her eyes glinted. She was not going to allow that to happen! She had made a solemn vow to help Joan make a success of things. She was not going to let anything defeat her, not even this.

'We've got to think of something, Joan.'

Surely there must be some way round the problem?

She left Joan's side for a moment and peered into the culvert. She crawled inside it for a short distance. She was looking into pitch darkness. The old tunnel ran under the wide country lane that lay beyond the school's boundary wall. It would once have carried the bubbling waters of the stream beneath the road, then out into open farmland on the other side.

'It's lovely and warm, just inside here, Joan!' she said, as she emerged. 'Come down here, a minute!'

'What are you doing, Elizabeth?' asked Joan, coming and crouching down beside her.

Elizabeth was on her knees now, moving rubble and fallen brick away from the entrance to the culvert. She cleared a space, then lay down in a bed of dock leaves, just inside. She was excited.

'I've had a brilliant idea, Joan!' she whispered. 'Let's go and get your sleeping bag from the tent. You can sleep in here! It'll be warm and cosy but you'll still be able to peep out and see the moon and stars above!'

Joan lay down for a moment in the space that Elizabeth had cleared. Suddenly, she looked pleased.

'I really think I could sleep here, Elizabeth,' she said. 'I really think I would rather like it!'

'Come on, then!' hissed Elizabeth, taking her friend's hand. 'Let's go and get the sleeping bag. You'll need the thick one. And – I know! When you've gone, I'll stuff your kitbag inside the other one! If anyone should chance to look at it in the early morning, they will think it's you lying there, sound asleep.'

'Of course!' said Joan, in delight. 'But I shall be sure to creep back to the tent, as soon as dawn breaks, and be safely back in my place by morning. Oh, Elizabeth. I can do this every night! What a glorious plan.'

'But now we must be as quiet as mice,' whispered Elizabeth, as they crept silently back up the bank. 'If Arabella wakes up, our plan will be ruined.'

Unbeknown to the two friends, Arabella was already awake. She was not only awake but up and about.

She was a light sleeper. The slight draught that had been caused by Elizabeth's leaving the tent had roused her.

Gradually, she had become aware that she and Teeny were alone in the tent. So she had scrambled into her dressing-gown and ducked out of the tent herself. Where were the other two? She would try to find out what on earth they thought they were doing!

'I can hear you!' she hissed, in a loud triumphant whisper. She was coming this way. 'I can hear you larking about down there!'

Just below the embankment, the two friends froze like statues. Arabella was coming. She knew they were there!

'I shall have to report this to Miss Ranger!' Arabella was saying.

Joan gazed at Elizabeth in dismay. Arabella had woken up. They were about to be discovered. Oh, what horrible luck!

JOAN TELLS ELIZABETH THE TRUTH

In her desperation, an idea came to Elizabeth. She whispered it into Joan's ear. This was an emergency. It was the only thing she could think of to do.

It was to be an example of the Naughtiest Girl at her most headstrong.

CHAPTER NINE

ARABELLA IS MADE
TENT MONITOR

ARMS OUTSTRETCHED, like someone in a trance, Elizabeth appeared over the top of the bank. She was moving at speed. She would have crashed straight into Arabella if the other girl had not jumped clear.

Arabella stared in surprise as the figure shot past her in the pale moonlight.

Elizabeth was walking stiffly, her eyes tightly shut, her arms as straight as pokers in front of her. She appeared to be walking in her sleep, marching towards the area where the tents stood.

Joan was following along in her wake.

'Hey, you two—!' began Arabella, as Joan carried straight on past her. 'What's going on—?'

Joan put a finger to her lips.

'Sssh, Arabella. Sleepwalking! Mustn't be woken up suddenly. Dangerous. Just trying to keep an eye on her . . .'

Elizabeth was playing the part with gusto.

ARABELLA IS MADE TENT MONITOR

She was striding past Philippa's tent now, her hands still outstretched as though feeling her way. Arabella frowned suspiciously and started to run to catch up with her. She must get a proper look at Elizabeth's face. Was she really asleep? Was it true that she was walking in her sleep? Arabella found it hard to believe *that*.

As Arabella came up alongside her, Elizabeth quickly screwed her eyes shut again. She quickened her pace. It was horrid not to be able to see where she was going! But she must get away from Arabella.

She strode on fast and then faster and then . . .

Whoomph! Crash!

She tripped over the guy ropes of someone's tent. She hit the guys with such force that the tent pegs came clean out of the ground!

As she fell heavily against the small, green tent there came a horrible creaking, crashing sound –

The smart little tent began to subside. She heard a strangled cry from inside.

'What is going *on*?'

The tent was lying on the ground now. Miss Ranger's angry face appeared from under the folds of limp canvas.

Elizabeth could only sit there and stare in horror. She had brought the teacher's tent down on top of her while she slept!

Miss Ranger struggled out from beneath the fallen

tent, found her dressing-gown and slipped it on over her pyjamas. She confronted Elizabeth, who had now got to her feet and been joined by both Joan and Arabella.

'What exactly is the meaning of this tomfoolery, Elizabeth?' she asked. 'What are you all doing out of your tent, may I ask?'

'I think Elizabeth may have been sleepwalking—' Joan began, desperately.

'You fibber!' exclaimed Arabella. 'Elizabeth was only pretending. And you were only pretending to be looking after her! You just did it because I'd come to see where you were! I heard you talking together before that. I heard you larking around!'

'Are you saying, Arabella, that Joan and Elizabeth were out of the tent at night?' asked Miss Ranger. 'And that you had to go and look for them?'

'Yes, Miss Ranger. And Elizabeth *can't* have been sleepwalking!' Arabella continued, triumphantly. 'Look, she's wearing her dressing-gown! Whoever heard of someone remembering to put on their dressing-gown before they start walking in their sleep?'

The teacher had only to look at the two guilty faces to know that Arabella was speaking the truth.

'I can see that camping has gone to Elizabeth's head,' observed Miss Ranger. 'I thought she was much more sensible these days. But I am shocked at *your* behaviour, Joan. That you, a tent monitor, should have been joining in Elizabeth's pranks! I am beginning to wonder if I did the right thing to put you in charge of Teeny Wilson.'

'Joan let Teeny go off and climb a tree in the woods this afternoon!' Arabella blurted out. 'And Teeny fell out of the tree and broke her glasses!'

Miss Ranger was taken aback. Telling tales was not encouraged at Whyteleafe School. But, occasionally, the teachers agreed, it could be justified.

'Is this true, Joan?' she asked.

Joan stared at the ground and said nothing. She was deeply mortified.

'It was only a low branch she fell off!' Elizabeth protested. 'And she didn't hurt herself at all.'

'Thank you, Elizabeth, that will do,' replied the teacher. 'I can see that what Arabella says is true, then.'

Miss Ranger gazed at all three girls, wondering what was the correct thing to do. To give herself time to calm down, she asked them to help her right the tent.

Only when that was done did she speak again. The teacher had come to a decision.

'The three of you will now return to your tent, in silence,' she said. 'I shall ask William and Rita to call a special Meeting for tomorrow afternoon, so that it can be decided whether Joan should remain as a tent monitor, or not.'

Miss Ranger then placed a hand on Arabella's shoulder.

'Until the special Meeting takes place I appoint you, Arabella, to be acting tent monitor. Until then, you are in charge of the tent and, in particular, I expect you to take good care of Teeny. Do you think you can rise to the challenge, Arabella?'

'Oh, Miss Ranger,' simpered Arabella, longing to gloat but somehow managing to look humble, 'I'll try my very best not to let you down.'

Joan's face was ashen.

And Elizabeth could have screamed with rage.

Elizabeth went to sleep feeling very sorry for herself. It was bad enough that Arabella had been appointed acting tent monitor. But she felt angry, too, at being in disgrace. She dreaded the special Meeting. She had not set out to be naughty, not at all. Everything she had done had been to help her friend. From the moment she had taken the blame for their being late back from the village . . . It had all been for Joan's sake! She had wanted nothing more than for Joan to make the grade as a fine tent monitor. And it had all been in vain, after all.

ARABELLA IS MADE TENT MONITOR

And now Arabella would tell everyone at the Meeting about the sleepwalking episode! She would be teased and laughed at and called the Naughtiest Girl again . . .

But then, shortly before daybreak, Elizabeth was awoken by Arabella's voice.

'I know perfectly well you've got your torch on, inside that sleeping bag, Joan. I can see the light from here. As tent monitor, I must ask you to put it out, please.'

At once, a lump came to her throat.

Poor Joan! Her troubles were so much worse than Elizabeth's own. It seemed that she had managed to snatch a few hours' sleep only by keeping her torch on inside her sleeping bag. Elizabeth heard the torch click off and its feeble light was extinguished.

She longed to protest but she knew that Joan would not thank her for it. How she would hate it if Arabella, of all people, knew about her fear. It would make her more superior than ever!

If only there were some way of *curing* Joan's fear, thought Elizabeth. Suddenly, she dimly remembered staying at a cousin's house. He always had to have the light on at night. 'He will grow out of it,' she had heard her Aunt say to someone. 'The doctor says when he is about ten or eleven.' Why, in that case, Joan should be growing out of her fear any moment now! decided

Elizabeth, hopefully. How wonderful if that happened and they could enjoy the rest of camp!

But how *could* they enjoy the rest of camp, she realized dully, with Joan suspended as a tent monitor and the insufferable Arabella appointed in her place? That, surely, was the only possible outcome of this afternoon's special Meeting.

At that moment, the first twittering of birdsong rose up outside. The dawn chorus was beginning. Soon, the pitch dark inside the tent was giving way to a softer gloom. Comforted by the thought that Joan would now be able to sleep, Elizabeth turned over and went back to sleep herself.

When she awoke, the sun was well up and the tent flap tied back.

Joan was outside somewhere.

Arabella and Teeny were up and dressed. Teeny was kneeling in the centre of the tent, in front of the mirror. Arabella was brushing her hair for her.

'Fifty strokes, morning and night, make your hair shine, Teeny,' Arabella was saying. 'It will make it shine like mine does!'

The little girl's spectacles had already been returned by Matron and were secure on her nose once more. Drowsily watching Teeny, Elizabeth noticed that she seemed to be preening herself in the mirror. She had buttoned her blue shirt up to the neck and had turned the collar up. She was staring at the image, dreamily, as though she liked it.

'Arabella's going to make Teeny as vain as she is herself,' thought Elizabeth, as the child fiddled with the shirt, unbuttoned it and turned the collar down again. Now she was asking Arabella why Joan was no longer in charge of her.

'Because Miss Ranger thinks I will make a better job of looking after you,' said Arabella, proudly. 'You'll hear all about it this afternoon. There's going to be a special Meeting.'

'Oh,' replied Teeny, looking disappointed.

But Arabella did not make a better job of looking after Teeny. She made a very bad job of it. That morning she forgot all about her and the consequences could not have been more dramatic.

CHAPTER TEN

TEENY IN DANGER

'WHERE'S TEENY?' asked Arabella, tetchily. 'I'm waiting to take her for a shower.'

Elizabeth and Joan stared at her in surprise. It was now noon. The two friends had spent the morning at the stables, helping Robert to groom the horses. After that they had been for a short ride. Now, as they returned to their tent, they found Arabella waiting impatiently outside. She was wearing a different outfit from the one she had worn at breakfast.

'How should we know?' asked Elizabeth rudely. It was a relief not to have to be polite to Arabella any more. 'You're the important tent monitor in charge of everything. You should know where Teeny is, not us.'

'But I thought she must have spent the morning with you!' said Arabella. 'When did you last see her?'

'We haven't seen her since breakfast time,' replied Joan, with a puzzled frown. What was this all about? 'You and she were washing up your breakfast things together.'

Both friends had noticed how forlorn the little girl looked this morning. She had not seemed to be enjoying Arabella's company very much. She had been gazing wistfully at Duncan and Kitty. Once again, the two boisterous juniors had been taking no notice of her. Elizabeth had commented to Joan how tragic it was that Teeny had been too cowardly to jump off that branch, the day before.

'How different things might have been!' Elizabeth had sighed. 'For all of us.'

'You mustn't call Teeny a coward,' Joan had replied, gently. 'We all have things that we're scared of.'

Now, a pallor was creeping over Arabella's face.

'Where is she, then?'

'Do you mean to say you haven't seen her all morning, either?' asked Elizabeth, accusingly. 'But where have you been? You were supposed to be in charge of her!'

'I had important things to do . . .' began Arabella, lamely. 'She was in the tent when I left her. I didn't mean to be gone very long . . .' Arabella pouted. 'In any case, Teeny said she had something *she* wanted to do.'

'What?' asked Joan, tensely.

'I've no idea,' said Arabella. She clammed up.

The truth was that Arabella had quickly become bored with Teeny's company. After breakfast, she had decided to slip up to school, taking some of her clothes back to exchange for others. She felt that she had brought the wrong outfits to camp and that she would look better in some others.

She had been only too happy when Teeny declined to come with her, saying that she had something of her own to do. And she had left the little girl sitting cross-legged in the tent, shuffling those silly playing cards, lost in thought.

Once in her dormitory, Arabella had soon forgotten about Teeny altogether. Admiring herself in a wardrobe mirror, she had tried on outfit after outfit and quite lost track of time. She had only just returned to the tent.

'You had better start looking for her,' said Elizabeth grimly. 'Hadn't you, Arabella?'

'Elizabeth and I will run to Camp Centre and see if she's there,' said Joan, anxiously. 'If we can't find her quickly, we must tell Miss Ranger.'

Leaving the frightened Arabella peering, helplessly, into empty tents, the friends raced off.

When they reached Camp Centre, they dearly hoped to find Teeny there. Had the loneliness of being left on her own all morning made her force herself to come and mix with her classmates? Perhaps they would find her playing happily with some other juniors, at last.

But there was no sign of her.

Most children had already left with their tent

monitors to have a shower before dinner. Duncan and Kitty were loitering about and chatting happily to two of their classmates. That was all.

'Have you seen Teeny, any of you?' asked Joan softly, as she and Elizabeth walked up. 'Arabella's waiting to take her for a shower.'

Joan spoke in a calm, quiet voice for she did not want to alarm the younger children in any way.

'Not since breakfast,' volunteered Kitty.

'We've been helping Mr Leslie build some plate racks this morning,' said Duncan. He pointed proudly into the Kitchen Area. A row of plate racks stood there, made from green twigs criss-crossed and lashed together. 'Now we won't have to do so much drying up. We can leave things to dry in the sun, Mr Leslie says. Do you like them?'

'Yes, very good,' said Joan, absently, at the same time gazing everywhere for some sign of Teeny. 'Well done.'

Elizabeth, however, was staring at the children in fascination.

All four had their sports shirts buttoned up to the neck and the collars turned up. It was the new fashion amongst some of the juniors, as Elizabeth was already vaguely aware. But today they also wore what looked like a fat sprig of grass tucked in behind the top button. It was worn discreetly, almost like a secret badge.

Then some tent monitors appeared in the distance, shouting to the juniors to come up to school with them for their showers.

'Well,' said Joan worriedly, as the four juniors went racing off, 'Teeny can't have been at Camp Centre all morning, or those four would have seen her. Oh, Elizabeth, it was very wrong of Arabella not to find out what it was Teeny wanted to do. If only we knew that, it would be much easier to find her.'

Elizabeth was thinking hard. A picture flashed into her mind of Teeny this morning – of her turning her collar up, admiring herself in the mirror.

'I thought the juniors' shirts were just some kind of fashion,' she told Joan excitedly. 'But now I'm not so sure. I think it might be some kind of club – and that Teeny wants to join it. And maybe being asked to jump from the branch yesterday was somehow connected with it—'

She stared at her friend.

'Joan, do you think she might have gone back there this morning? To try the jump again? On her own?'

'Why would she do that?'

'Well, hoping to be let into the club . . .?' mused Elizabeth.

'If you're right, we'd better go and tell Miss Ranger straight away,' said Joan. 'But why should the juniors have a club? You know they get crazes about how to wear things . . .'

'But the stems of grass they were wearing!' replied Elizabeth. 'It was those as well. They could be some kind of badge!'

'Grass?' asked Joan. 'Oh, you mean those green ears of corn? I noticed them wearing them last night, round the camp fire.'

Elizabeth gasped.

Green ears of corn. Of course!

Excitedly she told Joan what she had overheard Duncan say to Kitty in the woods yesterday. About Teeny.

'But she does like us so. Shall we just try the green ear . . .'

Joan now became very interested.

'So you think Duncan and Kitty are the club leaders and they decided to give Teeny another chance? They told her last night that she could go and get a green ear of corn, like theirs . . .? And that's where she's gone to this morning?'

'I'm sure of it!' exclaimed Elizabeth. 'But I'm sure they don't know about it. Teeny's made up her mind this morning, all on her own, to try and do it. To prove she's not a coward. That means it must be somewhere quite difficult . . .'

'But where?' asked Joan. 'Oh, we have to *think* . . .'

The whole camp had been to the woods yesterday. But there was certainly no corn growing there. Nor had they passed any on the way back. And, of course, there was no corn growing anywhere in the school grounds.

Yet at no time were members of the junior class permitted to go out of the school grounds on their own. So how had they managed to get those fresh-looking ears of corn?

'The only place I've ever seen any corn growing is over there somewhere,' said Elizabeth. 'On the other side of the lane.'

She waved a hand vaguely in the direction they had just come from. Out riding last July, she had seen a huge field of golden corn and men getting the harvest in. At the moment, of course, it would still be green. The field, she now realized, must lie opposite the high wall where their tent was pitched.

She gasped.

'I think I know how they did it!'

Joan had realized the same thing.

The two friends raced to the footbridge and swung themselves down into the dried-up stream bed. They ran all the way along the cutting, puffing and panting, until the mouth of the culvert came in sight.

'Listen!' cried Joan, as they neared its entrance.

From deep in the darkness came a faint whimpering sound.

Teeny was trapped somewhere in the tiny tunnel!

Remembering the pitch blackness in there, Joan hesitated. Only one of them would be able to squeeze in. But Teeny was in there. There was not a second to lose!

She wanted to do it. She had been Teeny's tent monitor. She *must* do it. But she knew that Elizabeth would stop her. And that would be more than enough to make her nerve fail . . .

Elizabeth glanced at her friend's face and saw everything that was going through her mind.

She ran forward, tripped and fell to the ground. She gave a cry.

'My ankle! I think I've done something!'

Now Joan could hesitate no longer.

'It's all right, Elizabeth. Don't try to move! I'm going in there to get Teeny!'

Joan dropped to the ground, dived through the gap, then crawled forward into the darkness and was gone.

Soon Elizabeth heard her voice, echoing from deep inside the culvert.

'It's all right, Teeny. It's Joan here. Don't be frightened. We'll get you out of here!'

Elizabeth got to her feet and tiptoed forward. There was nothing wrong with her ankle, at all.

Peering into the blackness, she could hear the clunk of rubble being moved. The roof of the culvert must have collapsed. Joan must be clearing a path for Teeny, with her bare hands. The child had been overcome with panic. She had lain there, not daring to move, convinced that she was trapped.

The little tunnel, like an echo chamber, carried their voices out.

'We'll just move these last few bricks, Teeny, and there'll be a nice gap and I'll be able to pull you through. We must do everything very slowly and carefully, so that we don't make any more disturbance.'

'Yes, Joan. Oh, Joan, I've been so scared.'

Only Elizabeth knew just how scared *Joan* must be and how brave she was being. Feeling immensely proud of her friend, she raced away to find Miss Ranger and Mr Leslie.

When she returned with the teachers and with Rita as well, they were just in time to see Joan's rear view appearing. Crawling backwards, Joan was gently pulling Teeny by the hands, out of the culvert, into the fresh air.

'We didn't feel there any time to waste!' Elizabeth explained to Miss Ranger. 'We were both so

frightened Teeny might suffocate.'

'I think the whole school is going to be very proud of Joan,' replied the teacher. 'She can take great pride in what she's done.'

'I think she does already,' replied Elizabeth, looking at Joan's happy, glowing face as she hugged Teeny close.

Teeny, in spite of her frightening ordeal, was also looking very proud. Her tear-stained face was, just like Joan's, glowing with happiness and a sense of achievement.

There was something clutched in her grimy fingers. She held it up to show Joan.

'Look! Duncan and Kitty will be friends with me now!' she blurted out. 'I shall be allowed to be a member of the Dare Club.'

It was a green ear of corn.

CHAPTER ELEVEN

A VERY GOOD SCHOOL MEETING

THE SPECIAL Meeting was about to begin. The campers sat on the ground sheets in rows, again. A low buzz of conversation rippled up and down the rows. It was always very exciting and interesting when William and Rita called a special Meeting. It meant that there was something important to discuss.

Sitting with her classmates, Elizabeth wondered what exactly was going to be raised at the Meeting.

It was no longer going to be about who should be tent monitor between Joan and Arabella.

There was Joan, at the front, seated with the other tent monitors. Elizabeth smiled and waved to her friend. Proudly, Joan waved back. She was back in her rightful place.

As soon as Teeny's rescue had taken place, Miss Ranger had stripped Arabella of her acting monitorship and asked Joan to resume her duties. Arabella was in deep disgrace for neglecting the little junior in her charge when it was well known that Teeny had no little friends to play with.

But Teeny certainly had friends now! thought Elizabeth, with a smile.

It had been wonderful to watch her at lunch-time, surrounded by the other members of the Dare Club. In clean clothes, after a hot shower, she had sat between Duncan and Kitty, in the place of honour at one of the junior tables. She was a member of the club at last, her collar worn turned up, like the rest of them, her green ear of corn displayed like a trophy in her top buttonhole. Having no idea of the danger she had been through, Duncan and Kitty were simply pleased that Teeny had finally proved that she was not a 'coward'.

She was still sitting with her new friends now, chattering happily in the front row, a child transformed.

Since arriving at Whyteleafe, the shy, nervous girl had longed only to be friends with Duncan and Kitty – she liked and admired them so. They had promised her that once she had proved her courage with a successful 'Dare', she would be allowed to join their secret club and play with them.

But each time Teeny had been given a Dare to do, her courage had failed and she had not completed it. With each failure, her confidence had ebbed away. The more desperate she became to join the club, the more scared and jumpy she was; dreading each new Dare, yet longing to succeed. Her greatest battle had been with herself. This morning, sitting in the tent and struggling with her fears, she knew that the challenge, to crawl through the culvert and pick a green ear of corn in the field that was out of bounds, was her very last chance. Duncan and Kitty would not give her another. And she had won the battle!

'Silence, please!' called William, banging the mallet on the table. 'At the Meeting this afternoon, we are going to talk about courage.'

There was an immediate hush.

Rita then told the astonished Meeting about the fall of rubble in the dangerous old tunnel. She told how it was only thanks to the alertness of Elizabeth and the bravery of Joan that no harm had befallen Teeny Wilson.

The two friends stood up and were given a round of applause.

Then William took over.

'We believe that Teeny's narrow escape had something to do with a Dare,' he said. 'If so, would the person or persons who made the Dare please stand up?'

Sitting in the front row, Duncan and Kitty had turned pale. They exchanged frightened glances but remained sitting.

'Would they please stand and own up?' William repeated.

The two juniors sat very, very still. They were frozen with fear.

William sighed.

'In that case—' He banged the mallet sharply on the table, making everyone jump. 'Duncan and Kitty, I must ask you to stand up at once and come out here to the front.'

Trembling slightly, the little boy and girl got slowly to their feet and went and stood in the front. Their faces had turned red with shame.

'I see,' said William. He surveyed them. 'How very interesting. So even you two are frightened of something? You are frightened of Rita and I.'

Now Rita joined in.

'William and I have made a full investigation. We have discovered, though not from Teeny, that all term you have been calling her a coward. You have been setting her Dares to do that were beyond her capabilities. In doing so, all her confidence was destroyed. You did not mean it to be cruel. You wanted her to succeed. But cruel it was.'

Duncan and Kitty, and some other members of the Dare Club, too, were beginning to feel extremely uncomfortable. Teeny's mouth was hanging open, in wonder, that the head boy and girl had found all this out.

A VERY GOOD SCHOOL MEETING

From the rest of the campers, there came not a sound.

As William continued, they hung on to every word he said.

'What you must all learn and understand,' he said, 'is that there are many different forms of courage and many different forms of cowardice. Let me give you an example. One Dare you set Teeny, when we all got to camp, was to play a joke on someone in her tent. Because she was discovered, you told Teeny that she had failed. But do you know why she was discovered?'

Kitty and Duncan shook their heads.

'She was discovered because another girl was blamed. So what did Teeny do? Rather than let the other girl take the blame, she owned up. Did that not take courage?'

Slowly, the juniors nodded.

'And not to have owned up – would that not have been cowardly?' prompted Rita. 'And should you not have owned up just now, when William asked you to?'

'So who are the real cowards, you or Teeny?' concluded William.

'We are,' said Duncan, looking deeply ashamed.

The lesson had been well and truly learnt. Rita spoke to them now, almost gently.

'It is not brave or clever to make sleeping-bag jokes,

or to break school rules, or do dangerous things. It must stop. But we want you all to put this behind you now and enjoy the rest of camp. And I think the monitors have decided that you must give your club a new name. Can any of you think of one?'

'Let's call it the Friendship Club!' exclaimed Kitty, taking hold of Teeny's hand. 'Would that be a good name, Teeny? Do you like it?'

Teeny loved it. They all did.

Afterwards, the whole camp agreed that it had been a very good Meeting. They had all learnt something from it, including Elizabeth.

'In a way, I'm as bad as those little juniors,' she confessed to Joan later, as they sunned themselves outside the tent. 'I thought Teeny was a terrible coward when she wouldn't jump off that low branch.'

'Yes, William and Rita were so right,' agreed Joan. 'There are so many different ways of being cowardly – and of being brave.'

'And still no one knows how brave *you* were, Joan,' said Elizabeth. 'Going into that pitch black tunnel. It would have meant nothing to me. But for you, of all people—'

'And nobody is going to know, either!' replied Joan, quickly. 'It was a private battle and I know now that I have won it. I am going to sleep without any light in the tent tonight, Elizabeth! You wait and see!'

Then she turned to her friend.

'It was so lucky that you fell, at exactly the right moment. I don't think I would have had the courage to go on, if that hadn't happened. I was convinced you must have twisted your ankle. Are you sure that it's really better now?'

'It seems absolutely fine,' replied Elizabeth solemnly. She bent forward, as though to examine it. In fact, she was making sure that Joan would not see the smile on her face.

After such a bad start, camp turned out to be wonderful. There was no more trouble with Arabella, certainly none with Teeny and, true to her word, Joan found that she could manage the darkness after that. Everyone was to agree that Joan turned out to be a very fine tent monitor, just as Elizabeth had vowed that they would.

Joan wanted to tell Miss Ranger that, for private reasons, she – Joan – was to blame for the visit to the village and for the sleepwalking episode. But Elizabeth refused to allow her.

'It would all be too complicated,' she said, with a shrug. 'And besides, the sleepwalking was such a terrible idea. I would rather we all forgot about it.'

It had not been one of the Naughtiest Girl's best.

The last one, the falling over idea, had been much better. Elizabeth was pleased about that. She could bear one or two black marks against her name, just to see her best friend happy again.

Elizabeth was not without courage herself.

THE NAUGHTIEST GIRL

Saves the Day

WHYTELEAFE

CHAO · ET · PERTINACIA

CONTENTS

CHAPTER ONE

ELIZABETH AND JULIAN ARE TOGETHER AGAIN

'PERHAPS THE train from London's running late!' said Elizabeth impatiently. 'Do you think so, Joan? Or perhaps the coach from the station has broken down! Do you think it could be stuck halfway up the hill with a flat tyre? Just imagine all the boys and girls having to sit inside the stuffy hot coach waiting for the wheel to be changed . . .'

Elizabeth jigged from one foot to the other, restlessly. She was at the top of the stone steps, outside the main doors of Whyteleafe School. Her gaze kept darting to the big stone archway through which the school coach was due to appear.

'. . . what do *you* think, Joan?' she finished.

Joan was Elizabeth's best friend at Whyteleafe School, although slightly older and in the second form. She was as calm and sensible as Elizabeth was excitable and impulsive. She shook her head and smiled at her friend.

THE NAUGHTIEST GIRL SAVES THE DAY

'*I* think you have a vivid imagination, Elizabeth. That's what *I* think!' she said quietly. 'The coach is hardly late at all yet.'

'But it was due at half-past one and that was five minutes ago!' protested Elizabeth. 'And I'm starving hungry, aren't you, Joan? And none of us can go into the dining-hall and have dinner until everyone's back from half-term!'

It was true that Elizabeth was hungry and regretted the fact that dinner would be late today. The delicious smell of savoury pies baking in the big ovens had wafted over to her from the kitchens. And, much earlier, she had seen the domestic staff preparing heaps of new potatoes and carrots from the school gardens. They would no doubt be steaming merrily away by now. There was always an especially good meal after a holiday, when many boys and girls were hungry at the end of a long journey back to their boarding-school.

But there was more to it than that.

'As a matter of fact, I'm really looking forward to seeing my class again, Joan,' she confessed. 'Especially Julian. I'm longing to tell him about the notice that Miss Ranger has put up on the notice-board. It's going to make our English lessons really exciting!'

Most of the first form had gone home for the half-term holiday, including Elizabeth's special friend,

Julian. Elizabeth had stayed on at school for a summer camp in the grounds. There had been lots of ups and downs but all in all it had been a wonderful adventure. Now she was looking forward to the second half of the summer term, sleeping in a proper bed again and life getting back to normal.

'Hello, Daniel! You're one of the last back!' she called out cheerfully, as an open-topped car cruised by. Daniel Carter was one of her classmates and only lived in the next village. As with any child who lived near Whyteleafe, he was being brought back to school by car. 'You should have been one of the first!'

The pale, fair-haired boy was sitting in the back of the open car, reading a book. He looked up briefly and returned Elizabeth's wave, then immediately turned his attention back to his book.

'Have you seen the coach?' she shouted. But the car had passed them now and her words were carried away on the breeze.

'It must be such fun to ride in an open car like that,' commented Joan. 'What an unusual boy Daniel is, nose stuck in a book as his father drives him along!'

'Yes, he does seem to prefer his books to the sights and sounds of the real world and to having friends,' agreed Elizabeth. 'I think shyness has a lot to do with it.'

'But he's a great one for complaining about people at school Meetings,' Joan pointed out. 'That's not the best way to make friends.'

'Yes, wasn't it funny that time he grumbled about Arabella making faces at him?' laughed Elizabeth. 'He makes himself sound such a baby when he stands up with silly grumbles and complaints. It's such a shame he can't learn to be a good mixer because then people would like him more.'

'I expect Whyteleafe will lick him into shape in time,' smiled Joan. 'You know that better than anyone, Elizabeth. When you first came here, you were the Naughtiest Girl in the School!'

'Yes. I've been trying to live it down ever since!' groaned Elizabeth. Her Naughtiest Girl nickname had stuck and no doubt always would! 'Oh, Joan, wasn't I horrid?' she sighed.

She stared across the green lawns to the trees beyond. A bird wheeled above them in the cloudless blue sky. It was so lovely at Whyteleafe, thought Elizabeth.

'I did everything I could think of to get myself sent home, didn't I?' she continued. 'From the best school in the whole world!'

'I'm so glad you didn't succeed,' said Joan quietly, giving her friend's hand a squeeze. 'I really am.'

A few moments later a large coach with

ELIZABETH AND JULIAN . . .

WHYTELEAFE SCHOOL on the front came nosing through the archway.

'It's here!' whooped Elizabeth. 'Hurray! Now *everybody's* back!'

The coach pulled up at the foot of the steps. All the boys and girls who had been on the London train came tumbling out. Elizabeth ran down to greet them. Joan, as befitted a second form monitor, followed at a more dignified pace to meet some of her own classmates.

'Julian!' squealed Elizabeth, her brown curls bouncing.

'Hello, Naughtiest Girl!' grinned the dark-haired boy, his cousin, Patrick, just behind him. 'How was camp then?'

'It was wonderful! But listen, Julian, such an exciting notice has gone up on the board. Wait till you see it! Miss Ranger's just put it up this morning. It's our form's turn to put on the Summer Play this year! It will be performed outside, in the school grounds! If we want to try for a part, we've got to sign up on the notice. The auditions are going to take place during English lessons!' Elizabeth had been bottling this news up for over an hour and it was now pouring out like a torrent. 'Oh, Julian, wouldn't it be fun if you and I could get the lead parts? The play's called *A Woodland Adventure* and it's been written by the joint heads!'

She tugged at Julian's hand.

'Come on, let's run. If we hurry, we'll be the first to get our names on the list—'

'Hey, steady on, Miss Whirlwind—' began Julian, looking amused.

'Yes, steady on, Elizabeth,' smiled Miss Thomas, as she shepherded the last of the children off the coach. She could see that the Naughtiest Girl was trying to whisk Julian away! 'Julian's not allowed to disappear off anywhere at the moment. Everyone from the London train's been given strict instructions to go straight to the dining-hall, as soon as they've washed their hands and faces. I suggest you do the same, Elizabeth. We're all very hungry. Whatever it is, it will have to wait.'

Elizabeth sighed and knew that she would have to be patient.

CHAPTER TWO

ELIZABETH'S HOPES
ARE KEPT ALIVE

JULIAN REFUSED to hurry through dinner. He was very hungry and wanted second helpings of everything. Elizabeth had to agree that the savoury pie was one of the tastiest that Cook had ever baked. The new potatoes and carrots were mouthwatering. And pudding was treacle tart and custard, one of their favourites.

It was a very jolly meal, with everyone catching up on everyone else's news. Some of the children had been to see shows in London. Ruth and Tessa had been taken to Regent's Park Zoo by Tessa's mother. Patrick had been at Lord's all week with his father, watching the cricket. Patrick was slightly boring on the subject but Elizabeth didn't mind at all, feeling happy to be surrounded by her classmates once again. Julian claimed that he had done absolutely nothing apart from laze around and go swimming once or twice.

Elizabeth, Belinda and Kathleen enjoyed telling the others about school camp. Arabella, who had behaved badly at camp and got into trouble, was suitably subdued.

'What's the matter, Arabella? Didn't you enjoy camping out very much?' asked Julian lightly. He was always very quick and shrewd. 'You don't seem to be saying very much about it.'

The spoilt girl screwed up her dainty, doll-like face and gave a little shrug.

'It was all right,' she murmured.

Elizabeth had no intention of telling tales on Arabella but she felt a quiet satisfaction. Arabella not saying much made a very pleasant change!

However, this happy state of affairs didn't last long.

At the end of the meal, the conversation turned to the exciting news about the first form play. Kathleen, like Elizabeth, had seen the notice that Miss Ranger, their form teacher, had placed on the notice-board and she had been spreading the news.

'Let's all go and put our names down for it!' she said. 'Oh, won't it be fun, doing the auditions in English lessons.'

'I've put my name down already,' announced Arabella. 'And I've read the play! As soon as Miss Ranger put the notice up, I asked to borrow a copy. It's absolutely brilliant.'

'It's all about a little girl called Fay who falls asleep in the woods!' interrupted Arabella's friend, Rosemary. She was very excited. 'When Fay wakes up, she's turned into a beautiful fairy queen and she has all these wonderful adventures with a goblin called Jonkin and they meet all these woodland creatures . . .'

'Miss Belle and Miss Best wrote the play themselves,' said Arabella, knowledgeably. 'They wrote it especially for us. Apparently it's five years since the first form had a turn of performing the Summer Play and they want it to be really special. Oh, aren't the joint heads clever to have written a whole new play?'

'And the part of Fay is just *made* for Arabella!' gabbled Rosemary. 'Can't you just see her as a fairy queen? I can. Of course,' she added, quickly, 'there will be lots of other parts for everyone and lots of things to do, like make costumes and things. I'm hoping to be chosen as prompter,' she added modestly.

Elizabeth listened to all this in stunned silence.

Arabella and Rosemary were now getting up from the table, keen to be off. Rosemary was still gabbling in excitement.

'Shall we go and get the play from your desk, Arabella? We'll take it outside as you suggested! I'm longing to hear you read bits out loud. It will be good practice for you! I wonder which boy will be chosen to play Jonkin? Oh, that's going to be a good part, too, isn't it—'

Arabella turned back and gave Julian a dazzling smile.

'I think Julian would make a wonderful Jonkin!' she simpered. 'Jonkin wears a mask in the play but he has green eyes, just like Julian, and he's very funny and clever. I do hope you'll put your name down, Julian!'

As the two girls left the dining-hall, Elizabeth bent her head over the last of her treacle tart, struggling to keep calm. In a blur she heard some of the others chattering as they started to drift away from the table . . .

'My goodness! Arabella's staked her claim quickly, hasn't she?'

'Trust her!'

'You have to admit she *might* make a good fairy queen. She'd look the part, at least, with that dainty little face of hers.'

'Too doll-like. Not vivacious enough.'

'Well, let's go and have a look at this notice.'

'Might as well put our names down. It's going to be fun.'

Before long, only Elizabeth, Julian and Patrick were left sitting at the long table, all on their own.

'I *knew* we should have rushed and put our names on

the list, Julian!' she said crossly, trying hard not to scowl. Arabella had got her name down first. Probably right at the head of the list! Not only that, she'd got hold of a copy of the play already. She'd read it through and was about to start practising for the auditions. 'Now Arabella's got a head start on everybody else!'

'Well, blowed if I would want to play the part of a fairy queen!' said Julian. He was laughing at her. 'And if *you* want to, Elizabeth, you'd better stop scowling and looking like a bold, bad girl and practise looking pretty!'

'I don't know *what* I want now,' said Elizabeth sulkily. 'Perhaps Arabella *would* be best. Perhaps I wouldn't be any good. And besides, she's got her name at the top of the list now.'

'You silly bumpkin.' Julian tweaked her hair. 'As if that makes the slightest difference to anything! Miss Ranger will just give out the parts to whoever reads them best when the auditions take place. I should think Arabella would be much too wooden. Now, you just run along, and sign up as you said you were going to.'

Elizabeth immediately felt cheerful again.

'I will, too!' she exclaimed, smiling and clapping her hands. 'But . . .'

She looked at Julian anxiously.

'. . . what about you, Julian? Surely you want to be in the play, too? It won't be half as much fun if you're not

307

in it. Arabella's probably right about you being the goblin. I can just imagine you!'

Julian yawned.

'I don't think acting's quite my line, Elizabeth,' he said gently.

Patrick, sitting further along the table and toying with the last of his treacle tart, suddenly looked up when Julian said that.

Elizabeth was about to start arguing with Julian. She knew perfectly well that her friend was a natural actor, brilliant at voices and imitations and altogether very funny. What he really meant was that the idea of being in the first form play bored him. How typical. How mean of him!

But before she could open her mouth to protest, Patrick spoke for the first time. He had been looking rather gloomy but now he had suddenly perked up. He couldn't help being a little jealous of his cousin, who was so full of talent, so good at everything he touched. To hear Julian being praised, even by Arabella, had made him smart.

'Glad to hear you've got some sense in your head after all, Julian,' he said. 'Wouldn't like to see my dear cousin make a complete fool of himself.'

'Oh, so that's what you think, is it?' asked Julian sharply.

He suddenly got to his feet.

'Come on, Elizabeth. Let's go along and sign up for this play then.'

Patrick watched them go, open-mouthed.

'I thought you didn't want to be in it!' he said crossly.

Julian glanced back over his shoulder.

'I've changed my mind,' he said, carelessly. 'It should be fun. A chance to make a complete fool of myself!'

As the two of them left the dining-hall and headed towards the school notice-board, Elizabeth felt rather sorry for Julian's cousin. She might have guessed that, whatever Patrick wanted, Julian would want to do the exact opposite.

As they wrote their names up on the list, she felt hopeful all over again. It would be wonderful to be chosen for the lead part and to play opposite Julian. He would make everything such fun.

Who else had signed up?

She looked at the names. There were slightly more girls than boys so far. But there was one name that was rather unexpected.

'Look, Julian!' she exclaimed. 'Daniel Carter's signed up.'

All through dinner he had, as usual, sat furtively reading a book under the table and not taken the slightest interest in the conversation about the play.

Daniel never joined in any activities that he could possibly avoid.

'What a surprise,' said Julian. 'Do you think he's hoping for the main boy's part, the goblin?'

Elizabeth laughed happily.

'With you around, Julian,' she replied, 'I'm afraid he'll just have to hope away!'

CHAPTER THREE

DANIEL DROPS A MYSTERIOUS HINT

IN THE English lesson the next day, Daniel hardly looked like somebody hoping to land a good part in the play. He looked rather glum about the whole thing!

'Here's yours, Daniel,' said Miss Ranger, brightly, as she finished handing out copies of the play to those who had signed up. 'When you read it, you will find it's a very good play. I want you to study it carefully over the next few days and decide which part to try for. You must learn some lines from your favourite part. And –' the teacher looked up and smiled round at the class '– the same thing applies to the rest of you. Please try to learn some of the lines you wish to speak when we have the auditions next week. You'll be able to act a part so much better if you do not have to read it from the script.'

'I've learnt some of my lines already!' piped up Arabella, smugly.

'Are you sure?' asked the teacher, kindly. She knew how much difficulty the oldest girl in the form had with memorizing things.

DANIEL DROPS A MYSTERIOUS HINT

Elizabeth was pleased that the auditions were still a few days away. They would be held during English lessons next week and the joint heads would be sitting in on some of the judging! Arabella had tried to steal a march but now they all had a chance to catch up. It was very pleasing.

Daniel, however, did not look in the least bit pleased. Elizabeth, sitting on the corner of Julian's desk and eagerly leafing through the play, had noticed how reluctantly the fair-haired boy had collected his copy, the last member of the class to do so. Now he walked back to his desk, opened the lid, and placed it inside without even glancing at it. Then he sat down and folded his arms.

As Miss Ranger addressed the class, he looked glummer than ever. She was telling them how, later on, rehearsals for the play would have to take place out of school hours – and in the fresh air. As the Summer Play was always held out of doors, it would be good practice for the children to get used to acting outside!

Daniel hated any form of outdoor activity. He was one of the few children at Whyteleafe to have his own tiny room, up on the attic floor above the main dormitories. Summer or winter, he loved his cosy little room under the eaves, where he could read his favourite story books to his heart's content.

'So be prepared to give up some spare time, those of you who are chosen,' concluded the teacher. 'We have so much other work to get through in English lessons. Remember, you have exams at the end of term and very important ones, too, for those who wish to go up to the second form in September. So now,' she clapped her hands briskly, 'stop talking everyone, please, and return to your desks and get out your spelling books.'

But by now Elizabeth was chattering away non-stop to Julian.

'Doesn't the story look fun, Julian? I *can* just see you as Jonkin! I don't in the least mind giving up my spare time if I'm chosen, do you? I'll have to skip some of my piano practice! But have you noticed something?' She lowered her voice to a whisper. 'Have you noticed how grumpy Daniel looks about the whole thing? I can't imagine anyone who would hate acting more, especially out of doors! So why did he put his name down?'

'I think there's probably a very simple answer,' Julian whispered back. He, too, had noted carefully Daniel's attitude. 'I don't think the poor boy wants to be in the play, at all. I think one of the teachers *ordered* him to put his name down for it. Perhaps Miss Ranger herself. It must worry them a bit, the way he never joins in anything.'

DANIEL DROPS A MYSTERIOUS HINT

'Oh, Julian! You are clever!' responded Elizabeth. 'Yes, that must be the answer—'

'ELIZABETH!' exclaimed Miss Ranger. 'Please stop talking and get off Julian's desk. Julian, please get your spelling book out as you have been asked to do. I think I will have to separate you two.'

The teacher looked around the room and then pointed to an empty desk, all on its own, at the back of the classroom under the open window.

'Elizabeth, please get your books and move to that desk at the back. You love talking so much that I think it will be better for you.' She spoke to the little girl quite kindly. 'You will be out of temptation's way there and I know I can trust you to pay attention and work hard, even right at the back there.'

'Yes, Miss Ranger,' replied Elizabeth.

Julian looked at his friend apologetically but Elizabeth did not mind in the least. She knew that Miss Ranger was acting for the best and besides, it was a lovely place, there by the open window. There were soft summer scents wafting in on the warm breeze. The last thing Elizabeth wanted to do at present was to blot her copybook by talking to her friends in class. Now any temptation to do so had been removed.

She pondered upon what Julian had said. 'Poor Daniel!' she thought.

But the very same day, at the end of the afternoon, Daniel caused them another surprise.

Once lessons were finished for the day, Elizabeth and Julian went for a short ride in the grounds on the ponies. Emerging from the trees afterwards, they dismounted and walked the horses back to the school stables. A boy was leaning against one of the stable doors, as though enjoying the sunshine. He waved cheerfully when he saw them and hurried forward to greet them.

'Hello, Julian! Hello, Elizabeth!' he exclaimed, whilst patting the horses' necks. 'Isn't it a lovely day! Have you had a good ride?'

It was Daniel.

The two friends unsaddled their horses and rubbed them down, at the same time glancing at each other in astonishment. It was such a surprise to see Daniel out in the fresh air! He looked so happy, too. His cheeks were flushed and there was an air of suppressed excitement about him. What could have happened to bring about such a change in him? It was most perplexing.

'Isn't it a grand day?' he repeated, once the ponies were unsaddled. 'Here, I'll put the tack away for you and shut the ponies up for the stableman.'

'Will you really?' said Julian, gratefully.

'That's sweet of you, Daniel,' said Elizabeth.

They dumped the tack and were about to leave when—

'Do you two know when the next school Meeting is?' the boy blurted out eagerly.

'Friday,' replied Elizabeth. 'Why?'

'Planning a complaint, Daniel?' asked Julian, teasingly. 'Or possibly a grumble?'

The boy flushed.

'No, not at all. Nobody's done anything to annoy me at present,' he said solemnly. 'I've got a special request to make to the Meeting, that's all. A *very* special request!'

'Whatever's that?' asked Elizabeth, fascinated.

'I – I'm sorry, I can't tell you. Not yet . . .'

'Oh, please do!' begged Elizabeth. 'Why can't you tell us?'

'I – I've got to see how things go,' mumbled the boy. 'I'm sorry. I shouldn't have said anything. I didn't mean to intrigue you . . .'

He looked apologetic.

'Fair enough,' said Julian, turning to walk away.

Daniel hurried forward and grabbed Julian's arm.

'But please, if I do . . . when I do ask the Meeting

this thing, I do hope you two will support me. Please.'

Elizabeth was more intrigued than ever.

'I'm sure we will if we can, Daniel.'

'Once we know what it is!' laughed Julian.

It was such a surprising episode. The two friends talked about it all the way back to the school building. Daniel had seemed so very different from his usual self.

'Whatever's happened to him?' wondered Julian. 'Can that be the same chap who looked so glum in English this morning?'

An anxious thought suddenly crossed Elizabeth's mind.

'You don't think it's because he's read the play by now? And he's realized what a brilliant play it is and how brilliant the part of Jonkin is, and how this is his big chance to shine . . . ?'

She hated the idea of anyone other than Julian having the part.

'Hardly! He'd be up in that little room of his, learning it off by heart, not enjoying himself in the fresh air for a change,' replied Julian. 'No, I'm sure it's not that. But something's transformed him, all right.'

'Can it be to do with this mysterious request he wants to put to the school Meeting?' pondered Elizabeth. 'I can't think what it's going to be.'

'We'll find out,' said Julian, airily, 'soon enough.'

CHAPTER FOUR

AN INTERESTING SCHOOL MEETING

ON FRIDAY, lessons over for the week, Elizabeth ran up to the dormitory and got ready for the school Meeting. She washed her hands and brushed her hair and decided that today she would wear her school blazer, even though it was still a bit big for her. As she did up the shiny silver buttons and looked in the mirror, she felt a happy, belonging sort of feeling.

She was proud to wear the blazer and to be a member of Whyteleafe School. She admired the way that William and Rita, the head boy and head girl, ran the Meetings with the pupils themselves making all kinds of important decisions about any problems that arose, without any help from the teachers.

As she filed into the hall with Belinda, Kathleen and Jenny she looked at her watch. They were early. But somebody else had got there ahead of them.

Daniel, usually one of the last, was seated very near the front at the far end of an empty bench. The girls took their places alongside him and Elizabeth noticed how spruce he looked. He was sitting upright, arms folded, waiting for the Meeting to begin. He seemed very alert. There was still the same air of suppressed excitement about him that had been there for some days.

Others, as well as Elizabeth and Julian, had noticed the change in Daniel. Although he still took a book with him everywhere, he was spending much more time out of doors. He looked happier and more lively. He had even begun to take an interest in the Summer Play. Apparently he'd learned bits from several different parts and had shyly asked Martin to test him.

'Well, now we shall find out more, at last, thought Elizabeth. He looks quite keyed up about this special request of his, whatever it is!'

The twelve school monitors came and took their places on the platform behind William and Rita, who were seated at a special table. There was a big book on the table. Important things that happened at Meetings were always written down in the Book. The scene never failed to remind Elizabeth of a court room, with William and Rita as the Judges and the monitors, the Jury.

The hall soon filled up as all the classes came in. Miss Belle and Miss Best, the joint heads, and Mr Johns, the senior master, slipped quietly into their special chairs, right at the back. They were there to observe proceedings but never joined in unless their advice was requested.

When everybody was seated and the hubbub of chatter was reaching a crescendo, William picked up a small hammer and struck the table loudly.

'Silence, please! The Meeting will now begin.'

As the gavel went down Elizabeth, as always, felt a frisson of excitement. There was an instant hush all around her. What would today's Meeting bring?

'First of all, finance,' said William. 'A lot of you will have brought money back with you. Thomas is passing the school box along the rows. Please place all your money inside.'

There came the rustle of banknotes and the merry rattle of coins going into the big box as the children cheerfully parted with their money. Some of the campers had been sent postal orders. They went into the box, too. It was a strict rule at Whyteleafe that all spending money was pooled and then shared out fairly, so that no pupil had an unfair advantage over another.

After that, every child in the school was handed two pounds. This was their spending money for the week.

'Now, are there any requests for extra money?' asked the head girl.

Eileen put her hand up.

'Please, Rita, I broke a string in my racket at team practice yesterday. We've got a match soon but Mr Warlow has had a look at it and he feels the racket's so worn that I really need to have a new one and just keep the old one as a spare.'

Rita had a quick word with William and they both nodded.

'That tennis racket of yours has had a lot of wear and tear this term in the service of the school, Eileen,' smiled Rita. 'No wonder it's worn out. You will be allocated some money to buy a new one.'

Patrick, who was in the second tennis team with Eileen, looked pleased for her sake. Now she would play even better.

The next request was rather more difficult to deal with.

A member of the junior class (which always sat cross-legged on the floor in the front of the first form benches) rose to his feet.

'Please, I'm getting very keen on tennis now we're starting to learn but I haven't got my own racket. There's one in the school second-hand shop and it only costs five pounds. Could I have some extra money to help me buy it?'

The head boy and girl went into a huddle with the monitors to discuss the request. After two or three minutes, they returned to the table and William called for silence.

'We don't think we can donate you any money from the pool, Henry, because it wouldn't be fair on any other juniors who don't own a racket. What we are prepared to do is to advance you your next two weeks' pocket-money. With today's money that would mean you have six pounds.'

The little boy looked very disappointed.

'But then, please William, that would only leave me a pound for sweets and things to last me three whole weeks!'

'Yes, Henry,' said Rita kindly. 'So this offer is a good test for you. It will help you to decide just *how* keen you are on tennis and how much you want your own racket, rather than using the school ones while you're learning. Think about it for a while. Then let us know at the end of the Meeting what you have decided.'

'Yes, Rita.'

'Any more requests for money, anybody?' she asked.

Elizabeth glanced sidelong at Daniel. But he remained silent.

So whatever he intended to ask for, then, did not require spending money.

The Meeting moved briskly on to discuss the school camp. William proposed a vote of thanks for the tent monitors, explaining that they had all done an excellent job. Sitting on the platform, Joan looked proud and gave Elizabeth a grateful wave. Only they knew about the problems she had had as a tent monitor and how they had been overcome.

After that came grumbles or complaints.

There were none at all this week.

'Good,' said William. 'We have just one more important matter to deal with. After that we will finish up with Any Other Business . . .'

'Nearly there, Daniel,' whispered Elizabeth behind her hand, smiling. 'You'll soon be able to ask what you want to ask.'

'I know!' nodded Daniel, looking eager and excited.

Elizabeth suddenly noticed how solemn William was looking.

'I'm sorry to have to tell you,' William was saying, 'that the matter we now have to deal with is a serious one. John, would you please stand up and tell the Meeting what you have told Rita and me?'

John Terry, the head boy of the school garden and one of Elizabeth's favourite people, rose to his feet. He was a blunt, straightforward boy who had great gifts as a gardener but none for public speaking.

'Some little idiot's been vandalizing the strawberry beds!' he blurted out, dark spots of anger on his cheeks.

'Somebody too greedy to wait for the fruit to get ripe! Pulling up the plants to see if any of the underneath berries are red yet, I daresay. Uprooting the plants with all the berries still green!'

There were shocked gasps around the hall. Whispers rippled up and down the rows of children. What a mean thing to do. Another month of ripening sun and the school gardens always produced big, luscious red strawberries – heaps of them. Strawberries and cream for tea . . . They all loved strawberry time! But any plants pulled up by the roots would die now before the fruit could ripen properly.

'How greedy and silly!' whispered Elizabeth.

'Greedy and silly and ignorant,' agreed Kathleen.

William banged the gavel for silence. There was more drama to come. He held something up between his thumb and forefinger. Everybody looked at it.

It was a shiny, silver blazer button.

'Here is something very interesting,' he said. 'The person concerned lost their blazer button while they were hunting for strawberries. John found this lying amongst the uprooted plants. Would the person responsible now own up,' he said, with heavy irony, 'and we can give them their blazer button back.'

There was silence.

'Stand up and own up, please,' repeated William.

They all held their breath and waited. A half minute ticked by. But still nobody moved.

'Very well,' said William, at last. 'Whoever behaved in this stupid way will no doubt have friends and classmates. *They* will notice that someone has a blazer button missing. Will they please persuade the person concerned to come to our study and own up? John has a great number of jobs in the garden waiting for them. Now, is there any other business, please, before we close the Meeting?'

In the drama of what had just taken place, Elizabeth had forgotten all about Daniel's special request. But she glanced at him now. He, too, seemed to have forgotten it! He was just sitting there, staring into space.

'Come on, Daniel!' she whispered, giving him a nudge.

The boy gave a start. Then, slowly, he put his hand up.

'Yes, Daniel?' asked Rita.

'I . . . I—' The fair-haired boy got to his feet, looking very self-conscious. Now that his big moment had come, he seemed embarrassed and tongue-tied. Poor Daniel! Elizabeth felt sorry for him. It was obviously something very important to him. It was daunting to have to ask in front of the whole school like this.

'Go on!' she encouraged.

AN INTERESTING SCHOOL MEETING

'Please, can I help with the horses and muck out the stables and things?' he blurted out. 'I know Robert helps sometimes and I'd like to as well.'

Rita looked at Daniel in surprise. This was hardly something that needed to be brought to a school Meeting.

'Well, only the stableman can decide that, Daniel,' she said, gently. 'I'm sure he'll be pleased to have some extra help and can find you some jobs to do. You must go and talk to him about it.'

Daniel sat down. His face was bright red.

Elizabeth stared at him in amazement. He had never taken the slightest interest in the school stables before. He was one of the few children in the class who never rode. But, above all, she felt cheated somehow. A sense of disappointment. Whatever had Daniel been making such a fuss about?

'What a let-down!' she said to Julian, after the Meeting. 'What was so special about that? Why did he beg us to support him, the other day? What a fuss about nothing! Oh, Julian, I do think Daniel is peculiar!'

'He's certainly a puzzle,' said Julian, with a shrug. 'But I'm more interested in this strawberry mystery.'

CHAPTER FIVE

THE AUDITIONS TAKE PLACE

'THE MYSTERY of who pulled up the strawberry plants? You're right, Julian,' nodded Elizabeth. 'That *is* rather interesting!'

It was annoying of Daniel to have been so tantalizing about something so tame. But now the Meeting had given them something different to think about! Poor John. What a shock it must have been to find some of his plants uprooted. She fully intended to spend some time in the school gardens this weekend and ask for some jobs to do. Could any of the plants be rescued?

'What puzzles me is why they didn't own up,' said Julian. 'People usually do.'

'Too scared, I suppose!' sighed Elizabeth. 'Too scared and cowardly.'

'But they must know they're going to be found out,' reasoned Julian, digging his hands deep in his pockets. He looked at the three gleaming silver buttons on Elizabeth's blazer. 'Our school blazers only have three buttons on them. If you've lost one of them, you can't exactly hide the fact!'

'Yes,' agreed Elizabeth. 'And wasn't it funny to be wearing a blazer in the first place? I know I wouldn't wear mine if I were just messing about in the school gardens.'

'That's exactly what I was thinking,' replied Julian.

'But it's lucky they were!' said Elizabeth, cheerfully. 'That blazer button is a wonderful clue. It's bound to catch them out before long. We could do some detective work ourselves, Julian. We'll start looking at everybody who's wearing a blazer.'

'Quite wrong, Elizabeth!' replied Julian.

'Wrong, why?' asked Elizabeth, indignantly.

Julian looked amused.

'We must start looking at everybody who *isn't* wearing a blazer. There will be somebody, somewhere, who never wants to wear their blazer for some reason!'

'Because they're too scared?' realized Elizabeth. 'Oh, of course.'

'Yes. And that's going to be much more difficult. An interesting challenge.'

They both agreed to keep their eyes open. They were not the only ones.

The mystery of the vandalized strawberry plants was a major talking point as they went into tea that day.

Everybody wearing a blazer was subjected to scrutiny, Elizabeth included! She quickly became tired of people making teasing remarks about her being the 'Naughtiest Girl', as they came up and counted the buttons on her blazer!

The following morning she went along to the school gardens. She found John Terry netting the strawberry beds. He was very pleased to see her.

'Hello, Elizabeth. How good to see my best little helper! This job can be done quite quickly now there are two of us.'

Elizabeth was relieved to see that the majority of the strawberry plants remained untouched and were bushing out well, with plenty of green fruit. The uprooted ones from the first row had now been tidied up into a small heap beside the path. They were already withering and well beyond being saved. They were mostly poor, thin things, she noticed, with not many berries on them. So the damage to the strawberry crop had not been as bad as feared, then. How stupid of someone to expect to find some ripe fruit in this way.

'I don't usually net the plants so soon,' explained John, as they unrolled the lengths of fine green netting and placed them carefully over the beds. 'They're to stop the birds getting at the ripe fruit – especially the blackbirds! They take not the slightest interest until they see a strawberry that's red and luscious and at its very peak! If you see a blackbird pecking at one, you can be quite sure that it has just reached its very moment of perfection!'

'How very clever of them!' laughed Elizabeth, her mouth watering as she remembered the days of strawberries and cream at the end of term last summer. 'I wonder how they know? So you've decided to prepare the defences well in advance?'

'Yes,' nodded John.

Once the nets were laid in place, they staked them down by driving small pegs in the ground all the way round the edges. The birds, John explained, would try to wriggle under them if they saw any good gaps.

'Then, as often as not, they can't find their way out again!' he explained. 'They get in such a panic before they manage to escape. Sometimes you find an especially silly one tangled in the netting and you have to release it. However that won't happen for a while yet.'

When they had finished, Elizabeth straightened up and arched her back. It had been hard work. She surveyed the covered beds with a sigh of satisfaction.

'Did you decide to net them early because of what one of the children has done, John?' she asked quietly.

He nodded.

'Yes. If anyone's ever tempted to meddle with the

strawberry plants again, it will remind them not to,' he said. 'Silly young idiots. I'm very surprised that nobody's owned up yet. But that blazer button is going to give them away.'

'It certainly is,' agreed Elizabeth. 'And I'm sure they won't dare to do it again!'

When she found Julian, later, she learned that he had been going round with Harry questioning people about blazer buttons.

'We've been getting lots of rude answers, I'm afraid,' he said, with a grin. He yawned. 'This could prove to be quite a long job.'

'The damage isn't quite as bad as John made it sound,' said Elizabeth. 'There should still be plenty of strawberries for tea when it comes to end of term time! Perhaps we should wait a while and see if the person owns up. Oh, Julian, surely they will?'

For by now Elizabeth's mind was turning back to the Summer Play.

On the way back from helping John Terry, she had seen Arabella, with the faithful Rosemary, over by the cedar tree, trying to say some lines off by heart while Rosemary held the script and acted as prompter.

Now that Elizabeth had read *A Woodland Adventure* through from beginning to end, she longed more than ever to be chosen for the leading girl's role. There were such sparkling lines for Fay to speak, especially in the scenes with Jonkin, the funny goblin who – surely! – could only be played by Julian.

And the two main parts would be auditioned first, on Monday! The joint heads were coming along and would give their opinions to Miss Ranger, although leaving her with the final decision. Later in the week, in other English lessons, the rest of the parts would be given out.

'Julian, we must decide which bits we want to act out on Monday,' said Elizabeth, 'and then we'd better learn the lines off by heart. Will you test me when I've learnt mine?'

'I'll test you tomorrow,' promised Julian, who had arranged to play tennis with Harry for now. 'Mind you learn them well!'

By Sunday evening, Julian had still not bothered to learn any lines of his own and treated the whole thing in his usual casual way.

'Stop fussing, Elizabeth. I haven't decided which bit I want to act out, yet. I'll get something together by tomorrow, I daresay.'

Elizabeth, on the other hand, had learned three different sections of Fay's part, skimping most of her prep that weekend in order to do so.

'I'll act out each bit in turn, Julian, and you tell me which one you think is best.'

Julian watched and listened attentively and gave her some good acting tips, too, as she went along.

'I liked the first one best,' he said, at the end. 'When Fay wakes up in the woods and finds that she's turned into a fairy queen and she thinks she's all alone until Jonkin peeps out from behind the tree! You do it very well. Do you know something? I think you could be a real star!'

He looked really proud of her as he said it.

Elizabeth's mouth went dry with excitement.

She could hardly wait for the auditions to begin.

When Elizabeth arrived for English the next day, she noticed Julian already in his place, casually flicking through the pages of the script. So he still hadn't learned any lines! By the look of him, he was only just starting to think about it. Elizabeth felt cross. But she knew that she must concentrate hard now and not let anything distract her.

'We will start with Fay's part,' the teacher was saying. 'Belinda, would you like to go first, please?'

Miss Belle and Miss Best, the joint heads, were sitting at the front with Miss Ranger. Belinda stood up and launched into her lines. It was all very exciting. Elizabeth watched and held her breath and wondered how well Belinda would do.

THE AUDITIONS TAKE PLACE

She had chosen a tender scene in the play where Fay finds the injured Mr Badger in the woods. She acted it out quite well, though she did forget her lines once or twice. When she sat down, everybody clapped her.

'Your turn now, Elizabeth,' smiled Miss Ranger.

'May I sit on the floor, under the window here, please?' asked Elizabeth. 'You will all have to imagine I'm sitting under the big tree, just waking up from a sleep, right at the beginning of the play.'

The joint heads nodded in approval. They were enjoying seeing their play start to come alive. Everybody in the class turned round to watch Elizabeth's performance. Somehow, she riveted the attention.

She began by stretching and yawning and then opening her eyes.

She stared all around her in wonderment.

'*Why am I here? Where have I been?*'

Then she stood up and ran her hands down her clothes.

'*Why am I dressed as a fairy queen?*'

Elizabeth continued her monologue, word perfect, acting it out as she went. She sighed, she gasped, she pirouetted, as she discovered the beautiful woods for the first time. It all seemed so real. She ended by subsiding back down to the floor again, once more under her 'tree', her voice a little sad.

THE AUDITIONS TAKE PLACE

'*. . . but when nightfall comes I'll be all alone.*
And missing my dearest friend from home.'
She gave a big sigh, as the script had directed.

Her performance should have ended at that point. But suddenly Julian stood on his chair, jumped off, hopped lightly over to Elizabeth's desk then ducked behind it. He peered at her round the corner, pretending the desk was a tree. Face screwed up like a goblin's, green eyes sparkling, he launched into Jonkin's part –

'*Alone my foot, alone my thumb,*
Come, my Royal Highness. Come!'

He pulled Elizabeth to her feet and danced her round the desk –

'*You'll meet new friends in this wood so green*
And all of them love their fairy queen!'

It was so unexpected that Elizabeth laughed in excitement. Her audition really was over now and her classmates were cheering and clapping. The teachers were smiling, too. But then Miss Ranger held up a hand for silence.

'Very good, Julian. But we're not auditioning for Jonkin's part yet. Your turn will come in a few minutes. Thank you, Elizabeth. Now let us see what Arabella can do, please.'

Arabella was the third and final girl asking to be

considered for the part of Fay. She rose to her feet, face pale with tension.

'Please, Miss Ranger, I've learnt the same bit as Elizabeth. The opening bit. And I was planning to sit and lean against the wall, just as she did.'

'That's perfectly all right, Arabella,' said Miss Ranger gently.

The fair-haired girl, looking as pretty as a picture, went and sat on the floor under the window – very much as Elizabeth had done.

Biting her lip in annoyance, Elizabeth had to watch and listen as her rival repeated all her actions. She stretched, she yawned, she opened her eyes . . .

'*Why am I here? Where have I been?*'

Arabella was striving hard to be expressive. It was a good effort – and there was no doubt that she looked the part.

But then, on her second line, she made a silly mistake.

Carefully imitating Elizabeth's action and smoothing down her clothes she said –

'*Why am I queened as a fairy dress?*'

Snorts and giggles broke out round the classroom and Miss Ranger had to bang the table for silence. Stumblingly, Arabella corrected herself and carried on through the opening monologue.

In spite of fluffing some more lines, and forgetting

one line completely, it was quite an impressive effort. The boys and girls gave Arabella a good round of applause at the end. The teachers joined in. As Arabella returned to her seat, pink with excitement, Elizabeth began to feel very tense.

'We will now audition for the part of Jonkin,' announced Miss Ranger. 'After that I shall have a private chat with Miss Belle and Miss Best and then at the end of the lesson the parts will be given out.'

Elizabeth could hardly bear the suspense.

CHAPTER SIX

ELIZABETH IS OVER EXCITED

SEVERAL BOYS wanted to be in the play, especially in the roles of Mr Badger and Mr Grasshopper. They were both such good characters! Those two roles would no doubt be fought over, later in the week. But only two boys wanted to try for the Jonkin part as it looked quite daunting.

The other one was Daniel. He was called first and even he seemed hesitant.

'I – I'm not that sure I want to try for it,' he said, awkwardly. 'Not really.'

'Oh, come along, Daniel,' chided Miss Ranger. 'You know you can do it.'

Elizabeth could see that the fair-haired boy was embarrassed. It was odd, how Daniel had returned to his old ways lately. He had been so different last week, lively and cheerful, even asking Martin to test him for the play! Since then he had become his usual self again. It was true that he was spending a lot of time at the school stables, after speaking to the stableman. But

Robert had complained that he was not really helping much. He read his books all the time, or simply lazed around, exactly as before. He might just as well have been in his room! What a funny boy he was, thought Elizabeth.

But now she felt uneasy. She remembered Julian's idea that the teachers had forced Daniel to put his name down for the play. Was it possible there might be favouritism?

Daniel began his first line, still embarrassed.

'Wait, Daniel!' said Miss Ranger, holding her hand up. Smiling gently, she rummaged in a bag. 'Look, this might help you. In the play, Jonkin always wears a mask. A lot of the animal characters will wear masks, too. Let's see you put this mask on, as you act out your lines. You may find that it helps you get into the spirit of things!'

The teacher handed the boy a face mask. It was not the actual goblin mask that would be used in *A Woodland Adventure*. That would not be ready until later. It was just an old mask from the school dressing-up chest but it was a funny one, with an upturned nose and rosy cheeks.

As Daniel put the face mask on, the children laughed and clapped. Elizabeth became even more uneasy. She was sure that Julian was right. The teachers wanted Daniel in the play; they very much wanted him to succeed.

Now, as he acted out the part from behind his mask, the improvement was very marked. He had learned his lines well and his shyness was dropping away. He was much more carefree.

His performance was not too bad at all.

'Congratulations, Daniel,' said Miss Belle, afterwards. 'You did that well. Didn't he, Miss Best?'

The joint heads looked pleased.

'Now, Julian, your turn,' said Miss Ranger. 'And you must wear the face mask, too, so we can judge you both fairly!'

Everybody cheered as Julian put the mask on and went straight into a goblin-like pose, crouching on his chair.

'I'm afraid I haven't learned any lines yet,' he said, carelessly picking up the script. 'Apart from the little bit I did with Elizabeth. But – let me see – there's a scene here that's rather good, I think.'

Before Elizabeth had time to feel angry with Julian again for being so casual, he had launched forth. It was a passage from the play where Jonkin has decided, secretly, to bake a cake for the fairy queen.

'Here's a pinch of aniseed
I'll find the other things I need

ELIZABETH IS OVER EXCITED

Flower where the sweet bees suckle
And honey from the honeysuckle
Butter from the buttercups . . .'

The class watched and listened in delight. It was hard to remember that Julian was reading from a script, so fluent was his performance. As he spoke the words, he did all the right actions as he went along! He ended up with a handstand, as required by the script.

Everybody clapped. It was a most excellent performance!

'Thank you, Julian,' nodded Miss Ranger, as Julian handed in the face mask. 'You should really have learned your lines, though, like the others.'

Then Miss Ranger told the class to get out their English set books and read them in silence. She wished to confer with the joint heads.

As the three grown-ups went into a huddle, Elizabeth strained her ears, trying to catch what they were saying. But they spoke in very low, soft voices. Soon after that, the joint heads departed from the classroom. Who had Beauty and the Beast liked best? she wondered. They, after all, had written the play.

Nevertheless, Miss Ranger was in charge of the first form and was the play's producer. The final decisions on casting must be left to her, for she knew her pupils best.

THE NAUGHTIEST GIRL SAVES THE DAY

After seeing Miss Belle and Miss Best out, Miss Ranger came back and stood in front of the class and made her announcement.

'Elizabeth will play the part of Fay,' she said. 'And Arabella will be her understudy . . .'

Elizabeth gave a gasp of pleasure.

'And we will try Julian in the Jonkin part as long as he behaves properly and learns his lines. Daniel will be the understudy.'

Elizabeth felt weak with happiness as her classmates crowded round and clapped her on the back. 'Well done,' said Belinda, sportingly. 'You were really good.' Julian was being congratulated, too. There was noise and chatter all round.

As the bell went for the end of the lesson Miss Ranger clapped her hands for silence.

'I can see you are all very excited,' she said. 'But remember, please, that this is school time. We have plenty of hard work to get through, if you are all to do well in summer exams at the end of term. The next lesson is geography. I am just slipping out to collect our weather map from Mr Johns . . .'

She looked at them sternly.

'When I return to the classroom, I expect to see you all sitting at your desks in absolute silence, please. You will have your geography books out and be ready to start the next lesson.'

It was rather too much to ask. As soon as the teacher had left, the buzz of chatter broke out afresh. Elizabeth, in particular, was rather over excited.

It had been such a strain, waiting to hear the results of the auditions. Now her dearest wish had been granted. She would play the part of Fay, Julian the part of Jonkin! With Julian cast opposite her, the Summer Play was going to be tremendous fun. She was already looking forward to rehearsals. It was going to be the best thing they had ever done at Whyteleafe School!

She noticed that Daniel was congratulating Julian. He did not seem to resent the fact that he would just be understudy. The same could not be said of Arabella. She was the only person in the class not to congratulate Elizabeth. She was sitting at her desk, head bent, looking out her geography books.

'Cheer up, Arabella,' she called out, boisterously. 'I might fall and break a leg!'

'Yes, you'll make a good understudy, Arabella,' giggled Belinda. 'You copied everything that Elizabeth did to perfection.'

Elizabeth winced. Nothing would have induced her to raise that herself. But she was touched that some of the others had noticed it.

Arabella looked up, sulkily.

'I did nothing of the sort! I had everything planned already. It wasn't my fault that I had to go last . . .'

Belinda just laughed and then Arabella lost her temper. She sprang to her feet and pointed at Elizabeth.

'She cheated! She got Julian to help her! I saw them practising together last night. They had it all planned. It's not fair! It was Julian joining in at the end that got her the part!'

'Rubbish!' exclaimed Julian.

Elizabeth felt a temper coming on. She would get her own back on Arabella for saying that. What a mean girl she was!

As Miss Ranger came along the corridor with the map two minutes later, she could hear a commotion in the classroom. What was going on? She stood in the doorway and gazed at the scene.

Elizabeth Allen was standing on her desk, declaiming loudly, her face flushed with excitement. She was imitating Arabella.

'Why am I here? Where have I been?

Why am I dressed as a hairy fiend?'

Some of her friends had crowded round, hooting and stamping their feet at Elizabeth's impromptu performance.

ELIZABETH IS OVER EXCITED

'SILENCE!' came the voice from the doorway.

The children all scrambled back to their desks. Elizabeth quickly jumped off hers and sat in her place. There was a hurried scuffling of paper and banging of desk lids as they all got their geography things out. Then came complete silence, broken only by muffled snorts as some children struggled hard to stop laughing.

But Miss Ranger's eyes were fixed only on Elizabeth, whose cheeks were still very flushed with excitement.

'I am surprised at you, Elizabeth. Do you not realize that anyone can fluff their lines in a play, even you? Do you not realize that you were being rather cruel and silly?'

Elizabeth opened her mouth to speak. She wanted to tell Miss Ranger how cruel and silly Arabella had been to her. Not just today, either, but from the very first moment they had met. That dreadful moment in the Christmas holidays when Arabella had come to stay at her house just because their parents knew each other. And Elizabeth's mother had informed her that Arabella was coming to Whyteleafe and would be a nice companion for her, with her beautiful manners and lovely clothes! Why, Elizabeth had hated the spoilt girl on sight.

But, with her mouth still open, Elizabeth remained silent.

'Do you not realize?' repeated the teacher.

'COR!' came the cheeky reply.

It was very loud and sounded deliberately silly and insolent.

There was a moment's shocked silence and then snorts of nervous laughter broke out. That *Cor!* coming from Elizabeth like that had been such a surprise. And now the Naughtiest Girl was looking all around her, pretending to be surprised herself.

'Who said that?'

'You did, Elizabeth,' replied Miss Ranger. She did not find it in the least bit funny. 'Stop showing off, Elizabeth. You have just been extremely cheeky to me. You will apologize at once, please.'

'It wasn't me, Miss Ranger!' protested Elizabeth, in bewilderment. She turned and looked out of the open window, which was right behind her. 'It must have been someone fooling around outside!'

She opened the window very wide and leaned out of it, looking right and then left. Several of her classmates rushed from their desks to the back of the room and crowded round her.

'That's funny, there's nobody there,' Elizabeth was saying.

'Ooops! Nobody there!'

'Can you see anybody, Martin?'

ELIZABETH IS OVER EXCITED

'Not a sausage.'

'Must have been a ghost!'

Some of the boys, in particular, were enjoying the distraction. This was the Naughtiest Girl as she used to be! It was good fun and better than geography.

'Sit down, all of you,' exclaimed Miss Ranger. 'Elizabeth, shut that window at once. Now turn round, sit down and face me.'

'Yes, Miss Ranger.'

The teacher spoke in icy tones.

'I see that getting the star part in the play has made you over excited, Elizabeth. You have got completely carried away. If you cannot calm down, I will have to think again about my decision. Now, for the last time, will you please own up and apologize for speaking to me in that rude way.'

The whole class fell silent. The joke was over.

They waited to see what Elizabeth would say.

CHAPTER SEVEN

A VERY BAD QUARREL

'I HAVE no intention of apologizing, Miss Ranger,' said Elizabeth. 'How can I, when it wasn't me?'

The boys and girls looked at the Naughtiest Girl in surprise. Of course it was her! Who else could it have been? They had all heard her. How silly of her to speak to Miss Ranger like that. Now she would lose her part in the play.

Elizabeth did not mean to sound ill-mannered but she had a very hot temper. It was really horrid, not to be believed like this. Even if it meant losing the precious part in the play, she thought angrily, she was not going to pretend she had made that cheeky comment when she had not.

'Really, Elizabeth,' began the teacher, in exasperation. 'You will leave me with no other choice—'

There was a sudden sound.

ZZZZZZZZZZZZ.

It seemed to be coming from Elizabeth's direction, near the window.

A VERY BAD QUARREL

ZZZZZZZZZZ.

There it was again. But this time it was over by the door. Was there a bumble bee flying round the room?

ZZZZZZ. ZZZZZZ.

It was buzzing here, there and everywhere. But where was it? Nobody could see it.

'Julian!' realized Patrick.

And suddenly Julian was grinning and everybody in the class remembered. Julian had done this before! He was absolutely brilliant at imitations. He could throw his voice, too. He could make sounds appear to come from anywhere, without moving his lips . . .

'Julian,' thought Elizabeth, in horror. 'Of course.'

She was not amused.

Nor was Miss Ranger.

'You have been misjudged, Elizabeth,' she said. 'I apologize for that. We had forgotten all about your friend, Julian, hadn't we, and the clever things he can do with his voice? However, I'm afraid there is one clever thing that Julian will *not* be doing with his voice in future. Please stand up, Julian. And take your hands out of your pockets while I am speaking to you.'

She lectured Julian sternly about disrupting the lesson and almost getting Elizabeth into further disgrace.

'I can see that you and Elizabeth are going to be very over excited and silly if you are in the play together,' she concluded. 'I'm afraid I have changed my mind about the part of Jonkin. It will be played by Daniel. You will be Daniel's understudy.'

'Yes, Miss Ranger.'

For the rest of the lesson, the class was very subdued, even Arabella and Daniel.

Elizabeth was subdued, too, but inside she was boiling.

She had briefly felt relief when the mystery was cleared up. She had been completely baffled as to where that voice had come from. She thought it must have come through the window just behind her but, of course, there was nobody there! She never dreamt it had been one of Julian's tricks. It would have been too stupid of him.

But it *had* been him! And if he hadn't let it be known, she could have lost the part in the school play.

Her relief quickly changed to anger, as she thought about his silly behaviour and his own part being taken away from him, which was no more than he deserved. Now she would have to play opposite Daniel, instead. How dull that would be. She had been so looking forward to acting in the play with Julian.

'How could you be so stupid?' she raged at him, after lessons, as soon as they were alone. 'Now Daniel's got your part! You and your silly voices. You've ruined everything!'

Julian's green eyes glittered for a moment.

'If that's what you think, Elizabeth, I don't call you much of a friend.'

'What else am I supposed to think?' exploded Elizabeth. 'Even friendship has its limits!'

'Somebody must have been trying to get you into trouble and it wasn't me,' replied Julian coolly. 'I was trying to get you *out* of trouble.'

'Oh, *really*? When nobody else in the class can throw their voice like that except you, Julian? Please don't make me any crosser than I am already!'

Now Julian's own temper snapped.

'In that case, there can be only one explanation, can't there? I mean to say, it's the only answer . . .'

'What?'

'Miss Ranger was right all along. You were completely over excited and you cheeked her yourself. So over excited you don't even remember doing it!'

'How dare you!'

Elizabeth turned her back on Julian and stalked away.

'If that's what you think, I have nothing more to say to you.'

'Nor I to you,' Julian retorted, as he turned on his heel and headed in the opposite direction.

It was a very bad quarrel.

In the days that followed, Elizabeth thought about it

many times. But she always reached the same conclusion. Julian *must* have been responsible for that silly voice. There was just no other explanation! He probably realized he had been very foolish indeed. Was it pride that stopped him owning up and saying sorry so that they could be friends again?

But it was mean of him to try to persuade her that *she* had been the silly one, so over excited that she didn't know what she was doing! That would make *her* responsible for his losing his part in the play!

She decided not to speak to Julian again until he apologized.

Julian felt exactly the same way about Elizabeth.

CHAPTER EIGHT

THE BUTTON'S OWNER IS FOUND

ELIZABETH WAS unhappy for the next few days. It was horrible not being on speaking terms with Julian. She had other friends in the first form but it was with Julian that she got on best. She would like to have seen more of Joan during this troubled time. But with the two girls in different forms that was not possible.

Arabella quickly took advantage of the situation. The vain little girl had no idea why Elizabeth and Julian had mysteriously fallen out but it gave her quiet satisfaction. She was tired of the way everybody liked Elizabeth and nobody liked her.

'We may only be understudies, Julian,' she told him, 'but that still means we have to learn out parts. It's a very important job being an understudy. If anything happens we could easily be called upon.' She gave him a winsome smile. 'I'm an absolute ninny at learning lines. Please help me. We can practise some of the scenes together. I'd love you to test me and I'll be only too pleased to test you.'

356

THE BUTTON'S OWNER IS FOUND

One evening, Elizabeth walked into the common room and found them rehearsing some of the play together. Rosemary was their prompter. Arabella was giggling happily.

'Oh, Julian, you are naughty. You're peeping at the script, I can see you. You still haven't bothered to learn it.'

Elizabeth turned on her heel and walked straight out again. It was infuriating. Arabella seemed to be having more fun just being an understudy than she was having in the real play! Julian was allowing her to help him over that blazer button mystery, too. It had still not been solved.

Much of Elizabeth's zest for acting had gone.

The other auditions had taken place and the full cast chosen. Rosemary had been made prompter. Elizabeth was pleased when Belinda, Kathleen and Jenny were all given good supporting roles in the play. John McTavish was picked to play Mr Grasshopper who had some very funny lines to speak. And Patrick, of all people, had landed the part of the poor, sickly Mr Badger. He seemed to be enjoying himself already, all the more so now that Julian had been kicked out of the play.

Elizabeth had vowed to put Julian right out of her mind and throw herself into the play with gusto. After all, Daniel had been rather good as Jonkin, once he wore that funny mask.

But from the very first rehearsal, her spirits sank. It was all Daniel's fault. He had memorized his lines well. He was good at English and had no difficulty with learning by rote. But his acting was so half-hearted! His mind always seemed to be elsewhere. She could strike up no rapport with him. In the scenes they had to act out together, he refused to meet her gaze but just kept glancing shiftily around.

Worst of all, he kept on apologizing.

'I'm really sorry you've got me, Elizabeth,' he said, at that very first rehearsal, which took place after school on the terrace. 'I feel terrible that Julian had the part taken away from him.'

'I shouldn't bother to feel terrible about Julian!' retorted Elizabeth, sharply. 'It was no more than he deserved.'

But the boy looked guilt-stricken, all the same, and the apologies kept on coming.

'I'm sorry, that wasn't very good. I'm sure Julian would have done it much better . . .'

By the third rehearsal, Elizabeth was ready to snap.

'If you mention Julian again, I'll scream! Stop being such a drip, Daniel. We've got to make a success of this! I'm begining to think we're going to make complete idiots of ourselves in front of the whole school. Put some verve into it, *please* . . .'

THE BUTTON'S OWNER IS FOUND

What was the matter with the boy?

It was the weekend and Elizabeth was feeling particularly irritable.

On her way to rehearsal she had noticed Julian, Harry and Arabella talking to some of the juniors. At this week's school Meeting, William and Rita had asked the assembled children to renew their efforts to find out who had vandalized the strawberry plants. Elizabeth would love to have been helping Julian track down that missing blazer button. Instead, he and Harry were allowing Arabella to tag along with them.

In fact, Julian was simply filling in time. Secretly, he was still very hurt and angry at Elizabeth's behaviour – and puzzled, too. As he saw her pass by, he wondered how long it was going to be before she finally came to her senses and apologized to him.

After the rehearsal on the terrace, Elizabeth trudged back into school, her spirits at a low ebb. She was sorry she had lost her temper with Daniel. It was the worst thing she could have said to him! It was silly of her to frighten him like that. At least he had managed not to mention Julian's name again. He had just acted like a frozen rabbit, instead.

'I don't think the play's going to be any fun at all,' Elizabeth concluded. She decided to go upstairs and read a book. She walked towards her dormitory when suddenly she heard her name being called.

'I've been looking for you, Elizabeth.'

Assistant Matron came out of the little sewing room and greeted Elizabeth in the corridor. She carried a small blazer over her arm. Elizabeth recognised the strawberry jam mark on the front! It was hers – one she had outgrown and handed in at the begining of term. She had a much bigger one now which would last longer, she hoped.

'I'm checking over all the second-hand uniforms this week, Elizabeth,' smiled Assistant Matron. 'I want to send it all to the cleaners next week. We need everything back in good time for the school uniform sale at the end of term!'

The school second-hand shop did a good trade at the end of the school year, when parents came to collect their children from Whyteleafe. New uniform was so expensive and the children grew so quickly. Some parents were always pleased to have the chance to kit them out in good second-hand items for the new school year ahead.

Elizabeth stared dreamily at her first blazer. She felt quite fond of it now. She remembered her governess, Miss Scott, taking her to the big store to buy the brand new uniform and, afterwards, reinforcing the blazer buttons with some extra strong blue thread. 'You treat your clothes so roughly, Elizabeth,' Miss Scott had said. 'We don't want the buttons coming off.'

Elizabeth had cheeked Miss Scott at the time, telling her that she would not be at Whyteleafe School long enough for that to happen. She did not *want* to go to a horrid boarding-school and would make sure that she was sent home as soon as possible! How silly and childish she had been, thought Elizabeth. She loved her school uniform now. She was very proud to wear it.

Elizabeth realized that Assistant Matron was looking at her expectantly. 'Did you want something, please?' she asked, politely.

'The button, Elizabeth! You promised to give it to me weeks ago.'

Elizabeth's hand flew to her mouth.

In her relief at handing in the uncomfortably small blazer, she had forgotten all about that button! It was the blazer becoming so tight that had made the middle button burst off, in spite of Miss Scott's best efforts. Elizabeth had put the button in a safe place but then promptly forgotten all about it. Now she apologized.

'I'll go and find it straight away. I think I remember where I put it.'

'I have to go to the village now,' said Assistant Matron, smiling. 'Just put it on my sewing table when you've found it, Elizabeth.'

361

'I will. I promise.'

She hurried into the dormitory and went to her cubicle. A white-painted chest of drawers stood there with pretty blue wooden handles. All the girls had one, next to their beds. On top of her chest of drawers, at the back, was a small china bowl in which Elizabeth kept oddments. A foreign coin, some hair grips, a mouldering bath cube. She was almost certain that she had put the button there for safe keeping, all those weeks ago.

But there was no sign of it now. Elizabeth poked inside the bowl, in puzzlement. Where *had* she put it then? She began to search through the drawers below, turning them out, one by one.

'Lost something, Elizabeth?' asked Kathleen, cheerfully, coming into the dormitory.

At the same moment, Arabella was passing the open door. She paused and peered inside, glancing at Elizabeth. She had just been indulging in a happy daydream. Her faithful friend, Rosemary, had told her what a poor performance Daniel and Elizabeth had put up at today's rehearsal; that Elizabeth had snapped at Daniel and Miss Ranger had not looked very pleased.

Surely it would only be a matter of time before she and Julian would be asked to step into the breach? Instead of being a flop, the Summer Play would be the most brilliant success! In her mind's eye, the sun was shining brightly. She and Julian, hand in hand, were being given a standing ovation . . .

Now, Arabella heard Elizabeth speaking crossly to Kathleen:

'Just a silly old button! I was sure I put it in my little bowl. Assistant Matron needs it! Oh, Kathleen, do help me look for it. It's a silver blazer button with some bright blue thread hanging from it.'

Arabella nearly gasped out loud.

She quickly tiptoed away down the corridor, feeling surprised and excited. She must tell Rosemary about this and they must think what to do.

Less than half an hour later, Jenny came up to the dormitory.

Elizabeth looked hot and bothered. It seemed to be one of those horrid days when *nothing* would go right. She and Kathleen had ransacked the cubicle. They had even pulled the chest of drawers away from the wall, no easy task, to see if the button could have slipped off the top and down the back. They had looked under Elizabeth's blue rug. They had even crawled under her bed. It was nowhere to be found.

The loss of the button somehow filled Elizabeth with uneasiness, although she could not think why. And now Jenny had appeared in the doorway and was looking at her rather strangely.

'Can you come down to the common room, please, Elizabeth?' she asked, unhappily. 'Something important's cropped up.'

When Elizabeth entered the common room, Arabella was sitting at one of the little tables. A few of their classmates sat nearby, watching with interest. There was a sense of expectancy in the room.

Something was lying on the table. Arabella placed it on the palm of her hand. Then, with a flourish, she held it out towards Elizabeth.

'Was this what you were looking for?'

Elizabeth stepped forward and examined the object closely. It was a silver blazer button with some bright blue thread hanging from it.

'My button!' she exclaimed. 'Where did you find it, Arabella?'

'William and Rita had it,' said Arabella, with a meaningful look. 'Rosemary and I heard you were looking for one. We've just been along to their study and borrowed it from them!'

'It's the button that John found in the strawberry beds!' said Rosemary solemnly. 'We were all asked to find out who owns it, remember? And now we have!'

Elizabeth looked at the button in complete astonishment.

THE BUTTON'S OWNER IS FOUND

'You surely don't think I was the person trying to steal strawberries?' gasped Elizabeth.

'We all like strawberries,' said Arabella, pursing her lips.

'I haven't worn my old blazer for weeks! Ask Assistant Matron if you don't believe me!' snapped Elizabeth, her temper flaring up. 'I'd never wear it to the school gardens, anyway. I've absolutely no idea how the button got *there*! I put it in the little bowl on top of my chest of drawers, weeks ago, and that was the last time I saw it!'

'Perhaps you just *meant* to do that,' suggested Arabella. 'Perhaps you actually had it in a pocket and it fell out one day when you were messing about in the gardens . . .'

'How dare you!' raged Elizabeth.

Before she could lunge at Arabella, Rosemary stepped between them. She spoke soothingly.

'Now, it's no use getting angry with Arabella, Elizabeth. William and Rita said that if you *did* recognize the button you were please to go and see them in their study at four o'clock. You can explain it all to them in the proper way.'

'Indeed I shall!'

She stormed out of the common room.

CHAPTER NINE

JULIAN MAKES IT FIVE

FOR ALL her bravado, Elizabeth felt scared as she tapped on the door of William and Rita's study at four o'clock. How had her button got there? It was dreadful to be under suspicion like this. Surely the head boy and girl knew her too well to believe that she would damage young plants? Surely they must know that although she might be tempted to pick the occasional ripe strawberry, she would never pull young plants out of the ground to look for fruit! It would be such a stupid and ignorant thing to do.

'Come in, Elizabeth.'

Still quaking, she walked into the cosy little study. William and Rita were waiting for her.

There was somebody else in the room with them, seated in the visitor's armchair. It was John Terry.

Elizabeth felt somehow reassured by the sight of John, as he stood up and offered the chair to her. She sat down. Everybody seemed very calm.

'John's just been telling us how you helped him net

all the strawberry beds, after the plants had been vandalized,' said William approvingly. 'But you do recognize the button, then?'

Elizabeth nodded.

'We know you're one of his best little helpers,' stated Rita. 'We thought we should have a chat with John first about this button business.'

'Don't look so worried, Elizabeth,' smiled William. 'None of us thinks for one moment that you pulled up those plants.'

'Oh, thank goodness,' replied Elizabeth.

'But have you any idea how your button could have got there?' asked Rita. 'Is it possible that you lent it to somebody?'

'Definitely not,' said Elizabeth, with a firm shake of the head. 'I mean, who would want to borrow an old blazer button? Besides, I had to keep it safe because I'd promised to give it to Assistant Matron. It was just that I'd forgotten all about it, until she asked me today.' Elizabeth explained about handing in the old blazer without it. 'The missing button should have been in the little bowl on top of my chest of drawers,' she finished.

At that, Rita smiled and shook her head.

'You must be mistaken there, Elizabeth. You really must! Now try to think very carefully. You *forgot* to give it to Assistant Matron. Is it not possible that you *forgot* to put it in a safe place, too? That you were just carrying it around in a pocket?'

'Well . . .' Elizabeth frowned. She was convinced that she had put the button in the bowl. 'I don't think so. But . . .'

'But it *is* possible, isn't it?' chuckled William. He was looking very relieved. 'Well, I think that's the beginning and the end of your involvement. John has told us how often you help in the garden. You must have been weeding the plants one day and the button fell out of your pocket! The whole thing is a complete coincidence and has nothing to do with the fact that, at a later stage, somebody vandalized them.'

'I – I suppose so,' said Elizabeth, reluctantly. She was still frowning. When had she ever worked in that part of the garden?

'You gave us a red herring when you produced that button, John!' chided Rita.

'It was wrong of me to jump to conclusions,' agreed John, with a wry smile. He scratched his head. 'I thought I'd found a grand clue and I'd found nothing of the sort.'

There was a thoughtful expression on his face as he tried to work it out. He had been so sure that the lost button and the damaged plants were closely linked. But if the two things were unconnected . . . why, perhaps he had been on the wrong track altogether. He must start to keep his eyes and ears open . . .

As Elizabeth left to go to tea, she felt pleased that William and Rita and John believed in her. It did make her feel a little better.

However, as she walked into the dining-hall, she could feel the tension in the air as many of the children glanced her way. The whispers had spread very quickly. The mystery of the blazer button had been solved! It belonged to the Naughtiest Girl. She had just been hauled up in front of the head boy and girl!

Her classmates were less chatty than usual. But her best friend Joan kept looking across from the next table and giving little smiles and waves, to show solidarity.

Elizabeth began to get a horrid feeling in the pit of her stomach. How very bad it must look to everybody, her blazer button having been found where the plants had been vandalized! Even worse was the feeling that somebody must have put it there deliberately. The more she thought about it, the more certain she became that she *had* left the button in the bowl and that things could not have happened in the way that William and Rita had suggested.

At the far end of the table, Julian was eating his tea. He was deep in thought, a moody expression on his face.

Elizabeth had lost her own appetite. She had to force herself to eat the tuna salad, usually a favourite. She left her raspberry yoghurt. She could feel a hot pricking sensation behind the eyes and just as soon as they were allowed to get down from table, she fled. She hurried out into the school grounds, her eyes blurred with tears. She was unaware of footsteps following her. She reached the lovely weeping ash tree, where the Summer Play was going to be performed. She crept under its secret canopy of leaves that almost touched the ground. She wanted to hide, like a wounded animal.

She sat down, leant against the tree trunk and buried her face in her hands.

Everything was going wrong!

It had all started with Julian putting on that silly voice! Since then nothing had gone right. And he *still* wouldn't own up and say he was sorry. How she wished that he would. She needed his friendship so badly now.

'Elizabeth?'

Startled, she looked up and saw Julian ducking under the cascading fronds and coming to join her.

'Hello, bad girl. Now, at last, I hope you will believe me!'

He sat down and put an arm round her shoulders to comfort her.

'There's nothing to cry about.'

'There is! There is! William and Rita and John believe in me and so does Joan. But that's only four people in the whole school. Nobody else knows what to think.'

'Only four?' said Julian. 'Don't you mean five?'

'Five?'

'Yes, you forgot to count me. I believe in you.'

She stared at him, in relief. She dried her eyes.

'Do you really? But, Julian, what did you mean just then—'

'Elizabeth, somebody is trying to get you into trouble. I told you that a week ago. Now perhaps – at *last* – you'll believe me!'

Elizabeth gasped as it dawned on her what Julian was saying.

'Listen, Elizabeth. I did *not* put on that silly voice! Somebody else did. And that button could hardly have *walked* on its own to the school gardens. Somebody placed it there. But do you believe me now?' he asked urgently.

'Yes,' replied Elizabeth, in a very small voice. 'Yes. I do.'

Her mind was in a turmoil. She still did not understand who else in the class could be clever enough to throw their voice in that amazing way. But now she was sure that it was not Julian.

I was trying to get you OUT of trouble was what he had

claimed at the time. And she had refused to believe him!

If that's what you think I don't call you much of a friend, Elizabeth he had told her angrily.

Now, she turned to him, her cheeks hot with shame.

'You were right about me not being much of a friend, Julian,' she admitted. She felt bitterly angry with herself for misjudging him so. 'You took the blame to save me from losing my part in the play – and ended up losing your own. And that was all the thanks you got from me! Oh, Julian, I don't know how you can ever forgive me. Why have I got such a silly temper? I'm not surprised if you like Arabella better than me. I can be such a horrid person!'

Julian looked at Elizabeth's grief-stricken face. He stood up, then took her hands and pulled her to her feet.

'Up you get, Elizabeth. Stop moping. It doesn't suit you. Not a bad, bold girl like you! Arabella? You must be joking!' he said cheerfully. He had waited so long for Elizabeth to apologize and now she had. Everything was all right again. 'Come on, let's see if the ponies are free and go for a ride. It will clear our heads and help us to think.'

As they strolled towards the stables, the warm breeze whispering in the grass, Elizabeth felt like a new person.

'It's horrid to think someone's trying to make trouble

for me,' she said, as they saddled up the horses. 'But nothing seems so bad now, Julian. Oh, I'm so glad we've made up our quarrel!'

'We'll soon get to the bottom of this peculiar business,' replied Julian confidently.

At that moment, Robert appeared with Daniel.

'As you don't ride, would you like to walk Captain round the meadow, to give him some exercise?' Robert was saying to the fair-haired boy. 'I've got to go and give Patrick some tennis practice now.'

'If you want me to,' replied Daniel, dully.

'What a strange boy he is,' Elizabeth remarked to Julian, as they set off on horseback. 'Let's take the bridle path, shall we? He still hasn't bothered to learn to ride. All that fuss about wanting to help at the stables. He doesn't seem to enjoy it very much! He doesn't seem to enjoy being in the play much, either! Oh, Julian, we've got to find out who really cheeked Miss Ranger – and then she'll have to admit she was wrong. About us not being sensible if we act in the play together! She'll have to give you your part back!'

'Oh, I'm not worried about that,' shrugged Julian. He had only put his name down to annoy Patrick!

'Well, I'm worried if you're not!' exclaimed Elizabeth. 'It's really hard work, doing it with Daniel.'

'I expect he'll improve,' said Julian.

They had a lovely ride together and talked a lot about the mystery. It was a very puzzling one. Elizabeth hated the idea that someone had a grudge against her. She could not think who it might be.

'The only person with a motive would be Arabella,' she mused. 'She would so love my part in the play. But I'm quite sure it isn't her.'

'So am I,' agreed Julian. 'She could never throw her voice like that. And she was really surprised about the blazer button, I could tell.'

On their return, they rode back through the meadow.

Daniel was sitting by the hedge, reading a book, while Captain grazed peacefully nearby. A bird was sitting on the old horse's back, pecking at Captain's coat.

'You're supposed to be looking after him!' scolded Elizabeth, as they rode past. 'Can't you shoo that crow away?'

'Captain likes it,' mumbled Daniel, without even looking up from his book.

'Isn't he hopeless?' grumbled Elizabeth, as they passed out of earshot. 'Anything rather than put his book down for a minute. How can he possibly say Captain likes it!'

'But he's right!' laughed Julian. 'Horses are really grateful when members of the crow family sit on their backs! I think that one was a rook.'

'Grateful? Whatever for?' exclaimed Elizabeth.

'The birds search through their coats and get rid of little insects and parasites for them, that's what,' replied Julian, still amused at her indignation. 'Elizabeth, I'm beginning to think you've got a down on Daniel. The poor boy can't do anything right.'

Later, as they rubbed down the ponies, Elizabeth said, 'I haven't really got a down on Daniel. He would be nice if he weren't so odd. But he is hopeless in the play, Julian! We've got to make sure you play Jonkin and not him.'

'You've got *your* part, Elizabeth,' replied Julian, contentedly. 'So that's the main thing. You're going to be a star, I tell you!'

But he spoke too soon.

That same night, the bane of Elizabeth's life struck yet again.

CHAPTER TEN

FIRE! FIRE!

IT TOOK Elizabeth a long time to get to sleep. She tossed and turned, listening to the gentle breathing of the other girls in dormitory six. She was so excited about the play and what Julian had said about her being a star. But she was also fearful. Why should someone be trying to get her into trouble? Who could it be?

Soon, it was dusk outside and every other child in the school was fast asleep.

At last she began to feel sleepy.

Her eyes closed.

She started to drift away into a light, fitful sleep . . . Then – a sudden raucous cry reverberated in her head –

Fire! Fire!

Was it a bad dream?

Fire! Fire!

There it was again! It seemed to be coming from outside. Someone was screeching a warning. The school was on fire!

Half asleep and half awake, Elizabeth tumbled out of bed in a panic.

'Wake up, everyone! Please wake up! I think the school's on fire!'

She stumbled out into the corridor and rang the fire bell.

CLANG! CLANG! CLANG! CLANG!

The fire bell rang out all over the building.

There was great excitement as sleepy children emerged from dormitories in dressing-gowns, rubbing their eyes.

'Fire!' cried Elizabeth. 'There's a fire somewhere in the school!'

They all formed orderly lines, as they had often been drilled to do, then left the building by the special Fire Exits.

Elizabeth led the way.

'Keep calm, everyone!' she cried. 'Make sure everybody's out of your dormitory.'

As they milled around on the lawns outside there was much chattering and ado. Where was the fire? They couldn't see any smoke! But there *must* be a fire somewhere. Elizabeth had rung the fire bell! Oh, thank goodness, it could only be a small one . . .

Now the teachers were appearing. None of them had gone to bed yet. They were still fully dressed.

'There's a fire somewhere, Miss Ranger!' cried Elizabeth. 'I heard someone screaming—'

FIRE! FIRE!

'Are you sure, Elizabeth?'

While the children waited outside on the chilly lawns, the teachers carried out a full inspection of the school premises.

There was no fire.

Mr Johns returned and spoke to the assembled pupils.

'Back to bed, all of you! A false alarm, I'm pleased to say. Form into lines and go quietly back to your dormitories. There is no sign of a fire anywhere. You are quite safe.'

When Elizabeth reached dormitory six, she found Miss Ranger waiting for her. The expression on the teacher's face gave her a feeling of intense foreboding.

'Go straight back to bed, Elizabeth. That was a very silly joke. I will see you in the morning, after I have had a chat with Miss Belle and Miss Best.'

The next day, in spite of all her protests, Elizabeth had her part in the school play taken away.

'I am extremely surprised at you, Elizabeth. I accept your word that you did not deliberately set out to play a joke. But your imagination is obviously in a feverish state. From the moment you were given the star part in the Summer Play you have been much too over excited. It is a great shame but I have decided to give Arabella her chance. I am sure she will be more sensible.

379

You will be the understudy.'

Tears came to Elizabeth's eyes. But this time they were tears of pure anger.

She went to find Julian.

'I know jolly well that I didn't imagine those cries. They were real as could be. Oh, Julian, don't you see? Somebody else must have heard them. Not just *me*.'

'Yes, surely,' agreed Julian. 'And somebody made them, too. Which direction did they come from? Can you remember?'

'I was half asleep . . .'

'Think hard,' coaxed Julian.

Elizabeth frowned in concentration.

'Well, my window was open. It was somewhere outside . . . but sort of *above*. As though there was a fire on the floor above and somebody was leaning out of their window up there and screeching down to me, in a panic.'

'The attic floor, eh?' said Julian calmly. 'Well, we'll question all the children who sleep in dormitory ten, that's the one upstairs, isn't it?'

'Yes,' said Elizabeth eagerly. 'And three or four children have their own little rooms, as well. Oh, surely *someone* up there will have heard something?'

'Lucky it's Sunday. No lessons. It gives us all day to

investigate. We're going to get to the bottom of this, Elizabeth, don't you worry,' he said, airily.

It was a great comfort to have Julian by her side that day. Joan, too, was very loyal.

'I am quite sure you will be vindicated, Elizabeth,' she said, sweetly. 'Somebody else must have heard something, as you say. Is there anything I can do to help? Would you like me to question everybody in the second form?'

'Oh, would you, Joan? That would be such a help. Julian and I are going to quiz everyone who sleeps on the top floor. I *think* the cries came from above. But, of course, I can't be certain.'

Most of Elizabeth's classmates were very impressed by her sincerity, as she went around with Julian talking to people. They were puzzled and bewildered by the whole affair, just as they had been about the blazer button. They hoped, for the Naughtiest Girl's sake, that everything was going to turn out all right for her in the end. It had been rather exciting, hearing the fire bell go off like that! But of course the teachers did not see it that way. And now she had lost her part in the play.

Arabella should have been in a sunny mood that day. But she felt oddly tense and irritable. It was extremely annoying that Julian and Elizabeth, who had mysteriously quarrelled, had now just as mysteriously made it up.

It had been such a triumph when Miss Ranger told her that she, Arabella, was to play the part of Fay in *A Woodland Adventure* and must do her very best to make a success of it. She fully expected some of her classmates to come and find her and congratulate her and wish her luck. But she waited in vain. They all seemed more interested in Elizabeth's predicament and the detective work that she was doing with Julian. As the day wore on, Kathleen and Harry joined in, too, trying to help Elizabeth.

'Did you hear anyone shout "Fire!", Arabella?' asked Kathleen.

'Of course I didn't!' replied Arabella scornfully. 'Elizabeth just made it up.'

'What a waste of time!' agreed Rosemary.

'We're having a play rehearsal soon,' said Arabella. 'Are you coming to support me? I'm a little bit nervous because Rosemary says Daniel's the most terrible actor. You won't find anybody who heard any shouts in the night because nobody did.'

On that point, at least, Arabella was correct.

One by one, Elizabeth and Julian tracked down all the children who slept on the top floor. It was a long task. They were all out and about, enjoying their various weekend activities. And it was a fruitless task, too. For, one by one, the children shook their heads when questioned.

'Think *very* hard, James,' urged Julian. His room, like Daniel's, was almost directly above Elizabeth's window. 'Did you hear someone cry out? In their sleep, perhaps? Someone having a bad dream about a fire?'

'I was dead to the world,' said James. 'I didn't hear a thing – except the fire bell. And I didn't even hear that at first.'

It was the same old story.

'Why don't you try Daniel?' he suggested. 'I often hear him moving around after Lights Out. I think he reads in bed.'

After that, Elizabeth and Julian went to look for Daniel. He was their last hope. But they had not seen him all day.

'I expect he's reading a book in the stables,' commented Julian. 'That's where he usually is these days.'

'Or else *under the haystack fast asleep*, like Little Boy Blue!' said Elizabeth, witheringly.

He was nowhere to be found.

'Surely he can't be spending all day in his room?' suggested Elizabeth, suddenly. 'He used to sometimes. Even lovely sunny days like today.'

Sure enough, they found Daniel in the small bedroom under the eaves. He was not even reading. He was lying on the bed, staring up at the skylight. His play script lay on the bedroom floor.

'Daniel!' exclaimed Elizabeth. 'You lazy lump!'

The boy sat bolt upright with a guilty start.

'I – I'm just learning my lines,' he said, feebly. He picked the script up off the floor and pretended to flick through it. 'What do you want?'

There seemed to be a strange pallor about his face.

'I didn't hear anything, no!' he burst out, as Julian questioned him. He seemed rattled and upset. 'I was fast asleep. Cross my heart and swear to die.'

Julian's interest quickened. He was sure that Daniel was speaking the truth. So why was he looking so upset?

'But you have an idea who it might have been, then?' he asked, probingly.

'It – it could have been . . .' he began to blurt out.

'Yes?' asked Elizabeth, eagerly.

The boy clammed up.

'I don't know,' he said worriedly. 'It could have been anything, I suppose.'

At that moment Rosemary burst into the room.

'So there you are, Daniel! Miss Ranger sent me to find you. You're supposed to be at play rehearsal!'

'Do I have to be?' he asked miserably. 'Can't Julian

FIRE! FIRE!

have a turn? I don't feel like it today.'

'Don't be silly!' said Rosemary. She grabbed him by the arm. 'You're keeping everybody waiting.'

As she hustled him out of the room, Julian and Elizabeth followed them downstairs. Julian was humming to himself, cheerfully.

'I think we're getting somewhere at last,' he said. 'I think Daniel knows something.'

'Yes,' agreed Elizabeth. 'So do I.'

Again she found it difficult to get to sleep that night. The dramatic events of the weekend were spinning round in her head. But now she was beginning to feel a glimmer of hope.

Arabella and Daniel were never going to last out in the play! She had heard from Kathleen that today's rehearsal had been a shambles!

Daniel's confidence had suddenly gone completely. And Arabella could not be of any help to him. She was a bag of nerves herself. She kept fluffing her lines. She had come back from the rehearsal with her face like a thundercloud. It was gradually dawning on her how much she was taking on and that failure stared her in the face.

Meanwhile, thought Elizabeth, she and Julian were getting to grips with the mystery. They had tried to pump Daniel again this evening, without success. But it was perfectly obvious that he suspected who the culprit was. He was shielding somebody! They would have to be patient but surely they would discover the truth soon? Then she and Julian would be able to clear their names. Their parts in the play would be given back to them!

Elizabeth was just drifting off to sleep when there came a sudden thump at the door. She sat bolt upright in bed. There was another thump, followed by a tapping sound . . .

This time she was wide awake!

Fire! Fire! came the choking cry. It was coming from the corridor. What an eerie sound!

'They're trying to trick me again!' she gasped. 'They're in the building this time. They're hoping I'll ring the fire bell again!'

Trembling, she slipped out of bed. She donned her dressing-gown and tiptoed towards the door. *Tap . . . tap . . . tap.* There was that noise again. She was frightened. But of one thing she was certain:

'I'm not going to be caught out a second time! I know perfectly well there isn't a fire!' she decided. 'I've got to catch them, whoever it is!'

CHAPTER ELEVEN

THE NAUGHTIEST GIRL
SAVES THE DAY

AS ELIZABETH edged open the door she heard rapid movements outside. She peered into the dimly-lit corridor. There was nobody there. They had moved along the corridor and disappeared round the corner. She could hear little bumps and thuds coming from the direction of the attic staircase.

She raced along in pursuit, turned the corner and bounded up the first few stairs in the gloom.

Suddenly, with a whoosh and a flutter, a black shape hurled itself at her legs and tried to peck at them.

Krrraaaa! Krrraaaa! Fire! Fire! it seemed to cry.

'A crow!' she gasped. 'A big black crow! How did it get indoors? Whatever's the matter with it?'

It was one of the most startling moments of Elizabeth's life. The bird was extremely agitated. It was still trying to peck at her legs.

Krrraaaa! Fire!

It was uncanny how human it sounded.

After that first shock, Elizabeth felt a sudden rush of relief. Her 'enemy' of the previous night had been no more than a silly black crow! A crow whose cries sounded almost like human ones. It must have alighted very briefly on her windowsill last night. Right by her open window. No wonder none of the sleeping children had heard the noise.

'I must get the teachers, quickly!' decided Elizabeth. 'They'll help get the bird out of the building. And now they'll see that I was *not* imagining things!'

As she tried to leave, the crow flew at her legs again.

'Do stop it—!' began Elizabeth, crossly.

Then she stopped.

A tiny wisp of smoke came curling down the attic staircase. Then another. And another.

She caught a faint, acrid smell . . .

'There is a fire up there!' she realized, in horror. 'There really is a fire!'

She went hurtling up the long staircase to the very top. The bird was fluttering and flapping around her head the whole time, in full cry. *Kraa! Kraa! Kraa! Kraaa!*

'The smoke's coming from Daniel's room!' she realized.

His door was only slightly ajar but, even from here, the smell was now becoming overpowering. It was the most horrid smell, like burning chemicals . . .

She pushed open the door and then reeled back. There were no flames but the room was full of suffocating smoke. The fair-haired boy lay prone on his bed, overcome by the fumes.

'Daniel's passed out!' she thought. 'I've got to get him out of there, quickly.'

But the acrid smoke was already filling her mouth and nostrils. She felt as though she would pass out, too. She closed Daniel's door for a moment and dived into the bathroom next door. She held a towel under the cold water tap until it was soaking wet.

Then, with the wet towel wrapped firmly round her face, she returned to the smoke-filled room and pulled Daniel to the floor. Her eyes were not covered by the towel and were already smarting painfully. She tried to ignore the pain.

Above their heads, the panic-stricken bird wheeled out of the open skylight. It flew high into the sky and away into the distance. The skylight – *so that was how it had got in!* realized Elizabeth.

'Get flat on your tummy, Daniel!' she gasped. 'So we're down below the level of the fumes . . .'

But the boy was still unconscious.

Slithering slowly backwards towards the door, Elizabeth dragged him, inch by inch, across the polished

389

wooden floor. It took less than a minute but that minute seemed like an hour. Several times Elizabeth started to choke. She was having to keep her eyes tightly shut now. She became scared that she, too, might lose consciousness before she could get Daniel to the door.

Then, at last, they were safely outside.

She slammed the door shut on the smoke-filled room. She knew that it would help to contain the fire. She rubbed the wet towel over her smarting eyes and then over Daniel's face, trying to revive him.

'Daniel. Daniel. Are you all right?'

His face twitched.

'Where am I? What's happened?'

'You passed out!' whispered Elizabeth, through her coughs. 'There's some horrible kind of fire in your room. This bird came and told me about it. A black crow—'

Daniel's eyes opened wide.

'You mean Rookie? He came and fetched you? Then, it *was* Rookie last time. I wondered if it could have been. And tonight there really *was* a fire—?'

'Rookie?' asked Elizabeth, in surprise. Daniel seemed to know all about the bird! 'Why do you call him that?'

'He's my pet. He's my tame rook. He's the brightest, best little rascal that ever lived.'

Daniel gulped.

'But I'm so ashamed, Elizabeth. He's brought you

and Julian nothing but trouble. And now I can't keep him secret any more, the teachers will send him away. He'll have to go, won't he?'

'I've got a funny feeling inside me that he's gone already,' whispered Elizabeth.

Suddenly she heard voices below and clattering footsteps.

The teachers had seen the plume of smoke coming out of Daniel's skylight. Now, armed with fire extinguishers, they came running up the stairs.

'What's happened? Are you all right, Daniel?' asked Mr Warlow.

'We'll soon put the flames out!' exclaimed Mr Johns, extinguisher at the ready.

'Please, Mr Johns, there aren't any flames yet,' warned Elizabeth, 'just these horrible poisonous fumes. You'll need wet towels round your faces!'

It was good advice. The two teachers were grateful for it as they charged into the room and squirted a smouldering toy on the bedside locker, then swiftly retreated. There was no risk of a fire spreading now. They had found the cause of all the smoke.

It was against school rules to have foam-filled toys but Daniel had brought a teddy mascot from home without knowing it was stuffed with the forbidden material.

It was also against school rules to read after Lights Out. It was even more strictly forbidden to read by candlelight. Daniel had been doing both. Nor had he remembered to blow the candle out. As he slept, the lighted candle had overbalanced. It had fallen against the teddy bear which had smouldered away, releasing the clouds of acrid fumes into the little bedroom.

'You won't be sleeping in there tonight, Daniel,' Mr Johns told the boy. 'It will take some hours for the room to air.'

Matron decided that both Daniel and Elizabeth should sleep in the sanatorium that night. She wanted to keep a watchful eye on them.

'Daniel has been very silly and Elizabeth has been very brave,' she stated. 'But they have both had a nasty shock. What they both need now is some medicine and a good night's sleep.'

By the following morning both children were fit and well again.

And James, who had been rudely awakened by the commotion on the attic landing, was soon spreading the dramatic news all round the school.

Elizabeth had heard those cries again! Why, he had half heard them himself. They had woken him up. And this time there really *had* been a fire. It was in Daniel Carter's room. Daniel had passed out in the smoke and fumes. He might have *died*!

Elizabeth had dragged him to safety.

The Naughtiest Girl had saved the day!

'You must have had a premonition on Saturday night, Elizabeth,' whispered Kathleen, in awe, when Elizabeth appeared for French. 'Isn't it weird?'

'Please do not talk in my lesson, Kathleen!' exclaimed Mam'zelle '*Silence, s'il vous plait.*'

Elizabeth and Julian exchanged secret smiles.

Over a delicious breakfast that Matron had cooked for them that morning, Daniel had told Elizabeth everything. After that, she had wasted no time in finding Julian. He had been so quick to spot that Daniel was trying to shield someone. Now she was able to tell him who it was!

Very soon, the whole school would hear about it, too.

CHAPTER TWELVE

WILLIAM AND RITA HAVE A STORY TO TELL

IT WAS very unusual for a school Meeting to be called in the dinner hour. But then this was going to be a very unusual Meeting.

'We may have to decide upon a punishment for somebody,' William told the rows of assembled pupils. 'But first we have a story to tell you.'

'Once upon a time,' began Rita, 'there was a boy who was not very happy at his boarding-school. He liked to read a lot and he liked to have privacy. In fact, his mother and father requested he be given a little room to himself. As things turned out that, perhaps, was not such a good idea . . .'

The audience listened, fascinated, as the head boy took up the thread of the story.

'He liked going home for the holidays and these Easter holidays were especially enjoyable. You see, on the first day of the holidays, he found a baby bird that had fallen from its nest. He took it indoors and nursed it back to health. It was a baby rook, so he called it Rookie. He hand-reared it. First of all he fed it with bread and milk. Soon it needed a richer diet and he went out every day and dug up worms for it to eat. It grew very fast indeed . . . Your turn now, Rita.'

The head girl smiled at the spellbound children.

At the very back of the hall Miss Belle, Miss Best and Mr Johns sat listening quietly. They had given their permission for Daniel's story to be told.

'Members of the crow family cannot really be tamed. Rookie was no exception. He was soon into everything, jumping into the butter in the kitchen, pecking at the soap in the bathroom. Outside, he would dive-bomb the bonfire in the garden, trying to attack the smoke! The family would cry *Fire!* to warn him. Unlike the magpie, or the jay, or the hooded crow, the rook can make a *great* variety of sounds if it wants to, not just the usual cawing,' explained Rita. She smiled again. 'Soon Rookie could scream *Fire!* himself. But he still kept attacking the bonfire smoke, in the same foolish way!'

'He was finally cured of the habit,' interrupted William, 'when he flew too close to the flames one day and almost singed his feathers. He had a healthy respect for smoke after that! By this time, his young owner was back at boarding-school for the summer term.'

'While the boy was away at school he often thought

about Rookie,' continued Rita. 'He did love his wicked pet so. He missed him. He could hardly wait for half-term. When he got home, he found that Rookie was now full-grown and was becoming very boisterous. In fact, unmanageable. He would wait for the postman in the front garden and try to peck at his legs! And, that very half-term week, something dreadful happened. Rookie took a liking to the young strawberry plants growing in the next door garden. He kept pulling them out of the ground. The next door neighbour would have been pleased to shoot him!'

Some of the pupils gasped. The story was getting very exciting. Strawberry plants! A bird with a warning scream! Now they were certain that they knew what this was all about.

'What happened next?' cried some of the juniors.

'What happened next,' said William, gravely, 'was that the boy's parents realized that they could cope with Rookie no longer. At the end of the boy's half-term holiday, before they took him back to school, they told their son that he must say goodbye to Rookie. For good. Very soon now, they would release the bird somewhere in the countryside, back into the wild.

'So for the first day back at school, the boy was very sad, as you can imagine . . . Until, by the stables the following afternoon, a bird flew down from a treetop nearby and settled on the boy's shoulder. It was Rookie! The bird had followed the car back to school. It had secretly taken up residence at its young master's school!'

It was Rita who brought the story to its conclusion.

'The boy was overjoyed. The bird loved him! It had refused to be parted from him! He plucked up his courage. At the first school Meeting he fully intended to beg for permission to keep Rookie at school. He was just about to put his request to that fateful Meeting. When . . .'

Rita looked round the hall.

'What happened?'

The juniors called out the answers.

'You said about the strawberry plants!'

'Daniel knew it must be Rookie!'

'He was scared Rookie would be sent away. So he made it up about helping in the stables, instead!'

'He knew Rookie was living down there and he wanted to be with him sometimes.'

The head girl nodded.

'The bird must have flown in through Elizabeth's window one day and stolen her button,' Rita explained. 'And then he saw the strawberry plants to play with instead.'

'So he dropped it!' concluded William.

A buzz of conversation rippled through the hall.

Sitting near the back, John Terry scratched his head and smiled to himself. He had been so sure that the button had been linked to the crime – and he was right, after all! When it had looked as though there was *not* a link, he had begun to wonder if a large bird or even an animal could have been responsible. He had been watching out for signs ever since but had seen nothing. So he had been on the right track both times – but had failed to make the vital connection!

As the noise level in the hall began to rise, William rapped his little hammer sharply on the table.

'Silence, please. Everyone be quiet now. You have all guessed who the story is about. And now Daniel himself wants to stand up and speak to us.'

Elizabeth saw the fair-haired boy nervously clench and unclench his fists. He rose slowly to his feet. Then he took a deep breath. He spoke timidly.

'I want to tell everybody I'm sorry for the bad things I've done. I know we're not allowed to have matches or candles and I could easily have set the school on fire. I'm very ashamed about that. I'm also *very* ashamed . . .'

He gulped and glanced at Elizabeth. His voice seemed to be drying up in his throat. She gave him an encouraging nod. *Go on, Daniel.*

'. . . that I was so deceitful. I wanted to have Rookie at school with me so badly that I kept quiet and let other people suffer. I *guessed* it was Rookie who made a noise outside our classroom window. I expect he was looking for me. It was one of his cheeky sort-of-human sounds. But I let Julian take the blame! And Elizabeth getting into trouble for ringing the fire bell was even worse! I couldn't be sure, but I guessed she must have heard Rookie. And I didn't own up. I was so miserable about it. I just sat in my room all day. And the worst thing of all has been play rehearsals! How could I enjoy being in the play when I had made other people lose their parts?'

He sat down hurriedly and buried his face in his hands.

William then asked Elizabeth and Julian to stand up.

'You two have had the worst of Daniel's behaviour,' he said. 'Especially Elizabeth. Can you, Elizabeth, suggest to the Meeting what *you* think his punishment should be?'

There was an expectant hush in the hall, as Elizabeth opened her mouth to speak. School waited to hear what she would say.

CHAPTER THIRTEEN

THE SUMMER PLAY – AND AFTER

ELIZABETH HAD already consulted Julian. The two friends had discussed things very carefully just before the Meeting.

At the end of morning lessons, they had gone with Daniel to the school stables to help him look for Rookie. But the glossy black bird with the white blaze above its beak was not there. It was so sad to see Daniel, walking around and looking up at the trees, calling out 'Rookie?' over and over again.

'You were right, Elizabeth,' he had said, tearfully. 'He *has* gone. And I don't think he'll be coming back.'

Julian had put an arm round the boy's shoulders as the trio walked slowly back to school for dinner.

'It's hard for you to accept, Daniel. But it will be good if he never comes back. Rooks are not meant to live on their own. No wonder he was so anti-social! They like to live with other rooks, in colonies. It will mean he's been accepted back into the wild.'

Now Elizabeth spoke up at the Meeting.

'Daniel *should* be punished for the fire in his room last night,' she said. 'But he already *has* been. The worst punishment of all. His bird was terrified. The fire and all the commotion frightened Rookie away! He's gone, you see. Daniel's been punished for everything else, too. He's not had a moment's peace since Julian and I lost our parts in the play. His own guilty conscience saw to that!'

She sat down, out of breath.

There was a moment's silence.

Then suddenly everybody was clapping Elizabeth's little speech. It was very fair of her. She had said exactly the right thing.

The head boy and girl both nodded in approval. So did the monitors on the platform. Joan felt very proud of Elizabeth.

William held up a hand for silence again. He fixed Daniel with a calm, kindly gaze.

'Love of books is a wonderful thing, Daniel. Favourite storybooks are like dear friends. But they must never be a substitute for caring for *real* people, too. Lost in your storybook last night, burning that candle, you gave no thought to all the real boys and girls here at Whyteleafe and the possible danger of fire.'

Daniel hung his head.

'And caring for birds and animals. That, too, is a

grand thing,' William ended. 'But neither should that ever be a substitute for caring for people. In your desire to keep Rookie, you allowed *people* to suffer. You caused Elizabeth, in particular, a lot of pain and unhappiness.'

'Please, William, I know you are right but it was just so amazing that Rookie liked me so much!' blurted out Daniel. 'The way he followed the car, all the way from our village, just so he could stay with me! You see,' he shook his head, 'the trouble with "real people" is that they don't seem to like *me* very much.'

Elizabeth leapt to her feet indignantly.

'That's not true, William. Julian and I like Daniel. We really do!'

She sat down embarrassed.

Then, languidly, Julian got to his feet.

'There's something else that needs clearing up,' he said, casually. 'About *my* having suffered over the play. That's not quite true. The part of Jonkin is such a long one. Surely I can't be expected to start learning it now? I would much rather Daniel kept it.'

'Only Miss Ranger can decide that, Julian,' replied Rita, pleasantly. 'She is the play's producer. Miss Belle and Miss Best will have a say, too. After all, it's their play.'

But the joint heads – and Mr Johns – were already

nodding their approval. It was what the teachers had wanted all along for Daniel. They were worried that he never mixed. Julian's surmise had been correct. Furthermore, Daniel should never have been allowed a single room in the first place, the joint heads decided. They would have to rectify the matter.

It was a disappointment to Elizabeth. Julian was not to be her co-star in the Summer Play, after all. Arabella was left with that consolation, at least.

But Daniel's performance just got better and better.

Although he was still pining for the bird, the boy started to throw himself into rehearsals. It was fun that John McTavish was in the play, as Mr Grasshopper. Since moving in right next to John, in the big dormitory, the two had become good friends.

Julian was in the same dormitory and gave Daniel a lot of coaching. There was no doubt that helped, too.

Most of all, Daniel did not want to let Elizabeth down.

She soon began to get over her disappointment.

The great occasion itself took place on a beautiful midsummer's evening. *A Woodland Adventure* was enacted in the prettiest corner of the school grounds. The weeping ash tree with its trailing fronds made a perfect stage set for Jonkin and the Fairy Queen.

THE SUMMER PLAY – AND AFTER

Everyone loved the be-masked 'woodland animals' that appeared, disappeared and reappeared amongst the greenery.

The whole school sat transfixed, not least Miss Belle and Miss Best. They had worked so hard writing a new Summer Play in time for the first form's turn this year. And how well they were doing it! What a success for their play.

Elizabeth was the star of the show. She had to make several curtain calls. But Daniel, too, had some curtain calls for a fine performance.

Beauty and the Beast were delighted with both of them.

Elizabeth lingered in the grounds long afterwards. She wanted this evening to last for ever.

So did Daniel. He was standing by the big sundial at the top of the lawn. Suddenly he looked up into the sky.

'Hello, Dan. What are you looking at?'

He pointed. A cloud of rooks was flying overhead but one of the birds had dropped back. It circled above their heads for a moment.

They both held their breath and waited.

Then, dipping one wing towards them, as if to say goodbye, it flapped away and caught up with its companions.

Elizabeth and Daniel continued to watch as the

cloud of birds headed for the distant horizon. Soon, the little cloud became no more than a moving speck against the lowering red sun. Then the birds were gone, and there was only the sun.